The Love Scam

The Love Scam

MaryJanice Davidson

ST. MARTIN'S
GRIFFIN

First published in the United States by St. Martin's Griffin,
an imprint of St. Martin's Publishing Group

THE LOVE SCAM. Copyright © 2020 by MaryJanice Alongi. All rights reserved.
Printed in the United States of America. For information, address
St. Martin's Publishing Group, 120 Broadway, New York, NY 10271.

www.stmartins.com

The Library of Congress Cataloging-in-Publication Data
is available upon request.

ISBN 978-1-250-05316-9 (trade paperback)
ISBN 978-1-4668-5544-1 (ebook)

Our books may be purchased in bulk for promotional, educational,
or business use. Please contact your local bookseller or the Macmillan Corporate
and Premium Sales Department at 1-800-221-7945, extension 5442,
or by email at MacmillanSpecialMarkets@macmillan.com.

First Edition: 2020

10 9 8 7 6 5 4 3 2 1

For my dear friend Jessica,
who suffered a great loss last year
but never lost herself

Polyglot: a person who speaks, writes,
or reads a number of languages
—DICTIONARY.COM

Polymath: a person of great learning
in several fields of study
—DICTIONARY.COM

There's nothing trashy about romance.
—PARRY, *The Fisher King*

Author's Note

This is the second book in the Danger series, which came about because my editor and I love romance tropes, and basically I wanted to write a love letter about . . . well . . . love. And tropes! (But also love.)

For those of you in a hurry, there's a trope list at the back.

Anyway. On to the various things that inspired certain parts of the book.

Dooneese Maharelle, a woman with absurdly small doll hands played by Kristen Wiig on *Saturday Night Live*, terrifies me. I have seriously had nightmares about her pattering after me on her teeny feet, calling for me with her waist cinched in and those little doll hands clawing the air as she gains on me . . . ye gads. I think I thought up a heroine with small hands as a way to deal with my terror of Dooneese Maharelle. I'm very, very sorry you have to be subjected to it.

(None of this is to say I don't like Kristen Wiig. I think she's wonderful. She's got more talent in a discarded fingernail clipping than I have in my entire body. Which makes Dooneese Maharelle no less terrifying.)

Polyglots are cool. So are polymaths.

Venice's Cruising Pavilion wasn't a thing until 2018, but for the purpose of this story, it was a thing in 2010, as well.

Like Rake, I love *lardo,* which is superskinny paper-thin slices of cured fat, often wrapped around wonderful things like pork chops. I know, I know—sounds a little *urrggh,* right? But it's so thin, it doesn't have that greasy mouthfeel, and it's cured with yummy herbs like rosemary and it was unlike anything I had ever put in my mouth and I instantly pledged all-consuming loyalty to my new overlord: *lardo.* Won't you join me? *Lardo*: It's what's for dinner! Except when something else is for dinner.

San Basso is a real building in Venice, a gorgeous deconsecrated church that is now used as a concert hall—think of the acoustics! However, for the purposes of fiction, I made it a church, then a haunted house, then a post office, and finally a charity.

The character of Ronald Kovac was loosely based on Eun Tae Lee, a resident of Virginia who bilked the Korean Central Presbyterian Church out of nearly a million dollars. He persuaded them to give him control of the church checkbook and wrote checks to himself (he was also a fan of buying wonderful presents for himself). When the church finally tumbled to what he was doing, he was driving a Porsche.

Bad enough people do these things; what's worse is that churches don't always report it. They're tax-exempt, so they're not required by law to release annual reports, and nobody likes admitting they were conned, especially if they need the community to trust their judgment. It's speculated that billions are scammed from churches in America every year. Also: ugh. C'mon, guys. If you're gonna steal, can't you steal from the bad guys?

Colomba di Pasqua is a thing! I'd never heard of it before I went to Italy. It's to Easter what fruitcake is to Christmas: disgusting, but traditional.

According to momjunction.com, Nedra means "secretive" and Naseef means "speaking in secret." I'm going through a phase where I make my characters have meaningful names, and if they were real, I doubt they'd thank me for it. Also, Lillith means "of the night."

Every family should have a nuclear option. I'm just saying.

The Love Scam

Prologue

Agh. Pain. And thirst. Painful thirst. Thirsty pain. Where? Was? Ow.

Rake Tarbell sloooowly rolled over and stared at a ceiling. (His ceiling? No.) His eyes were so gritty and the room so quiet, he could hear his eyelids sticking and unsticking as he blinked. And sometime in the last few hours, he'd eaten . . . a dead bird? And washed it down with another dead bird? One that had drowned in vermouth?

He tried to open his mouth and felt his gummy lips struggle to part. Had he been kidnapped? Hit over the head and kidnapped, then had his mouth and eyes taped shut?

No.

Worse.

Hungover.

He made it to the edge of the bed in a series of small wriggles, each one causing a wave of nauseating pain to claw up his spine and wash over his brain. When at last he was upright, he fought his gorge to a draw and buried his head in his hands, hoping for a swift death. He noticed he was in a black T-shirt he'd never seen before with the puzzling yet reassuring logo I DO ALL MY OWN STUNTS. No socks. No pants. By squinting very, very hard, he could just make out a pair of crumpled dark brown cargo shorts on the floor three feet away.

I keep telling you, Rake.

Shut up, Blake.

You can't party like a twenty-year-old forever.

Seriously, Blake. Shut. Up.

His inner voice, which sounded exactly like his tight-ass twin's, obligingly shut up, something the real Blake hardly ever did.

He managed to lurch to his feet and staggered toward a doorway leading to a sparkling clean bathroom—okay, mystery solved, he was in a hotel room. Bland white walls, bland tan carpet. De rigueur nightstand, two-drawer dresser, television. Shiny clean fixtures and various helpful signs his head hurt too much to even look at, much less interpret, but at least he had a vague idea of where he was.

He turned the tap on full and tried to kill himself: suicide by sink, glug, glug, ahhhhh. When he realized drowning would take too long, he cupped his hands under the cool flow and drank and drank and drank, then washed his face, ran his head under the tap again—thank God for roomy hotel sinks!—and slowly stood as he raked his fingers through his hair and slicked it back from his eyes.

He nearly screamed: He'd rarely looked so fucked-up. Even his inner Blake voice

(Kill it at once, and with fire!)

was horrified.

"Okay," he said, and winced. His deep voice reverberated around the small shiny white bathroom, which is how he found out it hurt to talk. "Okay," he whispered to his hideous, red-rimmed, ghastly pale reflection. Normally dark blond, his hair was now dirty blond. And his eyes, God, his eyes! Like the zombies in *28 Days Later* or, worse, *28 Weeks Later.* He was the before picture in an antacid ad. "Get out of the room. Don't think about the scary hotel room from *1408.* Figure out where you are, then get something in your stomach—no, you have to." His reflection was shaking his head and looking horrified; time to get stern. "You *know* you'll feel better with something in your stomach." Mirror Rake cringed, but Actual Rake was relentless. "You've got a day of crackers and ginger ale to look forward to, you horrible-looking shithead, and only yourself to blame."

Probably. He hadn't ruled out kidnapping yet; this might be someone else's fault. He'd been hungover before, though not as often as Blake assumed. He never did anything with the frequency Blake assumed—as a matter of pride, if nothing else. But he had no idea where he was or how he'd gotten to—to wherever he was. And the mystery wouldn't be solved from the bathroom. Had any mystery ever been solved from a bathroom? How often did Sherlock Holmes take a dump? The books never said.

He left the bathroom and managed to inch across the room to the shorts, gingerly step into them, and pull them on. These, at least, *did* belong to him, though they needed a trip through a washing machine. He felt the comforting bump of his phone in his side pocket as he zipped up, and the beat-up loafers at the end of the bed were also his. He figured he must have checked in (somehow—how had he managed to walk, much less communicate with a hotel clerk?), kicked off his shorts (but left his shoes on?), collapsed facedown on the bed, his absurdly long legs dangling over the end, and the shoes had fallen off in his sleep. Stupor. Coma. What have you.

After a few tries, he found the door to the hallway. The water *had* helped; he knew most of the pain of a hangover came from dehydration. That, and knowing he'd done it to himself and had no one else to blame. Fine. He'd get some fresh air, take stock of his surroundings, start Plan Ginger Ale + Ritz = Might Not Die.

Somehow he made it to the lobby, though for a minute he thought he was going to hurl tap water in the elevator. He closed his eyes against the killing glare of the fluorescents and focused on his breathing, then staggered out of the elevator with a real sense of accomplishment: no barf left behind!

He ignored the guest babble in the lobby, though normally he liked talking to strangers, especially female strangers. Not today. If he had to focus on anything besides falling down, he would fall down. *I'll give everyone in the hotel a thousand bucks if they just don't talk to me. Money well spent.* He made it through the revolving doors once . . .

"Agh! Mistake, mistake! Stop the ride!"

. . . then twice around. The doors spat him out onto the sidewalk, where the sun immediately set about frying him like a T-bone.

Aaaggghhhh, my retinas! Who knew the sun was so huge and hot? In early spring, no less!

Eyes squinched to slits, he shuffled forward, breathing in the, um, fresh air—hmm. There was an odd smell; not bad, but distinct. Familiar. Wherever he was, he'd been there before. That alone was enough to cheer him up, and he squared his shoulders and took a few jaunty steps to his destiny while ignoring the people who were shouting behind him. *Back off, strangers! It's my time to shine! Or at least gobble some crackers.*

Then he fell. Not far, thank goodness, but *ack* cold cold *cold*! The river/lake/ocean/what-the-hell-ever he'd plunged into was beyond bracing and well into hypothermia-inducing. He popped to the surface like a furious cork and wiped the water out of his eyes. *So that's what they were yelling about. Now would be a good time to start paying attention to my surroundings. Also, ninety seconds ago would have been a good time.*

At first he thought the strangers were going to bludgeon him with paddles until he went down and stayed down, the perfect end to a horrific morning. Then he realized they were all extending poles and paddles and

(why????)

bottles of water.

"Venice?" he sputtered, spitting a stream of foul water back into the larger stream of foul water that was the Grand Canal. *"I'm in fucking Venice?"*

Another Prologue

NEW CHARITY DIRECTOR

Venice, Italy*: The executive director of Support San Basso Families has announced the hire of a new director, Ronald Kovac.

"Mr. Kovac brings to SSBF a decade of running American charitable programs, and we are very excited that he is joining the efforts to raise money for local families in need."

Mr. Kovac, a native of Colorado, U.S.A., has announced that due to fund-raising efforts he undertook prior to officially taking the job, SSBF will be able to donate 200,000 euros to local families in need in time for Easter. The money will go toward housing repair and food.

"We are tremendously excited to have Mr. Kovac on board at our fine institution. We believe that, as San Basso was once a church and the building has been a part of our history for over a thousand years, SSBF is getting back to its roots, so to speak, by giving back to the community."

---

* Translated from Italian.

Kovac is a graduate of Harvard Divinity School as well as Harvard Business School.

Media Contact:
SSBF Executive Director
SSBFDirect@ssbf.org

Share what you have, for such sacrifices are pleasing to God.*
—Hebrews 13:16

One

Months before fucking Venice . . .

Rake rubbed his forehead and fought down a groan as his twin took the seat across from him. They hadn't seen each other in months, which was good for all: the two of them, their mother, the population of Las Vegas, society in general.

He sighed and tried to straighten. The movement sent a wall of pain slamming through his brain. "Not that I don't love being treated to your scowling face in the wee hours—"

Blake sighed. "It's ten-thirty in the morning."

"—but why am I here?" Beside his brother, who sat with perfect posture and was wearing a suit at oh-God-thirty in the morning (though he was his own boss and could lounge in jeans and a T-shirt), Rake felt distinctly rumpled. Possibly because he *was* distinctly rumpled.

Blake's dark blond hair was meticulously trimmed, his blue eyes meticulously not bloodshot. Savile Row on the man's back, Armani on his wrist, and no doubt something fancy on his feet. Rake slouched lower and looked: yep. Black and shiny. Definitely expensive. The two of them were a before-and-after picture.

Worse, Blake hadn't insisted on a meeting at dawn so Rake could admire his twin's dapperness. (That was a word, right?) Something was up.

He struggled upright. "Is Mom okay? Please say Mom's okay. A hangover plus Blake plus Mom is just exhausting to think about." He sighed and rubbed his temples. Sometime in the night, his tongue had been switched out for a wad of cotton. A dirty wad that tasted like booze. "My head *is* still attached to my body, right? It didn't blow up or anything?" He gingerly felt his skull, worried his fingers would sink into it like bread dough. "My brain feels really explodey."

Blake snorted. "Stop making up words, you hungover troglodyte."

Rake nearly spit all over himself; probably wasn't the best time to gulp his water. "I will if you will!" *Wow. That didn't sound childish AT ALL. God, why do I let Blake get to me like this? Why does he goad me? We're almost thirty!*

"*Troglodyte* is a real word!" Rake cheered up a bit to see Blake's famously even temper was splintering.

"God, why do I ever reach out to you?"

"Dunno." He did know, but would never say. They'd always been different, always fought, but underneath it all was something like love, or at least loyalty, or at least not hate. So Rake would think, but never say, *You reach out because you're lonely. Because you're a stereotype—the uptight rich guy who needs tru luv to loosen up. And I'm your screwup brother who occasionally needs guidance but never admits it, because I'm a stereotype, too. And around and around we go.* "But it makes you nuts, so I don't know why you don't quit it." Rake finished his water, and now grabbed Blake's. *Ah, water, sweet water of life. Wait. Water of life?*

"God help us when you become a father."

"Back atcha." At Blake's uncharacteristic silence, Rake tensed. "Uh—do you know something I don't?"

"Almost always."

"Or some*one* I don't?"

Blake waved away his brother's sudden attack of paranoia. "You mean do I know you have a bastard or five running around?"

"You're one to talk!"

"Fair point. But no. I don't have personal knowledge of your hypothetical bastards. Nor my own."

"Oh, thank Christ." Rake was so relieved, he nearly swooned out of the booth onto the floor. "So why are we here?"

"Unlike some, I cannot simply jettison my responsibilities when they become tiresome. Not that I haven't been tempted; surely I've done nothing to be saddled with you." Blake was pontificating, and Rake gulped faster. Maybe he'd drown. Or belch! Blake hated pretty much every natural bodily function, especially ones made by Rake's body.

"Did so. It's your own fault for insisting on being born first. You probably elbow-checked me on your way out of the womb. Now c'mon, why are we here? Why'd you call? What couldn't wait until our birthday?"

"Our mother is in Sweetheart and she needs us. She hates it, but she needs us."

The sarcastic retort died and Rake sat up so straight, it was like someone had rammed a broomstick down his spine. "Tell me," he ordered.

Blake did.

Two

Ten confusing minutes later . . .

"So Mom's stuck in her hometown, which is called Sweetheart for reasons both dark and hilarious, and she's too stubborn to leave, and she won't ask us to help her bail." Rake considered that for a moment. "Yep. Sounds legit."

Blake was nodding. "It's too much for her, too much for anyone, and she keeps getting in deeper and deeper." A short pause, which Rake knew meant *here comes the judgment.* "You wouldn't recognize her voice if you took her calls."

"Hey! World traveler, remember? Show me the cell tower on Lopez Island or the Travaasa Hana or the Aran Islands. I always call her back."

Blake waved Rake's return calls away: Shoo, return calls, be gone from me. "At three A.M. Sweetheart time, when she's semiconscious and barely coherent."

Oh, now that's too damned ridiculous. "She's completely coherent! It's our mom! She'd be coherent if she was dead!" *If she was— Wait, that makes no—no! Stand by your senseless statement! Double down on the senseless!*

Blake sighed. "You disappoint me." Rake didn't have to be a mind reader to hear the unspoken *again*. "If anyone could recognize barely coherent, little brother, I'd think it would be you."

Rake opened his mouth to let loose a devastating retort *(I'll coherent you, tightass!)* but Blake was well into lecture mode. Which was kind of like Marshawn's Beast Mode, only no one ever *ever* wanted to see it. "And the racket when you pulled in! Like this town isn't barely tolerable as it is. A motorcycle *and* a leather jacket? How original. Lovely periorbital hematoma, Marlon Brando."

I've gotta take this from Slutty McJudgypants? "Blow it right out your ass, Benjamin Tarbell 2.0."

There was a *crack!* as Blake slammed his fist on the table. "I'm nothing like our father."

Rake let out what he figured would be an eloquent snort, then embellished said snort with "What's the new one's name? Carrie? Terrie? Gerri? Fo-ferry? Fee-fi-fo-ferry? *Ferr-ee!*"

"*Ava.*" Blake inspected his fist. "And she's fine. I have reasonable certainty she's fine. As couples often do, we came to a mutual decision to give each other—"

Some breathing room.

"—some breathing room," they finished, and Blake's glare was a fearsome thing. "And you're one to talk, little brother."

No you don't. Rake had zero intention of letting that one slide. "At least I'm open about what I want from them and what they want from me. You, *you* think you're a gentleman because you insist they spend the night instead of calling them a cab while you're both still breathing hard." Frankly, his brother should just buy his own cab company and get it over with. It would save him a fortune in trouble and eons of time. "You're just fooling yourself, pal. And they know it and I know it and Mom knows it and everybody but you gets it."

His twin had his temper back under its usual tight control, and merely arched a dark blond brow. "Wanting the lady in question to spend the night rather than showing her the door once we've stopped sweating isn't a character flaw, Rake, though it's telling that you think it is."

The twins glowered at each other but, to switch it up, remained seated. Usually by now they would be chest-to-chest, with Blake enumerating Rake's many character flaws and Rake cordially inviting his brother to suck himself sideways.

After a long moment, Blake sighed. "This isn't helping our mother."

"No." *That's* why they hadn't come to blows yet. They loved irritating the piss out of each other, but loved their mother more. Rake, suddenly desperate to occupy his hands, started stacking Splenda packets. "It's not. So. What, then?"

"I propose we join forces. Hear me out!" he added when Rake shuddered. "You know she has a harder time dealing with us when we're united."

He snorted. "Truth. It's like the Roadrunner teaming up with Wile E. Coyote. You never see it coming, and when it *does* come, it's creepy and weird and everyone's taken off guard."

"Yes." Whoa! A smile! Rake sometimes couldn't remember if his brother even had teeth. "Creepy and weird is an outstanding way to describe the situation. Let's initiate a conference call and let her know we're going to work together to help her through this mess, no matter how complex."

That's . . . not an entirely stupid idea. "Yep, yep. That would

definitely disarm her into allowing us to interfere. Help!" At
his slip, he rapidly adjusted. "I meant help."

Blake almost laughed, and seeing the light of merry mischief in his big brother's eyes reminded Rake why he loved
the son of a bitch. When Blake loosened up, he was almost
human. "So: We will reach out at a time early enough that
she will likely be in her room getting ready, but not so late
that she has left to deal with the judgmental farmers' brigade.
Eight A.M. ought to do it. Can you be at my place in time?"

Ugh. Well, he'd just stay up extra late that night, avoid
going to bed altogether until after the call. Also, Blake didn't
seem to get that they didn't have to be in the same room to
make a conference call. Or even the same state, continent, or
hemisphere. "Sure."

Blake's eyes went all narrow and squinty, like when he
was constipated or thought Rake wasn't paying attention. "So
when would that be, exactly?"

Rake shrugged. "Fifteen minutes early to work out the
script. Say quarter to ten?"

Another put-upon sigh. "She is trapped in the central time
zone, Rake."

"Right." Time for some fun. "Center means more toward
the middle. Noon is the middle. So she's two hours closer to
the middle: Ten A.M."

"I don't understand." As Rake opened his mouth to con-
tinue torturing his genetic double, said double kept up with
the whining. "You have a high school diploma. You have a
college degree. You're a polymath."

He smirked. This was too good. His twin was brilliant,
and like all brilliant jerks, had peculiar blind spots. For in-
stance, he didn't see how very like their father he was, he was
incapable of having a sense of humor 95.999999 percent of

the time, potato chips made him constipated but he couldn't stay away from them, and he got *polymath* and *polyglot* mixed up. Rake never corrected him because, again: It was too good. "Not anymore. The doctor gave me some antibiotics and it cleared right up."

"Very funny." Yes! Blake was doing that thing where he was forcing words past tightly clenched teeth. You could actually see his temples throbbing. O, victorious day! "You are not a complete imbecile."

"Awwww. So sweet!"

"Hww oo ot nnstnnd tmm zzzs wrk?" Years of translating Blake's diatribes through clenched teeth allowed Rake to interpret that as "How do you not understand how time zones work?"

He shook his head, suddenly tired of it all. "Christ, Blake, will you back off my dumbassery for once?"

Blake had broken off to massage his jaw. "But it's so fascinating. Like studying a new mold spore no one knew existed."

"Aw, jeez." He rubbed his eye—the sore one, he remembered too late. "Just tell me what time to be at your place."

"Five-forty-five." At Rake's shudder, Blake added with no small amount of relish, "In the morning. Tomorrow morning. Morning is the opposite of evening. Not today. Tomorrow."

"What?" Rake's beloved beat-up leather jacket was just a bit too big, and he sometimes got lost in it. When he straightened, he popped out, Blake had once told him, like a turtle from its shell. "But I'll have just gone to bed!"

Blake had gone back to glaring. "So assist me with our mother, and *then* go to bed," he snapped. "It's not rocket science!"

Oh again with the rocket science! "You're just saying that because you studied rocket science!" So, so embarrassing.

Blake didn't even have the decency to wait until college, had started reading up on that stuff during freshman year. Rake could still see that first book in his mind's eye: *Fundamentals of Astrophysics*. Something a person who lost a bet would read but oh no, not Blake. He claimed it was *interesting*. Said it was *fun*. Did it on *purpose*. "You're forever running around telling people this isn't rocket science, that's not rocket science. Nobody elected you the namer of things rocket science!" Rake stopped himself; Blake was starting to look like a stroke was imminent. "What's wrong? Why is your face doing that?"

"I have no idea. I can't see my face." He rubbed his temples. "Either I'm getting a headache or my brain is trying to eject from my skull in pure self-defense."

"Bummer!" Hmm, too bitchy. "Need some Advil?"

"Advil is not what I need." He glanced at his brother's face, his gaze lingering on the black eye, then away. "You all right?"

Ah. That. Rake shrugged. "It's just sore."

Blake made a sound that was a cross between *hmph* and a snort. *Snnmph.* "I assume whatever damsel you rescued was appropriately grateful?"

"I dunno." He didn't. "Never got the chance to ask." It was true. One of those ninety-second things that seemed, in retrospect, to have lasted longer. "I saw a couple of assholes harassing the kiddo, and when I rolled up, one had her purse and the other was about to have *her*. So . . . you know."

Blake nodded and almost—but not quite!—smiled. Both boys had inherited their mother's moral compass, and her hatred of unfair fights. There had been times in high school when Blake had been the one sporting the black eye. Once, when fending off some football jagoffs after gym, they ended up with matching black eyes. Their mother had marveled at the phenomenon ("Unbelievable, unfortunate, but the symmetry is almost . . . soothing?") before grounding them for a hundred years.

"She took off before I could make sure she was okay," he finished. "The way she was moving, she was probably okay." She also might have been a track star. He'd seen her shoot an unbelieving look over one slender shoulder, then return to her full-on sprint to the parking lot. Rake didn't blame her for wanting to vacate, and he was glad to see she got to her car and peeled out safely, but a thank-you would have been nice.

"If you're going to let people smack you, you might at least tend properly to the injury." Blake made an imperious motion and the waitress trotted over. Aw, no. It couldn't be. He wouldn't. Not here. Not now. They were grown men, dammit!

"Could I get a clean washcloth and—"

He groaned. "Blake."

"—a bowl of water? And some ice?"

"First off, they're not bringing you bowls of water and cloths." He was pretty sure. She'd scampered off in a hurry. "This is not business class on a flight to Tokyo. Second, this happened two days ago." Even as he was speaking, he knew he was wasting his breath. "Anything you do now will be window dressing."

"And some duct tape for my brother's mouth," he called after her, then turned back. "If you sit still and take care of this, I'll schedule the call to Mom for an hour later, so you can get a nap first."

Rake tried, and failed, to keep the grin off his face. "Awwww. You *do* care!"

"Shut up."

He batted his eyes at his big brother, who looked uncomfortable at being caught giving a shit. "I feel safer already."

Blake groaned and covered his eyes. "Stop talking."

"Such big strong arms! To go with your big strong feet!"

Ah, *there* was the familiar glare of death. "I hope you get blood poisoning and die."

"No you don't." *You grumpy jackass.* Blake's love usually came wrapped in a layer of prickly fierceness, just like Mom's. How many times had Blake patched him up after a scuffle on the playground? The guy had learned to sew just so Rake could hide the rips from their mother. Money had almost always been too tight for new clothes. So eight-year-old Blake would be hunched over Rake's torn jeans, forcing a needle through the denim while muttering a constant stream of "idiot" and "moron" and "at least go for their balls first next time, they were all bigger than you."

"No you don't," he said again, just to be saying it.

"No." His twin sighed, and gave him a crooked smile. "I don't."

Three

Venice, now

When he finally flopped out of the canal and onto the dock like a furious, grossed-out fish, a single thought dug into his brain.

Time to question my choices. Which? All.

He let the patter of excited tourists wash over him like background music as he struggled to his feet. The people who'd helped him out of the canal were, understandably, reluctant to touch him, but still wanted to help. He was surrounded by locals, a *very* concerned gondolier, and the requisite Americans peering at him through their phones, keeping a safe distance even as they took pictures for social media. He and Blake agreed on one thing: American tourists were the Worst. He let loose with a raspberry in their direction, then shook himself like a dog.

"Eww!" one of the cuter ones shrieked, and fled, most of her tour group right behind her.

"It almost went in my mouth," one of her pals whined, trotting to catch up.

"It *did* go in *my* mouth," he muttered. "About a quart, I think." He spat. Spat again. Prayed his mother would never, ever hear about the time he fell into the Grand Canal and, worse, spit (a lot) in public. He'd pay a thousand bucks right now for a ginger beer. And then a shower. This day, which had started horribly, could not possibly get any—

"Oh, hey, there you are."

He blinked and looked up. Standing in front of him with her head tilted and one hand on her hip was one of the most oddly striking women he had ever seen. She was tall—the top of her head came to his nose—with the curvy figure of a fifties pinup star. Her face was a pale, freckled oval, her nose long over a wide, smiling mouth with a plush lower lip. Her eyes were a color he'd never seen before, like storm clouds, or dirty ice. Her hair was a light brown that shone with good health and fell in waves to her shoulders. Her neck was long, but her wrists were delicate and she had small hands. Her feet, clad in tan leather sandals, were extraordinarily long and narrow. She was wearing knee-length black linen walking shorts, a crisp khaki shirt, and a light linen jacket, also black and clearly tailored, with the sleeves shoved up to her elbows. But no jewelry, not even a watch.

It shouldn't have worked. None of it should have worked. She was a mass of contradictions: flawless pale skin but freckles. Tall, but curvy instead of athletic. Long narrow nose, but full lips. Mouth too wide, eyes too narrow and oddly colored. Small hands but big feet. Expensive clothing but no jewelry. And she seemed delighted to see him, the first person that day who was. "I was worried I wouldn't see you again."

Add another contradiction; she had the smooth low voice of a radio-show host or a phone-sex operator, but spoke in a sort of slur, where all her words ran together, with odd inflections on some of the vowels: *Wuz worr'ed I wouldn't s'ya 'gin.*

He stared at her, dripping. "Wait, you *know* me? Do—do I know you?"

"Not really. We weren't formally introduced." She was fighting a smile, and losing. "Why'd you jump in the canal, you big dummy? Blech!" *Why'dya jump inna canal, y'big dummy?*

Blech? Did she just say blech?

"I didn't jump," he whined, "I fell." *And some goddamned sympathy would be goddamned nice, thanks very goddamned much.*

This made her laugh, because she was probably a monster. "How can anyone fall in?" She made a vague gesture, which encapsulated the enormous canal, the vaporettos, the gondolas, the cruise ship passing by in the distance, and the several feet of docks anyone would have to obliviously wander past before plunging into the water. "It's—y'know. It's right there. I thoughtcha musta lost a bet'r something."

"I didn't lose a bet, I'm hungover. Possibly because I lost a bet." Somewhere, he knew, Blake was laughing his ass off. He could sense it. He could sense the mocking laughter.

"Yeah, not surprised, alla vermouth you put away."

"*We were drinking together?*" And he hated—fucking *hated*—vermouth. It had to be a lie. Vermouth, as any sane person knew, was the devil's urine.

"Naw." She was still grinning at him with her wide mouth and weird gray eyes. "*You* were drinking. I was buying, on account of how you tried ta help me."

"Help you? What the hell is going on? What happened last night?" His voice rose to a roar. "How the hell did I end up in Venice?"

"Got me. I tracked you down to introduce you to your daughter, maybe." She gestured to the child standing beside her, a slight brunette who was silently staring up at him with big dark eyes. Dickens orphan big. Victorian London match girl big.

"Jesus!" He'd been so busy gaping (and dripping), he hadn't even noticed the kid until what's-her-face drew his attention to her.

"Hi," the child replied.

"What is going *on?*"

"Don't play dumb," the woman advised. "Unless you're actually dumb. In which case you should try to hide it better."

He opened his mouth to really let her have it, then bent forward and threw up on her shoes.

"Ah hell," she sighed as the child beside her laughed.

Four

The smirking weirdo and the child
   (daughter?)
   (nuh-uh, wrong guy, honey)
helped him back into the hotel, which is when he realized he hadn't grabbed his key card, and had no idea what his
room number was. Or what his hotel was, for that matter; all
he knew was that he woke up in Venice with a horrible hangover, which had been the nicest part of his day.

"You're kidding!" his annoying escort said. "D'you remember the floor at least? No?" To the child: "Who does that?"

"I was trying not to puke," he snapped. "I couldn't be bothered with minor details like where I slept and what country
I woke up in."

"And it worked," she replied, "kinda."

Normally he would have apologized for ruining her sandals and offered to buy replacements, but that was when he
came to another sickening realization. "My wallet! I forgot
that, too!" He was patting his soaked pockets and realized
it was worse than that. Because now that he gave it some

thought, he wasn't sure he'd *forgotten* it. In fact . . . "I lost my wallet!"

"Naw, you didn't."

"The hell I didn't."

"Where was the last place you saw it?" the child asked helpfully.

"I. Don't. Know."

"I said you didn't lose it."

"How the hell would you know?" God, she was infuriating. Her good mood in the face of his very serious problem was aggravating—

Aggravating beyond belief, Blake's voice spoke up helpfully.

Well, it was!

It's like she has no understanding of the seriousness of your situation. Thinks your problems are funny.

Well, she did! The only time she stopped grinning was when he threw up on her. And even then she'd left the child with him, resulting in an awkward chat,

("You're having a bad day."

"I am having an *unfathomably* bad day, sweetie. Um. No offense."

"It's fine. Sweetie."

"It's nothing to do with you personally—"

"It's fine," she insisted.)

ducked into the *bagno delle donne,* and emerged a few minutes later with damp but clean(ish) feet while he and the kid set up camp in the lobby, near the enormous double beverage dispenser. Oh sweet, sweet beverage dispenser, one side lemonade, the other side cold water in which floated a dozen spring strawberries. He guzzled glass after glass, until he could no longer taste vermouth barf; the resulting Mr. Misty headache, in the face of his hangover

("Aaaaagggggghhhh—"

"Press your thumb against the roof of your mouth!"

"—ggggggghhhhh—hey, that worked!")

was no biggie.

Anyway, there was no, repeat, *no* parallel between this woman's behavior and how he related to the rest of the world in general and Blake in particular, and what was with this kid, anyway?

"C'mon," he said abruptly when the woman rejoined him, leaving a trail of wet footprints between the bathroom and the lobby. "Let's talk."

"Oh, goody."

"Let's go over here." He (gently) jerked his head toward the *ristorante* to the left of the lobby. He might be able to get a single slice of bruschetta down his gullet without dying. Once he scraped off the tomatoes and olive oil and garlic. And crumbs. And crust. Maybe. Maybe he wouldn't die. "Have a—" He swallowed a gag. "Snack."

Her ever-present grin reappeared. "My treat, I bet."

"I can pay," the child said quickly.

He could feel his face get hot. God, when was the last time he'd let someone else pay for anything? Years. "I'm not a chauvinist," he snapped. "It's got nothing to do with my penis."

"Thanks for clearing that up. In front of a child, no less."

"Well, it doesn't!"

"I'm only a kid if you count in years. And I can pay."

"That's not necessary, but thank you, hon."

The child didn't look convinced. "Are you sure?"

"I can't believe I'm— Look, it's just we were poor for a long time, so we hated when other people paid."

She blinked, neutral. "Okay."

"It makes sense if you know the background."

"I think it's nice that when you weren't poor anymore, you treated other people."

"*Thank* you," he told the kid, then glared at the woman. She was infuriating, standing there all calm and judgmental, judging him calmly with her judge face. "Look, let's just go sit down and you can tell me—"

"Nope."

God, she was infuriating! "Nope, *what*?"

"Nope, we can't just go sit down."

"Why not?" he (almost) yelled.

"Because of that guy." She pointed, and he turned and beheld a man wearing dark trousers, black belt, shiny black shoes, white shirt, dark blazer, name tag on one lapel (*Matteo*), small gold letters (*Sicurezza*) on a pin on the other. He was polite, he was professional, he spoke terrific English, and he made it clear that people who barfed and then drank half the lobby water could not linger in the bar scraping tomatoes off bruschetta unless they were paying guests.

"Well, you're not," she said once they'd been politely escorted back out to the sidewalk. "Guy hadda point, you gotta admit."

"I *know*."

"You're kind of a bum."

"Why?"

"How should I know? Poor work ethic?"

"No, I mean why do you— Do you find everything funny?" he managed through gritted teeth, his temples pounding with every syllable. God, was this how Blake felt when they argued? How could he stand it?

"Naw." Again with the smirk. "Just stuff you do, I guess."

"I don't think you're funny," the kid said earnestly. At one point, she'd dropped the woman's hand and was now clutching Rake's. He found it oddly flattering. "It's just, funny things seem to happen to you. A lot. Y'know, because . . ." She gestured at his (still) dripping clothes.

He blinked, sighed, and shielded his eyes from the spring sunshine. "I woke up in Venice, which is not where I was yesterday. I have no memory of the hotel. I lost my wallet. I don't know what I'm doing here."

"Yeah, I know." She nodded at the kid. "We both do."

"You know?"

"I mean, I got that. It's basically all you've been bitching about since they fished you out of the canal. Speaking of, don't take this the wrong way or anything—"

"Oh, this'll be good," he snapped.

"—but you're kinda ripe."

"Of course I'm ripe!" he all but screamed. "I fell in that cesspool of a *il Canal Grande*! *E sto incazzato!*"

"What?"

"It's Italian for 'pissed off'! I'm also a polyglot, which my twin brother thinks is a polymath!"

"Okay."

From the kid: "Why does he think—"

"Blake thinks he's so smart, but you know what?"

"Naw, but I bet you're gonna tell us."

"He's not!"

"Yep. Figured."

"Oh my God." He clawed his fingers through his wet hair and shivered in the breeze. "Nothing's gone right since I woke up."

"You said that already." Argh. Hateful child.

"Actually, things were going wrong with you last night, and prob'ly earlier," her companion pointed out with aggravating cheer. She had shrugged out of her light linen jacket and was now holding it out to him. He looked at it, puzzled

(Is she going to wave it at me? Like a bullfighter? It's not red! What kind of a bullfighter doesn't know the red rule?)

so she took it back, stepped forward, and started drying his hair with it with the impersonal efficiency of a hairstylist. "That's what I gathered from what you were saying, anyway."

"Ack! Okay, this is decent of you and all, but I'm ruining your jacket, seriously." And yet, doglike, he refused to move. He might have leaned into the jacket a little. It felt soooo nice to have that revolting water wicked from his hair. "You're literally using your jacket to soak up the shit and germs in my hair. *Thank* you."

"You say," she sighed, "the sweetest things."

"Aw, *stai zitto*.* That means—"

"No need," she said drily. "I can guess what it means. C'mon, let's find a new place to sit down."

"And I'll get ice cream," the child announced. "My treat."

"Right. We'll get comfy and get ice cream and I'll tell you what you forgot."

"Starting with your name." It finally occurred to him that she'd come to him when she'd recognized his voice, suffered to let him puke on her, stuck with him while he tried to gather his senses, came *back* to him after cleaning her weirdly long feet, and allowed the security guard to kick them both out. And all with a small, pale, black-haired child in tow.

She could have taken off at any time. Most people wouldn't have gone near *anything* that came out of the canal, much less came out of the canal spitting and swearing and just generally

---

* "Be quiet."

being an enormo pain in the ass. Yeah, her constant amusement as he struggled through the worst day of his life was aggravating, and the kid was weirding him out a little, and he was beginning to suspect karma *was,* in fact, a bitch. This woman, though, didn't seem to be one.

Like it or not, he was clueless

(and wouldn't big brother love to hear him admit that)

and she, at least, had some answers. And not just about him. The kid—what was the backstory there?

"Yeah, your name," he replied. "I forgot it. Along with everything else."

"No you didn't." She reached out and tucked her hand into his damp paw. "I never told it to you. And you never asked."

"I'm occasionally an asshole."

"No, just . . ." The child trailed off tactfully. "Um, stressed. And a smidge snappy."

"Now that I *did* know," she said, and laughed. He wasn't quite ready to find any of this amusing, but he managed to find a smile from somewhere.

Five

The night before . . .

She was in a strange city in a strange country, and the men following wanted to rob her, hurt her. She darted into a dead-end alley, then had to turn to face them. Nowhere to go.

She took the one with the knife first, reaching out as if asking for help, for mercy, got her hand around the back of his neck, and spun to her right as she yanked him forward, using the momentum to smash him face-first into the bricks. His friend was so startled, she had time to hook her foot between his ankles and toss him off-balance, and a kick to the hinge of his jaw

(ow! of all the nights to wear sandals!)

put him down for nap time.

In those few seconds, the first man had begun to stagger away, not at all happy with what was left of his nose, and expressed his displeasure with a series of nasal, blood-choked yelps. She listened and realized he was hollering for help.

"Seriously? You wanted to take me to Rapetown—or at least Robbedtown—and *you're* yelling for help?"

More yelps. Disparaging remarks about her mother. She was a twat, a whore, she should bugger herself with her own ass

"Uh, what?"

and choke on her father's cock and die and after that she should jump off a cliff

"How would that even work? Logistically?"

onto her worthless father's cock, etc., etc.

"You boys don't get a lot of second dates, do you? It's tough out there. Being single. Ugh, do *not* bleed on me."

She stepped back as he trotted past her, abandoning his comrade in arms/dirt. She bent, fished out the other guy's wallet, helped herself to the cash, cards, and IDs (either business had been booming tonight or his name was Matteas and George and Carrie and he lived in Rome and New York and was also a woman in Arkansas), and left the alley in a much more cheerful frame of mind. *Too bad there weren't a couple more of them; I might've broken a sweat. Self-defense counts as working out, right?*

Right.

Besides, it had been over a month since her last hit. Getting rusty was never smart. In her line of work, it could be fatal or, worse, a ticket to a prison term.

"S'okay, I got 'em!" an all-too-familiar slurred voice assured her, and then here came Rake Tarbell, grinning a big grin and hauling the broken-nose thug back toward the alley.

"No, no!" she scolded. "I just got him to get *out* of the alley; this is all wrong. Bad! You are *bad*!"

"Don' worry. N'one's gonna hurtcha while 'm 'round," he slurred, then promptly stepped on her foot.

"Ow!"

"S'okay, baby. Rake's here."

"You smell like you took a shower in vermouth."

"Nuh-uh, don' wear cologne. S'all me, baby. That's Eau de Rake you're likin'."

And the evening had started *so* well.

Even if she hadn't followed him, she could have found him by listening for the yelling and laughter and splashing and, very occasionally, the tiny explosions. It had been a long day, and the only thing she had to look forward to was a longer night.

And there he was, yukking it up at the bar, hip-deep in men and women, tourists as well as locals, all intent on having a good time while ignoring the gorgeous man-made beach behind them. Lake Como: playground of the rich who were sick of Saint-Tropez but had no interest in scuba diving in Bora Bora.

Eh, cut 'em some slack. It's dark out. Gotta be able to see to appreciate, right? Stop indulging your inner brat because you're still on the outside. Contrary to pop culture clichés, her job didn't always require lurking in darkness. Tonight, yeah. But sometimes she got to skulk in the daytime. She spent a whole day skulking in Boston once, occasionally stopping mid-skulk for strawberry Italian ice. That was a hack that never became a hit; the mark had seen sense, and agreed to her demands. Also: strawberry Italian ice! And the New England Aquarium!

This time of night, the sunbathing gazebos were used for, um, *not* sunbathing—though people were stripped down as though they were—so she kept walking, listening to the sighs and murmurs with not a little envy. How long since she'd been on a date? Or was hit on when not on the job? Or hit on during the job? Ages.

The beachside restaurants kept the drinks coming, from glass after glass of Valtellina-produced wine to *limoncello* to (ugh!) *grappa* to *cappuccino* ordered only by tourists who didn't know any better. She learned quickly the best way to make an Italian wince was to order a cappuccino after lunchtime. And as she got closer to the main bar, she could hear the American.

"I thought I didn' like vermouth, but it's good! Or at least not terrible. D'you know, it used to be medicine? I mean, people used it like medicine? Cuz it tasted bad, I think. S'not, though. Med'cine, I mean. Think I better switch, though. Somethin' not vermouth, so I'm not too hungover. Gotta fly back to the States. Hate flyin' hungover. C'n I have a Rob Roy? Or a Gibson?"*

Yep, that was him: Rake Tarbell, happily drunk off his ass at nine o'clock at night, cheerful and occasionally vulgar, generous with his money and a smile for everyone: the life of the party. She'd never seen someone try so hard to convince themselves they were having a great time. And she'd been to Disney World four times.

And ohhhh, boy, he was practically hanging a PLEASE ROB ME sign around his neck. He'd caught the attention of at least two of the locals, large men with big hands and small eyes, who smiled with their teeth while the rest of their face stayed slack. Dark shorts, dark T-shirts—it was unseasonably warm for spring—and one of them sporting a too-small T-shirt, which he'd probably lifted from a tourist.

Locals . . . or employees of the Colorado asshole. Or in-

---

* Drinks laden with vermouth.

dependent contractors. How much did hired muscle make, anyway?

The life of the par-tay was too blitzed to notice or, if he did, see them as a threat. She wasn't sure he had ever seen anything as a threat. Rake Tarbell was a determinedly happy fellow.

He flaunted his money

"Rob Roys! Like, all over the place! I want wall-to-wall Rob Roys for everyone! Who wants to suck down Roys with me?"

and had huge mother issues

"M'not sayin' she's evil, but she's really kinda terrible, but in a loving an' maternal way. So maternally evil. Meevil?"

which were only topped by his brother issues.

"I mean, he's always all 'Rake is terrible' and I'm all '*You're* the terrible one, you terrible brother who's all terrible because you're terrible!' You know how annoying it is when the biggest, most anal, uptight asshole you've ever known looks *zactly* like you? Guy's gotta lighten up. Gotta smile more and be a dick less."

No question about it, Rake Tarbell was a hot mess. The best part? He had no idea how much trouble he was in. Even if you discounted the Lillith factor.

"No, huh-uh! M'cards work, they've been workin' all day 'cause they work."

Though he might be figuring it out.

"Run the other card! One of 'em's gonna work. *Run all the cards!* Let's keep the party going!"

Hmm. Might take longer than she thought.

Alas. Denied of Rob Roys, he soon staggered out of the bar, beach-bound—though what a broke drunk could do at an Italian man-made beach when it was nearing midnight she hadn't a clue. She *could* imagine what the two grim fellas were going to do. Street crime wasn't terribly common in Lake Como, which wasn't to say it didn't exist. And that's assuming they were your average tourist rollers. They might be involved in something quite a bit darker. Hence, her contract.

Time to be a rodeo clown: "Thanks for the cash!" she called, knowing a shambling Rake wouldn't turn, knowing his followers would. "I'll just try to find our car and then we can hit the next bar! It's over here, right?" In other words, *Don't go after the rider, you big strong bulls, come after the clown. It's what I'm here for.*

Probably shouldn't have dropped out of college. Coulda been a doctor, a teacher. Something with dignity. Or at least a steady paycheck.

So they followed her and she took care of them and one of them had quite a lot of cash and cards, which was excellent.

And . . . she was reassessing her mark. He was a rich, careless jerk who didn't give a thought to anything beyond his own pleasure. Who loved being the life of the party and treated booze like it was some kind of elixir of life.

And had come to help her, though he was so drunk, he could hardly stand.

Dammit. *He's a mark. And a jerk. And possibly a father. Never forget.* She couldn't imagine what his reaction would be. Would he bother curtailing his lifestyle at all? Or just dump his daughter on a series of nannies? What about his brother, his mother, the grandmother? Would they help? Hinder? She had no clue. Families were not her forte.

"Toldja you'd be safe with me, hon." The father of the year belched gently, and swayed like a beginner learning the hula. Which was excellent; it made that whole "never forget he's a jerk" thing much easier.

"You didn't, but that's fine. Some friendly advice, pal? Maybe don't fan yourself with hundred-euro notes at night in the open in a strange country?" Hell, Rake was lucky that the men had been a random smash-and-grab team. Could have been a lot worse, as she'd warned her employer.

"S'not strange, it's Italy!"

"Even so."

"Spoilsport, you're jus' like my brother."

"That's not nice," she said reproachfully. "I know you don't like your brother."

"Cuz he's the worst!" For some reason, reaffirming his brother's awfulness seemed to cheer him, and as they left the alley, he again started toward the beach. This time, she fell into step with him. "Norm'ly I'd buy you a drink, but my cards are broken."

"Thanks. I don't drink. They're not broken."

"No, they are!"

"They're absolutely not broken. They've been canceled by a third party."

"An' I used up all my cash in that betting pool. It was a fas' pool! An' I thought I knew football, but they do it different here."

She smothered a laugh. "They sure do. Don't let the name fool you. The NFL has nothing to do with anything in this part of the world. You're lucky you didn't lose your shorts. What are we doing, Rake?"

"Hi, I'm Rake, s'nice to meetcha."

"Yes, I know. But what are we doing?"

He'd stopped on the shore, the water a foot or so away from his Gucci-clad toes. "You ever skip rocks across a pond? Me neither," he added before she could say anything, "but always sounded fun. S'broken anyway, can't use it."

He shook his wallet like it was a remote with weak batteries, wound up like Roger Clemens (if Clemens were simultaneously drunk and having a seizure), and let it fly. She heard the *sploosh!* as the wallet hit, and sank, and didn't know whether to laugh or laugh a lot. "Aw. Didn't even bounce once. Lame!"

She stared out into the darkness. "I can't believe you did that."

"Me neither. Totally overrated activity! Say, you're kinda cute in a—wuh-oh." Then he bent at the waist, as if bowing to the lake, and threw up what she assumed was a bellyload of Negronis.

Goddammit. If I'd known he was going to spray me with his DNA, I wouldn't have bothered breaking into his hotel room in the first place!

Not for the first time, she questioned the wisdom of introducing Rake to the girl who could be his daughter.

Six

"*I threw my own wallet into Lake Como?*"

"Stop screamin', I hear fine."

"I. Threw. My. Wallet. Into. Lake. Como?" he whispered, eyes big.

"Yep."

"Wow!" From the child. "And it didn't even bounce. No wonder you're upset."

"I'd like to say I can't believe it, but it sounds pretty believable." He sighed and rubbed the bridge of his nose. Then winced, no doubt because he caught another whiff of himself. They were sitting (alone, natch—the one other couple cleared off when they saw/smelled/heard Rake) in one of Venice's fifteen thousand outdoor cafés, Osteria al Portego. He was starting to dry out and, if anything, he looked worse. The spring sunshine beating down on him wasn't helping, either. He was drinking glass after glass of carbonated water (or *acqua frizzante,* as he insisted on calling it each and every time and, needless to say, she was paying), and looking beyond aggravated. "Because I was out of cash and my cards weren't working."

"Uh-huh."

"Then how'd I get to Venice?"

"I don't know." She didn't. She'd had other concerns—meeting up with Teresa to secure the kiddo, checking the progress of the Big Pipe Dream, laundry, etc. "I think you must have talked one of your would-be muggers into giving you a ride, and checked in with his card. Somehow."

She still couldn't figure it. He'd been so drunk, he could hardly stand, but he had tried to come to her rescue, then given her the slip and gotten a stranger—a thwarted mugger!—to give him a ride. Or one of Kovac's hired thugs? And talked him out of his shirt, apparently? Since he'd gotten barf all over his when he'd puked on the beach? Then stole that same bad guy's wallet? Or at least just a credit card? Perhaps he seduced the lobby staff.

Or maybe the men who'd been on *her* tail were now on his, which was disturbing to contemplate.

"I was kinda surprised to see you climbing out of the canal." Surprised, relieved, a little grossed out . . . she thought she'd picked the perfect spot to wait for him with Lillith, but her plan's shortcomings were instantly visible when he swan-dived into a cesspool. Who could anticipate something like that?

"Did not jump. Did not— Wait. So who are you?"

"Oh. Sorry. Claire Delaney."

"Nice to meet you," he said automatically, extending a hand. She shook it, shrugged. It wasn't nice to meet her, and they both knew it.

"And this might be your daughter, Lillith."

"It means 'of the night,'" Lillith said helpfully.

"Of course it does." Bemused, Rake shook her small hand. "Who's your mom?

"Donna Alvah."

"Ah-ha! Argh!" He clutched his temples. "Too soon for yelling—yeah, that's what I thought. I don't know any Donna Alvah. I don't know any Donnas at all. You've got the wrong guy, kid."

"Your DNA might beg to differ."

He snorted. "Sure it might, Claire. Which is— You don't look—I mean, that's an old-fashioned name. Nice, though," he added, as if worried she'd be offended.

"I'm named for my grandmother. But everybody calls me Delaney."

"Of course they do. Now *that* makes sense. Because you definitely look like a Delaney."

"Yeah? What's a Delaney look like?"

"Uh . . ."

"Too tall, with a big mouth and tiny eyes, and big feet with absurdly small hands?" But she said it matter-of-factly. There were roughly eight thousand more important things in life to worry about than her looks.

"Well . . . not *absurdly* small . . ." His gaze dropped to her hands anyway. "Not, uh, Dooneese on *SNL* small."

"Who?"

"Kristen Wiig? Played a character with a big forehead and a snaggletooth and tiny weird doll hands on *Saturday Night Live*?"

"Are we seriously talking about this when you should be worrying about having a daughter but not having money or an ID?"

"Hey, you're right!" At once, he was irritated all over again.

"So you just let me do all that stupid stuff? Agh, shit, sorry. You're not my babysitter."

Wrong. "Right."

"I'm normally way more charming than this."

"I don't doubt it." And she didn't. Even drunk off his ass, Rake had something that pulled people in. "Anyway, as the song says, you were once lost but now you are found. In Venice."

He frowned. "You saw me in Lake Como as well as here? Quite a coincidence."

"Yes," she agreed, straight-faced. "Americans never go to Lake Como and Venice."

"No, I mean . . . how'd you even know where to look?"

"Well . . ."

"Are you a private detective or something?"

"Um . . ."

Seven

"Y'know what city fuck—fuckin' rules? Fucking Venice! Okay, it's just like a regular city with roads, but see, the thing is—it's old! And no roads! Just water! All of it! Goddamned place is drowning, and they even have water buses, y'know, the vaporettos? Cuz, again: water! *C'est merveilleux!* No, wait, wrong language—*è meravigliosa*! That's it, right? So Venice, and all the water—I'm gonna—I'm gonna go there. I mean— I'm not s'pose to. There's kind of a ban, but who keeps track of that stuff? Cuz I like Venice, though it's weird. Maybe 'cause it's weird an' I wanna go back, I think. I like the water streets. And the guys who drive the boats! They always have the best stories. S'different, y'know? Venice! Fucking Venice, here I come!"

Eight

"Oh my *God*."

She had to give it to him, he sounded pretty appalled.

"Well," Lillith said, "you weren't wrong. Venice is great!"

"I hope you picked up on the irony of loving 'fucking Venice' because of the water—"

"I know."

"—and then when you got here—"

"I get the irony!"

"Plop! Into the drink with you."

"Just stop now. God, this, *this* is why vermouth is the devil's urine."

"Don't have to tell me. I've seen you barf."

From Lillith: "Twice!"

She glanced at her watch. Putting Rake at ease in a nice restaurant on a beautiful spring day while she picked up the bill was not on the itinerary. Her employer needed him foundering, lost, broke, and laden with child. *She* needed him (and the forthcoming payoff) safe.

And speaking of, the same pair of "tourists"

(fanny pack and *I ♥* ROME *T-shirt? this is what happens when the bad guys watch too many movies)*

were coming up on them for the third time.

Delaney got to her feet, and Rake was so busy glugging his fourth fizzy water that it took him a few seconds to notice. She cleared her throat with a delicate bark. "So g'bye, then."

"Wait!"

Delaney, already leaving, turned back and raised her eyebrows. "Yeah?"

"You can't just—" He made an all-encompassing gesture that indicated the table, the restaurant, the child, the city of Venice, the country of Italy, the planet of Earth. "Y'know. Leave me in the middle of all this."

"Don't worry," Lillith said. "I have money."

She figured she had another forty seconds before Frick and Frack were on them, and gave him her card. "I'm at the Best Western Olimpia if you want to get a drink sometime. They make a terrific Negroni," she teased.

"Not funny."

"It's a little funny." To Lillith, who was the way she always was, calm and quiet and noticing everything while the adults talked over her. And who had probably deduced Delaney's sudden need to depart. "So you two are all set. Gotta go."

"Thanks for helping me," she replied. She put a small hand on Rake's. "I'll take it from here."

"Good to know." She left, and this time he didn't call her back, which was just as well, because she was about to have her hands full.

Nine

He definitely didn't watch Delaney hurry away until he couldn't see her anymore. Well, maybe he did, but it didn't *mean* anything. He had to look somewhere, right? While he figured out his next move? He didn't want to freak out the kid. And staring after the shapely weirdo who walked into his life, wove a tale of vermouth-fueled shenanigans, dropped a child in his lap, then trotted out (almost sprinted out, TBH) was something to do while he pondered.

But! To business. First things first, he'd check his phone. Call his bank, have them wire money, and maybe FedEx new credit cards. He'd promise a four-figure check to whoever could get funds to him the quickest. Then he'd—

He'd—

No. No-no-no.

No.

"Fuck!" he roared, then felt himself flush as Lillith jumped. "Sorry. I'm not that guy. Well, maybe sometimes."

"Lost your phone?"

"Are you a witch?" he asked with honest curiosity. "That's totally fine, by the way. I'm just curious."

Lillith giggled, dark eyes squinching almost shut in her mirth. They were her most noticeable feature, followed by her short, straight black hair, the bangs cut ruler-straight just above dark brows, with dark blue streaks running through the strands. She was pale and slender except for the swell of her tiny tummy beneath the yellow T-shirt (I'M MY OWN SAFE SPACE!). The same message was on her backpack, and blue jeans and battered sneakers completed the look. "No," she replied. "Not a witch."

"Then how'd you know?"

"You're lost in a strange city with no money and no wallet, which you already knew. What *else* would you freak out over so hard?"

Witch or not, she'd put her finger on the problem: He'd lost his phone. No. That wasn't right. He knew where it was: the bottom of the Grand Canal. He'd had it on him from the moment he slipped it back into his shorts. And it would have taken some real flailing to dislodge it from the secure side pockets designed by the good people at—Cargo? Was that the name of the company, or just what they called pants and shorts with those nifty side pockets that, normally, cradled his belongings (and his balls) in secure comfort?

Focus, moron.

His bitchy Blake inner voice was right. No time to get distracted (again). It wasn't difficult to figure out where he'd lost the thing. But that was a big, big problem. His *life* was in that phone, now marinating in the canal. His numbers. Everyone else's numbers. Account stuff. All his passwords. His *Deadspin* app. Not to mention the means to contact—who? The

Italian version of Social Services? Did he call the cops and report . . . what, exactly? How to get rid of this kid, who definitely wasn't his? He hadn't the vaguest idea how to begin.

Fine. Fucking *fine*. He'd find a café or a library, somewhere with free Wi-Fi, and he'd access his bank that way. They could still move money for him. Amex could still FedEx a new card; he'd be a real person again by 10:00 A.M. local time tomorrow.

Where are you going to sleep tonight? Correction: Where are the two of you going to sleep tonight?

He'd worry about that later. First things first: stealing Wi-Fi. He had to find a place that would (a) let him in so he could (b) borrow someone's phone or laptop in order to (c) use their free Wi-Fi. All this without (d) buying anything, or (e) showing ID. He could eliminate every hotel right off the bat. Oh, and it had to be somewhere close, because he had no money for a vaporetto. Which was too bad, because he loved the vaporettos.

And he had to do it all with a kid in tow.

Normally, none of that would be a problem. Well, maybe the last part. But even then, not much of one: Rake was a vain realist. But normally he didn't start his day by taking a bath in a toilet.

Several humiliating rejections later (Who knew the word *ew* translated into so many languages?), the kid stepped up, grabbed his hand, and put those big dark Matchbook Girl eyes to work. *My daddy and I are lost, his phone was stolen, they threw him in the canal, can we please use your phone to call for help?*

Damn. She was good. Worked on the second guy she tried it on, and—

Wait. That was Italian. Had she been speaking Italian the entire time and he'd only now noticed? The question must have showed on his face, because Lillith replied, "We're in Italy. What else would I speak?"

"But . . . *you're* not . . ."

"No, I'm a 'Merican." She paused, then added helpfully, "I was born in Las Vegas. Then we moved to Colorado. But Mama talked Italian to me as much as English; *her* mama came from Sicily."

"Hey, I was born in Las— *Grazie*," he said fervently, clutching the proffered phone.

The person who lent him his was, ironically, still a kid himself. The dark-skinned teen, who could have been central casting's dream Roma Gypsy but for the blue eyes, was probably a pickpocket—he kept a wary eye fixed for cops—and Rake most certainly wasn't going to judge. Neither was Lillith, who thanked him prettily and got an amused "*Sei la benvenuta, sorellina*"* in response.

He nearly fell on the teenager's neck and wept with gratitude, but contented himself with taking the phone and logging in to his bank's site, which took a hundred times longer than usual without his apps. *You're putting your name and password into a stranger's phone, moron.* Yes. He was. Whatever. He'd move everything but a thousand bucks, fuck it, let the kid take it. He'd never miss it.

Except.

"Fuck!"

The kid laughed at him. Rake supposed he couldn't blame him. If it had been happening to someone else, he probably would have laughed, too. Or at least giggled.

The good news? No need to worry about being robbed when someone's already taken all your money.

---

* "You're welcome, little sister."

*T*en

I might be in real trouble.

The thought had little weight. It was more like an intellectual puzzle, a mental Rubik's Cube. He felt faint concern

(how am I going to figure this out?)

and sometimes his brain got stuck in a confused loop

(the money's gone? the money's gone? the money's gone?)

and Lillith kept intruding

(what am I doing with this kid?)

but that was all. Like he was watching a movie. A great movie with a handsome yet cool star everybody rooted for, including him. *Go, Team Rake!* Was it because he was normally a cool customer, unmoved by the ups and downs of life? Someone who kept his head no matter what was going on, and thus could tackle any problem that came his way with collected, quick confidence?

Nope; that was Blake. Rake tended to roll with the punches (or drunken Lake Como shenanigans). Even now he kept thinking, *I'll just grab my credit card and— No I won't. I can just use my phone to— No I can't. I've got enough cash left to—*

No I don't. His brain, used to using money to solve everything since he was a teenager, was having trouble keeping up with current events: There were no cards. There was no money. There was a kid, though. For some ungodly reason.

He explained this to Lillith, who was heroically unperturbed. "I told you," she said. "I have money."

"I'm not taking your babysitting money, hon."

"I'm too young to babysit."

"And I'm too old to take a loan from a kid."

"Possible daughter," she corrected politely.

He bit back a groan, found them a small bench in the Giardinetti Reali, and tried to think of his next move, tried to think past the drumbeat of *your money's gone your money's gone your money's gone,* tried to squash the panic.

Okay. First. It probably wasn't gone. His bank was half a planet away; it was likely an electronic snafu, or their system was down, or something that was completely explainable during business hours—what time was it in Las Vegas, anyway?

Whatever the problem was, he was worth about twenty million, and that much money doesn't just disappear overnight, not for real. If nothing else, his mother and/or Blake would have warned him, since their names were on all the paperwork, too: When his father had died playing *9 1/2 Weeks* foodie sex games with his cutie of the month,* their mother had overseen the trust until he and Blake came of age, and now they all shared the fortune. They weren't *all* broke, ergo Rake wasn't broke. Not for real. Not—y'know— permanently.

But what to do in the meantime? Borrow another phone

---

* The sordid details can be found in *Danger, Sweetheart.*

(and oh God what fun *that* would be) and reach out to Blake for help?

Except Blake was one of the seven people in America who didn't do Facebook. At all. Not even ironically. He barely did email; he sure as shit didn't tweet. He preferred phone calls and—yeesh!—snail mail, and he'd only started texting two years ago, the goddamned Luddite. Thought social media "encapsulated all the ills of the world" and wanted nothing to do with it.

Okay, then: Mom.

Except his mother was stuck in Sweetheart, North Dakota. Yeah, he was stuck, too, but he wasn't stuck somewhere that sounded like a place you were sent if you lost a bet, somewhere they'd outlawed dancing in the fifties, and where there was only one streetlight. She had problems of her own—boy, did she!—and he sure as shit wasn't going to add to them. Was this selflessness? Or just the pure natural instinct of a grown man not wanting his mommy to know he was in such a weird dumb mess?

Hey, Mom, you know how I only call you when I need something, and maybe on your birthday? Listen, sorry you're hip-deep in family problems, here's another one: Someone stole all my money and I'm stuck in Venice. That's Italy, not California. Come get me, Mommy? Bring cash and Snickers. Yeah, that was a whole world of *no. Also, you're maybe a grandma! Some stranger dumped a kid on me we don't know is mine and then ran off. So there's that.* Which needed to be straightened out ASAP.

There was the nuclear option, but he'd have to be a lot more than broke and stranded in a foreign country with shit drying in his hair and saddled with a cute second-grader before he'd take that step. Maaaaaybe if he was in the ICU. Or had lost the use of his legs, brain, and dick. If he was hanging off the edge of a cliff by one hand and his fingers were slipping. *Maybe.*

The consulate? Nope; they were the reason he'd been appalled to wake up in Venice in the first place. Venice was beautiful, the food was incredible, the gondoliers had the best stories, and still he'd had no plans to come back after his last visit. The misunderstanding had been . . . extreme. The kind where grim men in uniforms held on to your passport and asked questions ad nauseum, then finally gave it back, only to immediately provide an "escort" to the airport.

The cops?

Maybe. But only if the consulate mess hadn't spilled over to the local police, and he wouldn't know that until he talked to them. Which would be a bad time to find out the knives were still out for him at the Consular Agency: when he was surrounded by cops. "You guys better treat me right! I was rich yesterday!" Pass.

He couldn't linger in the park much longer, either; loitering was frowned upon when you smelled like he did, and there were laws against begging here. Maybe he could find another friendly homeless person. *Thanks for the phone, I don't suppose you can arrange lodging, too, right? Sorry about that whole homeless thing, by the way. Oh, a sandwich? For me? No, I couldn't. Well, maybe just one bite. And one for the kid on my left.* Ugh.

Rake plunged his hands in his pockets past the wrists and tried to think. There had to be something he—

"We could ask Delaney for help."

He jumped. The kid had a near-uncanny ability to fade from his consciousness; she didn't fidget or hum or kick her feet or any of the things kids did when they were bored (and which he still did on occasion). No one would ever feel the need to buy Lillith a fidget spinner. She just sort of faded into the background, blending like adorable chubby-cheeked camouflage until . . .

"That's an idea." He felt for the business card he'd absently tucked away after Delaney left, and now he pulled it out and looked at it. Plain white, neat black lettering, nothing embossed: I. C. Delaney. Exactly the kind he'd have if he ever had business cards. Well, maybe with everything in a kind of shrieking red font. And I. C.? What was that supposed to mean? Didn't she say her name was—God, what was it?—something from one of the hotties in *The Breakfast Club*. No, not Judd Nelson. Definitely not the geek who grew up and turned psychic—Claire! That was it, Claire Delaney, who for some reason called herself Delaney, except when she was handing out business cards, when she called herself I. C. Delaney.

She'd even told him where she was staying, probably just trying to be nice—never in a hundred years did he think she was trying to pick him up, not after the horrors she'd endured in his company—but still: He had that info in his brain somewhere.

Somewhere he'd never stayed, somewhere cheap, relatively speaking. He even remembered feeling mild sympathy for anyone who had to stay somewhere less than luxurious in a city with the Ruzzini Palace and Palazzina G. Not that her hotel sounded terrible; it simply wasn't the best—the best—best—Best Western Olimpia! Yessss! Finally things were going his way! His brain was actually engaging and being helpful! He'd actually figured something out without Delaney's help! For the first time that day! Suck it, Blake!

"We should probably get going," Lillith the Uncanny was saying. "Her hotel's a couple of kilometers from here."

"How d'you even know— Never mind." He flipped the

card over and saw she'd written the name of the hotel on the back, like she knew he'd have trouble remembering, and where it happened to be at the kid's eye level. Like Delaney figured he'd need a mental nudge. Which was annoying, and not just because she was right.

"You think you're soooo smart," he told the card, then put it back in his pocket. "And you . . ." To Lillith, who once again put her small hand in his. "You're *really* smart. C'mon, let's go to I. C. Delaney."

Eleven

Fifty miles! Fifty fucking miles from point A to point B, all because Delaney had a hard-on for Best Westerns. Well, okay, three. Three miles in a city that offered at least a dozen ways to get lost with every turn. Three miles during which every step made him worry the top of his skull was going to implode until his brains squirted out of his nose. Three miles during which Lillith never once complained, though she offered to pay for a vaporetto. (He'd been tempted for a few seconds, but then pride—stupid, nauseating pride—won out.) Three miles during which he cursed Past Rake for leaving Present Rake in such a mess. Future Blake needed to get busy on a time machine so he could go back and beat the shit out of Past Blake, and oh thank God here it was.

He couldn't help but note the irony; the hotel was in the Piazzale Roma, the one place in Venice accessible by car, if he'd had one. And just a few feet from the vaporetto stop, if he'd let Lillith use her lawn-mowing money (was she even big enough to mow lawns?) to buy them tickets. *Venice, you cruel, ironic bitch.*

He tried not to stagger as he entered the lobby

(dignity, man! where'd you hide yours?)

and almost succeeded. He definitely didn't look around in desperate hope for a drink dispenser full of water and lemon slices as he didn't limp up to the front desk and explain what he was doing there. He let his eyes

(I'll give you a thousand bucks if you don't throw me out. I just don't have it on me right now.)

do the abject begging and sniveling for him. And Lillith's eyes.

But the clerk was ready for him. Them. "*Ciao, Signor Tarbell. La signorina Delaney ti ha chiesto di incontrarla presso dietro l'angolo al nostro ingress di carico.*"*

"She knew I was coming?" he asked, dumbfounded, and got a polite smile and a shrug in reply before the clerk turned away and picked up a ringing phone. "She knew I was coming," he said to Lillith, and it was still hard to process. Then: "Did he say loading entrance?"

"Yes."

Every time. Every time I think this day can't get weirder . . . it's like the day keeps hearing that and accepts it as a personal challenge. STOP accepting the challenge, weird day!

And Lillith doesn't just speak Italian. She's fluent—she knew he said "loading entrance," which is not an expression commonly found in remedial How to Speak Italian *texts.*

What a cool kid!

"You're an unnaturally calm child," he told her. "Which is not a criticism at all." He'd tried asking her about her mother

---

* "Hello, Mr. Tarbell. Miss Delaney asked you to meet her around the corner at our loading entrance."

and how she'd come to Venice and where Delaney fit into the mess, but Lillith had just blinked up at him and politely said, "I don't want to talk about that right now, please." He took the hint.

"Thanks. I have really low blood pressure." When he just blinked, she elaborated: "Hypotension?"

"I know what low— Never mind." He led her back out and around and found the loading area, and there she was, helping a few other women load boxes into an SUV, I. C. Delaney in the yummy flesh. "Oh, hey," she said with a wide smile when he limped up to her (except he definitely didn't limp). "Was wondering when you two were gonna swing by. Hey, gorgeous."

"Hi, Delaney!" Lillith waved as if she were afraid Delaney couldn't see her from three feet away.

"You sound relieved." He looked around. "What *is* this?"

"Charity" was the reply as she heaved the last box into the SUV.

"Oh, like a marathon?"

An inelegant snort greeted that. "Marathons aren't really charities. Well, technically they are, because technically they raise money, but still."

He grinned, both at her disgruntled expression and her matter-of-fact delivery. And God, that felt good. He hadn't felt like smiling much today. "So, the literal textbook defini-tion of *charity*, then."

She puffed a hank of hair out of her eyes. "Sure. But run-ners will always run. It's just, occasionally they'll do the thing they love to do and would do anyway to also raise money."

"What, they can't have fun? They have to raise money *and* be miserable?"

She blinked and straightened, patted the roof of the SUV,

and then stepped back as it cruised off, waving once. None of the women had spoken, just quietly went about loading until they left. "Huh. Well. Didn't think of it like that." Then she giggled. Giggled! The delicate sound should have sounded strange coming from the lanky woman, but it was just charming. Like her grin.

"How's your day been?" she asked Lillith, who shrugged.

"He still thinks I'm a horrible mistake."

"I do not!" Shocked, Rake stared down at her. "You're worlds from being a horrible *anything*. I'm just not your dad, and you shouldn't be with me. Not that there's something wrong with me. It's just—you should be with your mom, uh . . ."

"Donna Alvah." This from Delaney and Lillith in unison.

"Yeah, about that." He fought the urge to jab a finger at Delaney. "How do *you* know the kid's mother but I don't? And where *is* her mother? Why are you even here with her? Who are you? Are you some sort of one-woman international child-placement agency? What the hell is going on?"

"It's a long story."

"I knew you were gonna say that."

"What other kind of story could it be?" Lillith wondered aloud. "If it was a short one, she could have told it to you by now."

"Good point. See, Delaney? Lillith's got your number."

"Literally," the kid added, holding up a card identical to the one in Rake's pocket.

He laughed. "I'm pretty sure she's one of the smartest people I've ever met. And I've met Blake Tarbell."

"Fair enough. We're finished here, so." She spoke briefly with the three remaining women, hugged one of them, then turned back to Rake and Lillith. He was morbidly aware that Delaney's—friends? coworkers? sisters?—were staring at him. "C'mon with me."

They fell into step beside her as she left the loading area and headed to the front of the hotel. "You don't seem surprised to see me," Rake pointed out. "Us."

"Nope."

Now that he was under her steady gray-eyed gaze, he was having trouble finding the words to explain how his day had gone after she'd run off. *Am I seriously trying not to sound pathetic? After throwing up on the woman? Twice?* "This is going to sound incredible—"

"Try me."

"—but I've been robbed."

"We've been over this. You threw your own wallet into Lake Como. You mugged yourself."

"Not that!" he snapped over Lillith's giggles, then had to grin because, yeah, the whole thing was absurd, but he could see the humor in it. Sort of.

"Listen, my bank accounts are empty. I don't know if it's an online snafu or an accounting screwup or just a mistake, but technically, I'm broke."

"And he won't borrow from me," Lillith put in. "Out of a misguided notion of—uh—actually, I don't know why he won't borrow."

Because, among other things, you couldn't go anywhere or do anything in Venice for less than twenty euros. He wouldn't embarrass her by asking for money she didn't have. "Keep your snow-shoveling money." To Delaney: "Like I said, technically, I'm broke."

"Technically, that must suck."

"It does suck," he agreed. "I'm sure it'll get straightened out in a day or two, but in the meantime I can't reach my family and . . . I . . . we . . ." He glanced at Lillith, the hotel, and Delaney. The sun was setting, turning the canal gorgeous shades of orange and pink and cream, and tourists rushed around and past them, intent on dinner and, later, the night life. He wanted to be one of them very, very badly.

Come on, Delaney. Pick up on the hint. It's been the most humbling day of my life, and that's counting the time I fell asleep in Bio and fell face-first into my dissected frog. I had frog kidneys stuck to my cheek until lunch! Nobody told me!

Nope. No joy. She was opening the lobby door now, and walking toward the elevators. He hesitated, having no clue what to do next, and nearly wept in relief when Lillith said, "He hates borrowing and he's too proud to ask if we can stay with you tonight. He doesn't know you'll say yes."

"Oh my God I love you," he muttered under his breath, earning another giggle from Lillith the Great and Powerful.

Delaney glanced back and said, "Well, come on, then."

"Nice work," he whispered, and Lillith smiled at him, then let out a yelp as he practically lifted her off her feet as he galloped to Delaney.

Yessssss! She was leading him to her room! Her bed! Oh dear God, her *shower*! He might never come out. He might sleep in the shower, eat in the shower. He might vacation in the shower, grow old and die in the shower.

Of course, if Delaney wanted him in her bed, that was completely fine. Yes, she spent an annoying amount of time laughing at his troubles, but she was also the only real help he'd had since he woke up (besides the homeless teenager who'd lent him a phone). And he'd be lying if he said he didn't like the look of her: those long legs, those clear gray eyes, that wide, pretty mouth, that . . . um . . . that *mouth* . . .

Oh, but . . . Lillith.

Right. No nooky with a kid looking on. No *anything* with a kid looking on.

First things first. He'd beg a shower, they'd figure out sleeping arrangements, he'd eat something, and he'd get the scoop on the kid and finally hear about the sequence of events that led to three strangers bunking in a Venetian Best Western for the night.

Then: He'd get his life back.

Y'know, eventually.

Twelve

"What the hell is all this?" he asked, staring so hard that he thought his eyeballs might dry out.

"Cover," Delaney said shortly. She had brought them up to her room and, while Lillith used the bathroom, had gone straight to a safe underneath the coffeepot. She keyed in the combo, checked to make sure something was in there

(passport?)

then rummaged around and closed it again; when she stood, her hands were empty.

"What?"

"Cover," she replied. "Did you lose your hearing along with your money?"

"No, but the way this day's been, it wouldn't surprise me if I spontaneously went deaf from full-body exposure to toxic canal water."

Delaney snorted, because she was a heartless wench.

Rake looked around her room, which was too big to be a standard and too small to be a suite, at the serviceable desk and chair, a lovely big bed with the de rigueur padded headboard, a small kitchen area, and a great big window overlooking the hotel garden. All of which was eclipsed by the Easter baskets, toys, candy, and school supplies on every surface save the bed. And Peeps. Loads and loads of Peeps, pink Peeps and yellow Peeps and blue and lavender Peeps, Peeps as far as the eye could see, a goddamned rainbow of Peeps. He had drowned in the canal and this was Hell.

"Cover for what, exactly?" Was Delaney some kind of rogue Easter bunny? With a Peep fetish?

"Never mind."

"Oh, okay. Not *too* mysterious."

The toilet flushed and Delaney lowered her voice. "Have you thought about what you're going to do about Lillith?"

"I haven't the faintest idea," he replied, and he was pretty sure he'd never uttered a truer statement. "And why would I? We don't even know if I'm her dad! Which I'm probably not, since I never knew anyone named Donna. Where's her mother? Surely she can straighten this out."

"Ah. That. It's a long story."

"And a mysterious one, too, I'm betting. Because that's the way things are going."

"It hasn't been fun and games for Lillith, either," she snapped. "You could try thinking about someone who isn't *you*. Just for a change of pace. Just to see if you like it."

He made a concerted effort to stomp on his temper. "This is the third time I've asked for details about her and/or her mysteriously missing mother and been put off."

"Third?"

"I asked Lillith while we were walking over here."

"You—you did?"

"Well. Yeah. It was a three-mile walk. The conversation was lagging."

Delaney looked and sounded—could it be?—tentative. "What'd she say?"

"That she didn't want to talk about it."

"Oh. What'd you say?"

"I said okay, and we didn't talk about it. Then I took a break to dry-heave into a bush, and we continued on until we got here, where we're still not talking about it."

"Well." She leaned against the dresser, knocking packs of Peeps onto the floor as she did so. "You can't blame her."

"I have no idea whether or not to blame her, because I don't know what's going on! You can't pop up out of nowhere—twice—and then dump a kid on me you *think* might be mine and expect me to have her enrolled in Meadows by the end of the day. Especially since, hello, I'm not exactly equipped to do the dad thing, especially today."

"Enroll in what?"

He waved away the Meadows School. "It's a pricey private school in Vegas. Although it wouldn't be my first choice, 'cause I wouldn't want her to grow up into an entitled rich d— We're getting off track."

"That's a fair point about my word," she admitted. "But you won't have to take my word for it much longer—"

"I'm not taking your word for it at all."

"—because we'll have the DNA results in a couple of days."

What

the

fuck?

When he was sure he wouldn't scream, he said, "It sounded like you said you're waiting on DNA results. But that can't be right, since I haven't submitted DNA for such a test."

"Now, don't turn this around on me," she began, and he groaned.

"Literally every time someone says that, it's because they want the focus off whatever horrible fucking thing they *just did*."

"Hey, it's my job."

"It's your job to hang out in Italy to procure DNA for a test you arranged without the subject's permission?"

She shrugged. "Kinda."

He pressed his fingers to his temples and rubbed. *Squash . . . urge . . . to strangle . . . gorgeous nutjob . . .* "Okay, first? That's weird. You're a weird girl, Delaney. Second, how the hell did you manage to get your hands on my precious, precious DNA, annnnnnd now I'm remembering that I barfed on you a couple of times. It's my own fault," he admitted. "I was practically giving it away!"

Delaney made a strange noise, like she was trying to turn a laugh into a cough. "The point is—"

"You have a weird job that requires you to do weird things."

"—you won't have to take my word about Lillith when the results come in. So."

"So . . ."

"So you'll know she's yours—or not—and you can arrange your life accordingly."

He could only stare. "Just like that."

"Yep."

"It's just that easy."

"I don't think it'll be easy at all, but that's how it is."

"And if I'm not her father?"

"Then you're not her father and I go to the next guy on the list. That's why I'm here. I was hired to track down and test the candidates, and give the lucky winner custody of Lillith."

"Right, but . . . if I'm not the proud papa, what happens next?" Not that it was any of his business, but from where he was standing, this looked like a barely contained mess. So once he was out of the picture, where did that leave Lillith?

Not that he cared.

"Then it's no longer your problem."

"And I'm one of the names on your list because . . ." He'd bet the money in his wallet in the canal that the safe held her list, and probably some other goodies, too.

"Because her mother said so. And in nine years, Donna Alvah never lied to me."

"Ah-ha!" He felt like jumping up and down but was wary of crushing Peeps and chocolate Easter eggs. "Now we're getting somewhere. Except we aren't, because you've said that name before and weren't forthcoming either time." A pause while her words sank in, then: "You've known Lillith's mom for almost a decade?"

"We served together."

"Like, in the army? You look like you're in your early twenties. Are you a veteran? And—"

She cut him off with an impatient gesture. "We were friends and then we weren't. She went for a different life and that was fine. But then she got into trouble and her default kicked in, which was to make a big mess and then disappear. And that's when everything went tits-up," Delaney finished with more than a hint of bitterness.

Whoa. "You're mad at her," he realized aloud. At least that's what it sounded like. Christ. Even when he was getting details, he wasn't really getting details. "Wait, this Donna person, she went into hiding? Like a WITSEC thing?"

"No, Lillith did."

"Why? And when?"

"That's where it gets murky—"

"Oh, *that's* where?"

"—because the thing is—"

"The thing is, Mama hid me and got run over, so it took a long time to find me," Lillith said from the bathroom doorway, and then burst into tears.

Thirteen

Five minutes later, Rake was putting yet another freshly wrung-out washcloth onto Lillith's forehead. "There. And when this one stops helping, I'll get you another one. If you want it."

"Why do you keep doing that?" Delaney asked impatiently.

"Because he doesn't know what else to do," the child answered. She patted the washcloth. "It's okay. I'm better now."

"I'm so sorry about your mom. And that you got upset. Can I get you anything else?" Rake glanced around the suite for something to give her and cursed his lack of funds yet again. The Bible? No. The room service menus? No. The tiny shampoo? "Do—do you want a hundred Peeps? I could probably make it five hundred if you needed it. Just wait until I leave before you start gobbling them up. I couldn't bear to watch."

Lillith sniffed. "You can't leave. You're my dad, maybe."

"It was—uh—I was only joking. About leaving." Probably. "Do you—do you feel like talking?"

"No. But I will anyway." The child sighed and sat up, and Rake deftly caught the washcloth as it fell. She fussed with her shirt, smoothing it over her belly, and then speared him with that disconcerting direct gaze. *When this kid isn't going totally unnoticed, she can glare into your soul. It's . . . kind of awesome, and now that I think about it, Mom does the same—*

He cut off that line of thought. Fast.

"My mother," she began, as if reciting a book report, "did bad things for good reasons. She took things from bad men. And sometimes she found out they did something bad, and they'd do nice things for her so no one *else* would find out they did something bad."

Jesus Christ in a handcar. "So she was a thief and a blackmailer. Ow!" Rake rubbed his now-throbbing foot and glared at Delaney. "Really? I'm the one who's out of line in this story?"

"And one day," Lillith continued loudly, sounding like an aggrieved elementary school teacher, "she found out something *really* bad about someone who lived in Colorado, too. Something much, much worse than what she was looking for. And while Mama was making a plan for us to run, she . . . she died."

"Please don't take this the wrong way, honey," he begged, "but where do I fit into this story?"

"Nowhere. That's the problem." This from Madame Spoilsport in the corner. Well, near the corner. "I didn't know any of this until it was almost too late. It might still be too late. And nobody counted on your coming to Venice."

"Yeah, including me."

"But here you are. And that's very curious. But, ultimately, it's not as important as Lillith's safety and well-being, which are the top priority."

There was an expectant (insulting!) pause, which Rake defensively broke. "What? I'm not gonna argue that. Why would I argue that? She's a kid who lost her mom and people have to look out for her. A mom I didn't know, by the way. Just to reiterate. Again."

"That's because she changed her name after the Noodle Incident."

For a second, Rake thought he was going to have a stroke. Half his body seemed to go numb and the other half heated up, like he was some kind of weird Iceman/Human Torch Marvel hybrid. He opened his mouth and let out a tiny croak, all the noise he could muster, since his saliva had dried up.

Finally: "The Noodle Incident we promised each other we'd never talk about. Which is why she changed her name to Nedra Naseef," he said, and if he'd had any doubts, Lillith's beam was answer enough.

Fourteen

Eight years ago

"This is no way to live," the woman who was going to change her name from whatever it was

(*Debra? Dana?*)

to Nedra Naseef commented. "I'm not reliving my childhood. The first time was bad enough."

"Guh," Rake replied, because he was too exhausted to attempt words of more than one syllable. Armed with an out-of-date Fodor's, he and the cute brunette he met at the Bridge of Sighs had decided to find the infamous Cruising Pavilion and christen it. And by "met," he meant "was bowled over by." In fact, he'd heard her

("It's called the Bridge of Sighs because it was the last thing prisoners saw before they were locked up! For years! And sometimes tortured! Brutally! It is not romantic in the *slightest*, morons!")

before he saw her. One thing about American tourists,

you can always spot them. Or hear them. Often without trying! His admiration only increased when he saw the petite brunette with the curves of a courtesan and the mouth

("Oh, *I'm* out of line? You're the shithead who thinks it's romantic to take a selfie where dead men were chained up! So go fuck yourself!")

of a Red Sox fan.

"Bad enough I'm falling back into bad habits," Nedra was saying, pulling her woefully grass-stained shirt back over her head, "but the Cruising Pavilion isn't even a club. It's an exhibition. A closed one," she added in a mutter, as if an art exhibit should be open at 1:30 A.M. on a Tuesday.

"Toldja." Hey, two syllables! Maybe his heart rate was starting to come down. "But I like how this little park served as a handy substitute."

"Not to mention," she continued, as if he hadn't spoken, "it's an exhibit about homosexual cruising."

"*What?*" He sat up from where he'd sprawled on the grass. "But that means we did it all wrong!"

She gaped at him for a moment, then let out a string of giggles. "We'll never be able to hold our heads up in high society again. Or low society."

"Oh, the humanity," he agreed.

"And don't take this the wrong way, but we're never to speak of this again."

"The screwing-up gay sex part, or the—"

"All of it. Any of it. It's gonna be the thing we know about but never talk about, like the Noodle Incident trope."

"Weird. But fine. But I think you're overreacting. It's not like we've done anything wr—"

"*Polizia! Sei in arresto per aver commesso un atto osceno in un luogo pubblico!*"

"Oh hell," she groaned. "It's my senior prom all over again."

"*Osceno?* Obscene?" Rake yelped at the cops coming forward. "It was beautiful, dammit!"

Fifteen

". . . so then we paid the five-hundred-euro fine and went our separate ways and I never saw her again. And we were sort of . . . uh . . . banned."

"Uh-huh."

"From the city of Venice."

"Oh."

"For life."

"Ah."

"Our kids, too. They were pretty mad—the cops, the mayor, the guy in charge of keeping the park sex-free . . ."

"That's not fair," Lillith protested. She tossed the latest wet washcloth on the floor for emphasis. "I didn't do anything. I don't want to be banned. What if I want to go to the Accademia di Belle Arti?"

All Rake could do was shrug an apology and wonder, yet again, when he was going to wake up.

"So you did know Donna," Delaney said, blatantly ignoring the beauty of the tale of tender lovemaking to hone in on one teeny insignificant detail.

"Briefly." He wasn't sure how much of this was appropriate in front of Lillith. None of it would be his first guess. "Okay, so—I was wrong, I did know your mom." And to Delaney, because it was time to face up to the inevitable: "You said the DNA results will be back in a couple of days?"

"Yep. But that's not your only problem."

"My missing money," he said glumly.

She waved away the looming problem of his vanished fortune. "Not that, either."

"There are bigger problems than a mystery kid—no offense, Lillith—and finding myself broke in a forbidden city with dried shit in my hair?"

"Yes. Because we don't know if Donna's death was an accident. Myself, I'm not a fan of coincidences. But I don't like conspiracy theories, either. Here it is: Donna found out something, either by accident or because she was falling into old habits. That I can tell you for sure. But I don't know what it was. She sent me some paperwork the week she died. . . ."

"What kind of paperwork?"

"Some letters, and the fact that she thought you might be Lillith's father. She also referenced a flash drive . . . but that's it. I don't know where the flash drive is or what was on it. And I couldn't make that my first priority, because finding Lillith was my first priority. And now that she's with me, there are still questions to be answered. And if Donna's death *was* an accident, that still leaves the issue of Lillith's minority."

"I can take care of myself." The child sniffed.

Delaney smiled. "I don't doubt it, but that's not what your mother would have wanted. Right?"

"Right."

"All that sounds bad," Rake observed.

"Tell me. So we have to figure out what's going on pretty

damned quick, because we're *way* behind. *And* we have to keep Lillith safe, because she could very well be in danger." To Lillith: "Sorry to be so blunt."

"You don't have to apologize. Mama always said it's worse to keep quiet about trouble. . . ."

Oh, is that what the thieving blackmailer taught you?

". . . and *pollomerda* to pretend it's not there."

Rake blinked and wondered if society's rules against children saying *chickenshit* in casual conversation applied if the child in question swore in another language.

Best not to dwell.

"And that's where I come in," he guessed.

"Unfortunately."

"Hey!"

"You're plan D," Delaney continued, "the backup plan to the backup plan's backup plan."

"I'll have you know I've never been plan D in my life," he said hotly. "I'm always plan B!" *Huh. This is a weird thing to brag about.*

"And we need you both for this." She gestured to the room with candy on literally every surface. Even the windowsills!

"You said it was cover."

"It is. But that doesn't mean there's not work to do. Don't worry, the charities are real, and we really will deliver the Easter baskets."

"I can honestly say I wasn't worried about either of those things."

"But we need the bad guys looking in the wrong direction."

"If there *are* bad guys." He knew it was childish to cling to the hope that the people who might or might not have murdered Lillith's mother didn't exist and this was all some odd misunderstanding culminating in his reversal of fortune, but he couldn't help hoping.

"While my friends and I are investigating, you'll be here doing this, which, while tedious, is safer than you and Lillith being out and about on your own. Now listen, Rake—this is important."

"As opposed to all the unimportant stuff you've already told me?"

She ignored the sarcasm as well as Lillith's giggle. "You have to look like you're doing anything but protecting someone incredibly valuable. You have to make people believe you're an oblivious American idiot who's just in town to have fun and you aren't worried about a thing except getting everything in your wallet replaced because you jumped into the canal—"

"Fell!"

"—like a typical American moron. And you lost your passport during your drunken shenanigans in Lake Como the night before. And you can't go to the cops because you defiled—"

"Hey!"

"—a public park. So you're earning your keep by filling and delivering Easter baskets and just killing time until your paperwork's replaced."

"This sounds like the plot of a terrible on-demand series."

"Tough nuts." Delaney shrugged. "It's what we've got."

"But that'll take—" All the chocolate and pastels and Peeps

(they're STARING at me)

were making it hard to think. "Hours."

"Longer."

"Maybe a couple of days, depending."

"Yep. And remember: Lillith is the priority, and you don't exist."

"I totally agree." *Wait.* "Of course I exist!"

"Nope."

Were he and a woman he'd just met really debating his existence in a room full of eggs and baskets and fake Easter grass and Peeps while his possible illegitimate child looked on? And, speaking of that, wasn't it past Lillith's bedtime? What *was* her bedtime? And shouldn't she be in school, instead of hiding in hotel rooms? Who was in charge of that stuff? Given how self-possessed and mature she seemed, Rake wouldn't have been surprised if Lillith was in charge of that stuff. "Delaney. I absolutely exist."

She shook her head so hard, long dark waves of hair tumbled into her face, and with a flick of her head, she jerked them back. "Not without paper. Not without plastic, not these days. You're officially a nonentity—at least as far as the Italian government is concerned."

"You leave them out of this. And what the hell is with that accent, anyway?" he demanded, aware that he was deflecting even as he deflected like crazy. "Where are you from?"

"Minnesota."

"Oh." That explained it. Not really a twang, and not quite Canadian. A drawl, but not really. A twang, but not quite. It was like the people there couldn't make up their mind, and the only news that ever came out of Minnesota was weird news. Or updates on the Mall of America. "I really don't get *Fargo.* The movie or the show."

"Yeah, I'm not surprised, but see, the thing about the movie— Wait. Really? This is what you want to talk about?"

"No," he admitted.

She'd leaned forward to discuss *Fargo* but now settled back. "Besides, even if you weren't persona non grata, even if you had tons of ID to show the consulate, which you don't, which is your own fault, which they'll think is hilarious—"

"I wouldn't tell them the truth, *duh*." God, what was it about the woman that brought out his inner middle schooler? He only used *duh* with Blake, and then only under enormous provocation. Like when Blake spoke. Or breathed. "I'd say I was mugged."

"So your very first instinct, when dealing with the Italian consulate, is to lie like a rug. When you're already in their black books for defiling—"

"Hey!" He nodded toward Lillith. *A little respect, please, for the child who might have been conceived during the defiling.*

"Fair point," she said and, to his surprise, dropped the subject. Except not really, because the follow-up was, "And think about this: Even if you had lots of backup ID to prove you're who you say you are, which you don't, it would still take a while for them to get you a new passport. What would you do in the meantime?"

"Starve and die?" he guessed.

"Or work for your room and board, help me with Lillith, and help us figure out what's going on. And if all three of those sound like too much, at least the first two."

"Fine. I'm in."

She smiled, an utterly wicked grin that was as charming as it was off-putting. Off-charming? "Wise choice. And I'll tell you something else—you can use the shower first. In fact, I'm gonna have to insist on it."

Lillith coughed politely. "Me, too."

He grimaced. By now the vile water had dried and his hair was in clumps he was afraid to touch. The thought of a shower was almost enough to make him sob. Or shout—but a glance over at Lillith, who had somehow dropped off to sleep in the middle of the negotiating—put paid to that idea.

Poor kid, he thought, almost knocking Delaney over in his haste to get to the bathroom. *Tough breaks. Tough life.*

A sad story, sure. But hopefully not his problem. From a genetic standpoint, anyway.

Sixteen

Drunk Rake was annoying yet fun, and Canal Rake was smelly yet bitchy, and New Dad Rake was intense yet flighty, but Desperate Rake was adorably/selfishly clueless.

There had been, as her employer had warned, considerable whining. But not as much of it after the shower and new clothes, both of which had delighted him. The minute the shower spray hit him, she heard him let out a long, rumbling groan of pleasure, an amazing sound that she felt in her belly, of all places. Gotta give it to him, that voice was verbal velvet, and if his adventures that day had hidden his appeal, they hadn't obliterated it.

When he's on his A game, guy's prob'ly a force to be reckoned with. Good thing for me he's not, then, huh?

And, of course, the night before he'd tried to help her, though he'd been falling-down drunk. Cripes, she wished she could get that out of her head. She was not a damsel, and certainly not in distress. And Rake Tarbell was no prince.

She dug up the clothes she'd brought for him, then went to the bathroom door and rapped on it.

"Ohhhhhhhhhh myyyyyyyyyyy Gaawwwddd that's sooooooooo goooooooooo—eh? Delaney?"

"I've got clean shorts and a T-shirt for you. Okay if I put them on the counter?"

"You're an *angel*! Ahhhhhhhhh." This followed by sputtering as he once again submerged himself. And he was also . . . gargling? Then: "You shouldn't have to lend me your clothes."

I'm not. "S'okay, they're not mine." Or his. Rake would probably catch on if the American stranger happened to have a set of his clothes on hand. On the other hand, it was Rake, so who knew? "You want some supper?"

"Ohhhhhhhhh myyyyyyyyy G—yeah, that'd be great."

She heard the expected rap on her door and opened it to see Elena framed in the doorway. They'd been friends for years, but Delaney could never get over how Elena always looked sixteen. Odd enough when she was twelve, downright spooky now that she was in her twenties. But it came in handy when they needed to lure in a pedo, or a bully in search of prey. That was how they'd met, actually—Elena was fighting off the worst bully in the school, who was a head taller and had thirty pounds on her. None of which mattered after Delaney came up behind him and drove her foot into his balls.

So satisfying. Like punting a football.

"She's asleep," Delaney said, following Elena into the room.

"As expected, poor thing." She scooped Lillith up and nodded toward the bathroom. "Ooof! How's *that* going?"

Delaney made a face.

"It will be over soon."

"It better. We're on a tight deadline." To put it mildly. This job had to go perfectly, which had sounded fine on paper, but

Rake in real life was a walking, talking monkey wrench. She had exact parameters to stick to, and the family was counting on her. If she pulled this off, she'd have more money than she had made in the last ten years. If she pulled this off, the Big Pipe Dream was a certainty, and not only would *they* be safe, they could make others safe, too.

"It will be fine. And you're not alone."

You're not alone. The siren song the Big Pipe Dream was based on.

But Elena chewed her lip when she said it, aware that well-meant platitudes weren't a guarantee of a positive outcome. Delaney held the door for her—they'd agreed earlier that Lillith would sleep with the girls so she could have eyes on Rake—and out they went.

Fifty minutes later

(man am I glad we're in a hotel; I would not want that water bill)

Rake emerged, dressed in the dark shorts and navy blue T-shirt she'd left for him and rubbing his dark blond hair with a towel. Clean underwear in his size would have been *way* too much of a coincidence, so she knew he was going commando. She also knew she should stop thinking about his commando charge, so to speak. And absolutely stop thinking about the dark blond treasure trail she caught a glimpse of before he'd tugged the shirt down.

Clean and sober Rake was thoroughly yummy Rake.

"Ah, man, I feel . . ." A pause while his face disappeared behind the towel as he rubbed. ". . . almost human, or at least a rough facsimile."

"You look like a hedgehog." And he did; his damp hair was standing up all over in wet spikes that somehow made his eyes even bluer.

He grinned, bent, and shook his head in her direction; she had to bring up her arm to block the droplets.

"Real mature. Gah, you got my forehead *and* my knees, how'd you manage that?"

"Don't know, don't care, and mock my hair and drying method all you like—"

"Great, thanks."

"—because I don't give a shit what I look like right now, clean, I'm clean!" He twirled around, channeling Mary "I'm gonna make it after all!" Tyler Moore, and she leaned back to avoid being inadvertently smacked; the room was jam-packed with junk from corner to corner. "Finally finally clean!"

"I'd hope so, you were in there almost an hour."

"Where's Lillith?"

"My friend Elena took her to her room."

"Oh. Good." Rake brightened. "Well, whatever you guys think is best, and have I mentioned how thrilled I am to be clean? Never did generic hotel shampoo make such a sensual, cleansing lather."

"God, listen to you, I think you may have lost your mind—listen, if you want, I can send your old clothes down to the—"

"No! They must be burned," he announced. "Then burned again. And then the ashes should be sprinkled on Blake's morning oatmeal, which should also be burned."

Her good humor at his antics vanished. *Wow. Keep not learning, rich guy.* It's funny how this was exactly the kind of guy she'd hack and, if he didn't fall in line, would put a hit on. But her employer's instructions re Rake Tarbell were pretty clear. "You don't want them back. Got it."

"No, I do not." He was checking himself out in the full-length mirror hanging on the bathroom door. "Huh. These look like a pretty close fit." He tore his gaze away from his reflection to look at her over his shoulder. "And you just happened to have them lying around?"

Excellent observation. She rolled her eyes. "I have a life outside of you, Rake, and I wouldn't be the first tourist to hook up on vacation." *True, and true, and don't notice that I didn't actually answer your question. Don't notice much of anything about me, really. Instead be a little abashed. Enough to offer up a small apology.*

"Sorry, sorry," he said, turning back to check himself again. "I'm the last person who should be judging you on that one. It's none of my business and I really appreciate it and whoever he is, he's a lucky guy."

Well, that would be the salesclerk at Kohl's who sold them to me, so I'll pass that on to her.

"So." He tore himself away from his shiny clean reflection. "Now what?"

Now what turned out to be room service, and for a few seconds Delaney and the room service guy wondered if Rake was going to burst into delighted tears.

"I've—I've never been so happy to see a garden salad in my life," he whispered, then fell to his meal with all the delicate finesse of a starving goblin. "Oh God, it's even got cherry tomatoes in it! Beautiful, luscious cherry tomatoes! I hate cherry tomatoes!"

The waiter wasted no time heading for the door, and seemed disinclined to turn his back on Rake, and who could blame him? Rake didn't seem to be eating so much as jamming the food into his yawning mouth hole at roughly the speed of light. She gave the waiter a tip she hoped would soothe his frayed nerves, then fell to her own supper: more bruschetta than you could shake a stick at, followed by a plate of melon and prosciutto and a big-ass glass of milk—the latter surprisingly hard to find in Italian hotels. Who knew that stint on a dairy farm her fourteenth year would lead to a life-long love of dairy products?

She watched Rake eat, because looking away was not an option. If she only heard the noise and had no context, she might think he was strangling a dying pig. But nope—he just really, really liked *lardo*. Especially *lardo* wrapped around pork chops and snarfed down with green beans so thin, they looked like a pile of green Pick-Up Stix.

Later, when he'd collapsed into a delirious full-belly food coma, they discussed terms.

"So manual labor?"

"Yes."

"For what charity?"

"Does it matter?"

"I guess not." He settled on the end of the couch and fixed her with a dark blue gaze. "You must've been pretty upset when you heard Donna was dead."

"We had grown apart," she replied carefully. "But yes. It was terrible news." *Terrible.* Yep. That was one way to under-state it. *Horrifying,* that was another. *Devastating, shocking,* and, most of all, *infuriating.* She'd never get the chance to apologize. Donna would never get the chance to admit she shouldn't have left the family.

"Went your separate ways after prison?"

What? Idiot. "No."

"Oh. Um." She could actually see him trying to cast around for another subject. "So how long have you known Lillith?"

"Not long." Hell, it had taken her ages just to *find* Lillith. She hadn't seen her since she was a baby, and tracking down an extraordinarily self-posessed girl with a mind like a razor and Donna's eyes was . . . disconcerting. Donna had been in the ground less than a year, but Lillith kept her grief to herself for the most part. She got that from Donna, too.

"Well, she's a helluva kid." To his credit, Rake seemed genuinely admiring. "Smart and funny, and she doesn't ever seem to lose any equilibrium."

"Is this an attempt at a humble brag?"

"What?" he asked, astounded. "No! Even if it turns out I'm her father, I can't take credit for her general awesomeness. And I've been wondering—if I'm not her dad, what's going to happen to her?"

"Why d'you care?"

"Good God, I'm a jackass, not a sociopath. But I see by the look on your face that you're reserving judgment."

She laughed; she couldn't help it. He'd caught her fairly.

"What I mean is, is there any family on her mom's side? I hate the thought of her being alone in the world."

Delaney shook her head. "No. Donna's folks were only children and they died when she was a kid. No grandparents, aunts, uncles." *Just us. And if Donna's fate is an example to go by, we're not fit guardians. At all.*

"Poor kid."

"We all have that in common," she said drily. "Literally and figuratively."

"Well, I hope it works out for her," he said, shifting uncomfortably. "One way or the other."

"It will." She grinned at him, but it couldn't have been a nice grin, given how his expression faltered. "One way or the other."

Seventeen

At first, it wasn't terrible. It wasn't fun, exactly, but it wasn't like he was expected to shovel shit, an idea he mentioned to Delaney, who just smiled and said, "I've shoveled shit. It's not so bad. Second hour's the worst." In fact, the most innocuous comments he made would provoke the weirdest/coolest/ what-the-hell responses from her. It could be addictive if he wasn't careful.

She hadn't been at all worried about sharing a hotel room with a stranger, for example. He'd heard about the Minnesota Nice thing, and it was apparently true, even if it meant putting their own safety at risk. She'd explained that there was a sofa bed under one of the piles of Peeps, and he was welcome to sleep on it once he cleared it off. And like every sofa bed ever engineered, the bar hit him square across the middle of his back, because furniture designers are psychopaths. Still, it wasn't a park bench, which, while more comfortable, would have been much colder.

He'd liberated the spare blanket from the closet, ("Ah-ha!"

"What? You thought it was a treasure hunt? Putting a spare blanket in the closet isn't hiding it."

"Don't spoil it! This is all I have right now!")

slid between the blanket and the bar, got comfy, then glanced over. "Delaney?"

"Hmmm?" She'd changed into a pair of tattered black cotton shorts and a purple T-shirt with the logo I JUST WANT TO DRINK WINE, SAVE ANIMALS, AND TAKE NAPS.* She'd climbed into bed ten minutes earlier and was working on a laptop. "What? You want another pillow? They gave me eight, I'll never use 'em all."

"No, I'm fine. Listen, you don't, uh, have to worry. About anything happening. I mean, about my trying anything."

"I'm not," she replied without looking up from her computer. "At all."

"Please don't take this the wrong way—"

"Oh boy." She sighed and rubbed her eyes. "Here we go. No one ever says that and then *doesn't* follow with something jerky."

"—but *why* aren't you worried?" He sat up, giving his back temporary relief. "You don't know me, not really. I could be anybody."

"But you aren't anybody. You're Rake Tarbell."

"Well, yeah." *When did I tell her my last name?* He tried to remember, but mostly the only thing that came to mind was the canal and being broke and the hangover and Delaney helping him and Lillith. He couldn't remember when he'd introduced himself, but he must have. *Probably while I was drunk.* "But I could have any kind of background."

---

* This is a real thing from Etsy!

"You conceived a child—"

"Maaaaaybe. We don't have the labs back on that one."

"—in a public park. And you had money until last night. And you can swim, apparently?" She smirked, and it had either been a long day or she was growing on him (or both), because the smirk was less aggravating. "And you hate vermouth, except when you're getting crazy drunk on it. And your brother, pretty much all the time. And you're a bewildered father—perhaps," she added when he opened his mouth. "That's your background."

"I don't hate Blake, he just bugs the shit out of me, and you only know those things because I told you. It could've been all lies. Blake could be a lie. The vermouth thing *has* to be a lie," he added in a mutter.

She laughed. "Who'd lie about that? Any of it?"

"Look, you're missing the point." He wriggled to get comfortable, which was exactly the waste of time he'd predicted. "What if I got up in the middle of the night and was craving a bed without a bar and sex without a condom and tried to start some shit?"

"I'd handle it," she replied. It was a little startling how calm she was while they discussed her possible potential sexual assault, and his stealing of her bed. Not like she was in denial, but like she'd actually have no trouble handling it. Him. Like she'd weighed the variables and thought about the odds and found them decidedly in her favor. "It'd be fine, by which I mean *I'd* be fine."

"But how do you know?" he persisted, even while his inner Blake voice was cautioning him to shut up already and stop looking a gift sofa bed in the mouth (bar). "You can't know. Not really."

"No, but I know myself. I had an eventful childhood," she

said with a small, strange smile. "Donna, too. And there's nothing like an eventful childhood to prepare you for an eventful adulthood. I know you won't try to rape me, Rake— that's what we're dancing around, right? So let's just say it. I know you wouldn't, but if you lost your mind and tried, you wouldn't succeed."

"Oh." Now what to make of *that*? "Well. That's good." Puzzling and vague, but good. "Thanks, you know. For helping me."

"You shouldn't thank me." She was still looking at him, her work forgotten for the moment, and she wasn't smiling. "Because you don't know much about me, either. We ran into each other last night and again this morning and that's it, that's all you've got. Maybe I'm a terrible person. Maybe I set you up so I can creep on *you* in the wee darkest hours."

He spread his arms and flopped back. "Creep away, woman named Claire who calls herself Delaney. Consider me extremely open to creeping." *I've got no problem if a pretty brunette with wonderful eyes wants to get into my pants. Creep into my pants. Whatever.* "You don't scare me."

"Yes, well. You're an idiot." She shrugged. "So."

Weird (but nice!) how that didn't sound bitchy, unlike, say, every time Blake said it, starting when they were three and Rake gobbled the green Play-Doh so Blake couldn't finish the landscaping for his Play-Doh castle. The vomiting had been worth it. *Nontoxic, my ass.* "G'night, Delaney."

"Good night, Rake."

Weird. All of it. But not especially troubling, though perhaps it should have been. Frankly, he was too exhausted to fret much longer. He was clean, and full, and (almost) comfortable, and the headache was gone, and the nausea was manageable.

He was also broke, cut off from his brother (the dictionary definition of a mixed blessing), and had promised to stuff what looked like a thousand Easter baskets over the next few days. And he just couldn't worry about it much longer, any of it.

He was asleep in moments, and didn't dream.

Eighteen

If he had to look at another Easter basket, he'd puke.

"Only five hundred more to go!"

Rake shuddered and swallowed back the nausea. They'd been loading the SUV for the last hour. Before that, the stuffing. After that, as Sofia had just reminded him, more stuffing. And what was with the pencils?

"What's with the pencils?" he asked, following Sofia back into the hotel. "Is that a thing here? Jesus came back from the dead, so the Easter bunny hides eggs and gives out pencils? They're not even pastel."

Sofia giggled. She was teeny, her head coming to the middle of his chest, with masses of bright carrot orange hair that had to make up at least 15 percent of her body weight. She was in a lavender sweatshirt that clashed with her hair, jeggings, and scuffed flats. She'd been delighted with his Italian

("Senza offesa, la maggior parte degli americani non sono fluente, anche in inglese."

*"Nessuna presa. Tutto quello che hai sentito parlare di ameri-
cani è vero. Noi siamo i peggiori."*)*

and her chattering should have helped the time pass, but
it didn't.

"The pencils are for the poor children," she explained. She
had asked if she could practice her English on him, and he'd
been happy to oblige. Like virtually every European he'd
met, she spoke excellent English while apologizing for what
she thought was poor English. "Many people donate school
supplies at the beginning of the school year, but this time of
year those supplies have been used up."

"Oh." That made sense. He knew that when money had
been tight, his mother never bought anything that wasn't on
sale, including school supplies. That was fine in late August.
In the spring, not so much.

"In fact, we should have had more than pencils this time.
But some people, they promise and then they take back their
promise. So we have to—" She cut herself off and jabbed at
the elevator button, and finished as the doors closed. "Never
mind. Do not bring that up with Delaney."

"Bring what up?"

She beamed. "Yes, like that."

"You and Delaney, you've worked together for a while?"
Sofia looked to be in her late teens; maybe they went to the
same church or something? Volunteered for the same organ-
izations?

"Oh, yes. Her work is my work."

---

* "No offense, but most Americans aren't fluent, even in English."

"None taken. Everything you've heard about Americans is true. We're
the worst."

"Partners, huh? You should tell her you want to trade jobs—she can haul baskets and you can hang out in the hotel room, goofing off on social media."

"I will always do what Delaney asks of me" came the surprising and emphatic reply. "And she is not 'goofing off.'"

"Yeah, yeah, the old 'social networking *is* work' excuse, I've heard it before. You should ask for a raise at least."

"I would never take her money." Sofia sounded shocked, as if Rake had suggested they steal Delaney's panties and throw them in the Trevi Fountain. Dammit! Now he was thinking about Delaney's panties floating in the Trevi Fountain. "She has given me everything. Even when she was small and had nothing."

"Yeah? She must have set up a great dental plan. I mean, I've heard of employee loyalty, but you guys *commit*, you know?"

"You are a dolt of a man," she said, not unkindly.

A minute later, they were back in her (their?) room and he was saying hello to Elena and Teresa, still hard at it, and Lillith, who was elbow-deep in Peeps and furtively chewing while she "helped." He grinned at her T-shirt (BE YOUR OWN SAFE SPACE. OR BE BATMAN.).

And while it was great to see that a third of the baskets/candy/Peeps/supplies had been cleared out, it was awful to see that two-thirds remained. Still, there'd be a lot of happy kids on Easter Sunday, though he'd rather have written a check. And speaking of checks, he was that much closer to reclaiming his life, so the morning hadn't been an entire waste.

He glanced over at Delaney, working at the desk, and told himself he definitely wasn't hoping for a smile, or praise, or cash, or a kiss. (Or an antacid.)

Whoa. Keep it in park, pal. You've established this is purely a slave/master relationship, and not the kinky kind.

"Son of a bitch."

He started. Delaney had spoken so quietly, it was more a hiss.

"Aw, hell, you're not talking to me, are you?"

"Fuck." She looked up. "Sorry, Lillith."

"*Fanculo,*" the child put in helpfully, earning a snort of appreciation from Rake.

"Are you okay?" Rake asked, partly out of concern, and partly to be doing something, anything, besides more baskets. "Did the hotel change the Wi-Fi password? Try today's date."

Delaney appeared to notice him for the first time. "C'mere." When he obediently trotted to her side, she turned her laptop around to show him the screen. "D'you recognize these men?"

He squinted, shook his head. "Never seen them before."

"You have, you just don't remember."

"Vermouth is the real villain here."

Delaney didn't smile at his (admittedly lame) joke. "They keep popping up. I don't like that at all."

"Popping up?"

Delaney was glaring at her laptop. "Lake Como. Yesterday outside the hotel. Then later outside the café, which is why I split us up. And now this morning." She looked up at the others. "What do you think?"

"I think it's like Renner in Sardinia last year. And London two years ago—we simultaneously know too much and too little." Sofia had crossed her arms in front of her chest and was shaking her head like a disappointed parent. "I think if you try to take them, we might learn something—or nothing, and it gets worse as you've forced their hand."

"Wait, 'take them'?" Rake asked, startled. The thought

of it made his nausea, which had been in reluctant remission, surge back. And why did the room feel fifteen degrees warmer? "Maybe they're tourists with the same itinerary. Maybe they're deeply determined census takers. Maybe we've won a contest and they're waiting for the right moment to hand us that giant cardboard check. Maybe you're paranoid?" He stifled a burp. "And how many cameras do you have around here? Or are you tapping into the hotel's feed, you sneak?"

Meanwhile, the kid had been decorating each of her arms with about half a dozen baskets. "I'm going to take these down to Teresa's van," Lillith announced.

"Hmm? Yeah, okay, hon—give me a minute, I'll come with." It was almost certainly warmer, and he had a sudden longing for fresh air. Even if it meant stuffing more Peeps into more baskets and handling those same baskets. Or steering Lillith down the hall, to the elevator, and outside to breathe the sweet air of the loading dock. He turned back to the women. "What about walking up to them and asking them what they want?"

Sofia snorted something, and he would bet his nonexistent fortune that it was "amateur."

"We've found it works better if they don't realize we've tumbled to their surveillance," Delaney said, like this was a regular Tuesday morning for her. Which it clearly was.

"So then," Sofia prompted, "watch them watching us?"

"Tell me again why we can't call the—damn, Lillith didn't wait. I'll go with her. Don't confront anybody before I get back!" He was through the door in a couple of strides and hung a left toward the elevators just in time to see a strange man clamp Lillith's elbow and haul her up so high that she was on her toes.

Oh hell *no.* "Hey!" he said sharply, and they both looked. The man's irritated expression was not lost on him. Neither was Lillith's look of relief. "Hands off the kiddo."

The short, heavyset man with thick curly hair and a dark beard—Rake recognized him from the surveillance vids—loosened his grip but didn't let go. Instead, he pasted on an ingratiating grin. "Excuse me. I think this young lady might have stolen something."

"That's nice. Leggo my Lillith." Was it just him, or was the hallway receding? And who was shutting the lights off? "Right now."

"*Ich bin kein dieb,**" Lillith muttered in— Wait, was that German? She tried to plant her feet but was still on tiptoe. And was the bearded goon—he was! He was dragging her to the elevator.

Maybe Delaney & Co. aren't so paranoid. Damn, I hate apologizing. Rake decided it was past time to stop fucking around, and he broke into a clumsy run. "Last chance," he warned, then grabbed the man's shirt, yanked him close, and threw up all over him.

"Jesus Christ!"

"Warned you," he managed before passing out.

---

* "I'm not a thief."

Nineteen

Delaney was talking, but she was at the far end of a cavernous ballroom, God knew why, with her volume set to Murmur. But as she came closer, he was happy to see the room shrink and brighten as the volume came up.

"'Don't confront anybody until I get back.'" She was standing over him with a wry expression. "That's what you said."

"Should've taken my own advice," he managed, then saw she was holding a cold can

(condensation has never looked wetter or sexier)

of ginger ale. "I'll marry you if you give that to me right now."

"Yeah, I'm gonna pass on the proposal, but you can have a drink anyway." She cracked it open and held it for him while he lurched up on his elbows and took greedy, slurping sips. "Easy! You're just going to throw it up again if you don't take it easy."

"If this is Hell—and I'm almost positive it is—does that make you Satan?"

"Nope. I'm just a low-level demonic functionary," she deadpanned.

"Lillith! Is she okay? Ohhhhhhh," he moaned, slumping back and slamming his eyes shut. "I sat up too fast."

"See? She's fine. Sofia's helping her make you a tray."

"No trays. No traaaaays. Unless there's something on it I can use to kill myself, like a thirty-eight. Or enough dental floss to fashion a noose."

"No, just crackers and broth. But I have to admit, I'm impressed."

He cracked one eye open to look at her. This sounded promising. "Yeah?"

"I had no idea your superpower was the ability to vomit at will on anyone you confront."

"Only in Venice. Where'd the asshole scamper off to?"

"Are you kidding?" Delaney sounded equal parts amused and admiring. "He was horrified and dripping and got the hell out of there. We were too busy with you to go catch him."

"And can I assume calling the cops isn't an option because of all the secret weirdness and the weird secrets?"

Delaney stopped smiling and (wonders!) looked uncomfortable. "Yeah, pretty much. We can't have them looking at us, just like you don't want the local government to know you're in town."

"Or the Parks and Rec guys." He had no idea if Italian civil servants held grudges, and no wish to find out.

"But I don't like it. And I'm starting to think there's gotta be a way around it."

"Okay, so . . . figure something out, and is it just me, or do you have tunnel vision, too?" he managed before sleep grabbed him and hauled him under again.

Some amount of time later, he swam back to soupy semiconsciousness, reached out, groped, and accidentally

"Ow!"

poked someone in the eye.

So he opened his. "Oh, Lillith, thank God. If you love me, you'll kill me. Kill Daddy, please. Right now."

"Oh, now you acknowledge me?" She was looking down at him and nibbling her lower lip. "I'm sorry you're sick. I googled and I think it's gastroenteritis. That's why you're throwing up and have a fever, from jumping—"

"Falling."

"—into sewage and vomit and *merda* and other yucky stuff."

"There's no need to specify," he groaned. "You could have stuck with yucky stuff."

"Do you want to go to the hospital?"

"No. I want to die in this bed. Preferably within the next ten seconds."

"Because I'll take you, if you want to go. I know I'm supposed to listen to Delaney, but I don't care what she says on this one. Not everyone in authority is out to get her family."

"Her what?"

"Shall I take you to a doctor?"

He blinked at her. Lillith looked as earnest as she sounded as she stared down at him. "How?" He didn't actually want to go; he was just curious about the process. "You're little. How would you even get me to an ER?" Borrow a cell phone? Berate one of the others into obeying her command? Steal an ambulance? He felt confident she was capable of all that and more.

"Don't know. But I'd think of something."

"I believe it."

"Thanks for coming to get me."

"You should have waited," he reminded her gently.

"Yeah. I should have done a lot of stuff. Pulled away. Kicked. Yelled! But I just froze like a *manichino*."

"Or like someone having a perfectly normal reaction to . . ." He paused, stifled a belch. Waited. Apparently the ginger ale was staying put on a trial basis. ". . . to stress."

"It wasn't that. I started thinking about Mama and wondering what she'd do. And then I thought maybe I should go with him, try to figure out what they want. Or let him get me outside and yell for help until the *polizia* came. But before I could make up my mind, you drove him off with your vomit."

"Possibly my finest moment," he agreed with a chuckle.

He felt her small hand curl into his. "But you didn't know I was thinking up a plan. And you came to get me anyway."

"Yeah, course I did."

"So are we friends now?"

He blinked at her. "Well." He'd saved her. She was saving him. "Yeah. I suppose we are. Which is a bit of a new thing for me."

"How come? You're nice. And usually rich. You prob'ly have lots of friends."

"Fair-weather friends," he corrected her. "The kind who disappear if they think I'm not picking up the bill. This is gonna sound dumb, but I'd say Blake is probably my best friend."

"But you hate him."

"No." He shook his head at her. She looked earnest and focused, like this was the most important conversation of her life; the least he could do was be honest. "No, I complain about him—"

"A lot."

"—occasionally, but I love him and he loves me. If he were here, he'd be kicking ass all over the place on my behalf. And he's the same way—I'm probably *his* best friend, though he'd choke before admitting it."

"Well, now you have two friends. Right? Rake?"

"Yes, absolutely. It's a tiny elite group and you're now a member in good standing. Okay?"

"Okay."

He stifled a yawn. Ginger ale staying inside? Check. Roof over his head, however temporarily? Check. Delaney amused and Lillith safe? Check-check. "Think I'm gonna sleep some more. Don't go off with any weirdos without coming to get me first."

"Define *weirdo*."

He was out before he could oblige.

Twenty

Later that day

(night?)

over a robust meal of clear vegetable broth and stale *taralli,* Delaney remarked that he looked slightly better than half-dead, which she termed "a remarkable improvement."

And it got me out of filling more Easter baskets, which made it almost worth it. Almost. That, he figured, was best kept to himself.

"Still, I got a *lot* of work done for you guys before I came to Lillith's rescue," he pointed out. "Which also should be worth something. What do bodyguards get paid in this country?"

"About sixty euros an hour."

"You— Whoa." He was so surprised, he thought he might fall off the bed. "I thought that was rhetorical. Oh my God, so many new questions now. But getting back to me—"

"Of course. Don't we always?"

"—you wanted me to help with your cover, which means I'm probably halfway to a new iPhone at least." At her glance, he added, "What, I have to provide cover for whatever it is *and* work for free? I figured I'd use my wages to get a new phone. This can't be news to you. Besides, don't you want me off of your hands? Y'know, eventually?"

"Well . . ."

"Can you believe it? I actually can't wait to call Blake. Blake!"

"Rake—"

"This, knowing I'm in for one of his nine-hour lectures on growing up and taking responsibility. Who'd have thought that Italy could make me love cherry tomatoes? And my twin?"

"Rake, yesterday morning you earned just under a hundred bucks."

"Yep. And I'll be sore tomorrow. Hell, I'm sore now. Mostly from the throwing up, though." He let out a satisfied sigh, then stretched. "Your family—"

"Friends. I don't have any family."

"Bullshit, I've seen how you interact. You've known each other for years, defend each other when not bickering, and you get up to all sorts of criminal mischief together. Literal definition of a family."

She laughed. "It's really not, but I kind of love how your mind works sometimes."

"Anyway, Sofia and Elena and Teresa liked to hang the finished baskets on me like I was a tree and the baskets were my weird fruit. Exhausting! Lillith restrained herself because she is a charming child of uncommon dignity. Anyway, no need to thank me."

"A new iPhone," Delaney went on, "will run you about six hundred bucks. Minimum."

"Oh," he managed. "Shit." He'd never really thought about

it before. He'd always upgraded when the new one came out. The old one went . . . somewhere . . .

(iPhone purgatory?)

and the new one was his lifeline until the next generation hit stores. It was almost automatic, and the price had always been irrelevant. Maybe a burner was an option—those were still a thing, right? "That's . . . shit."

"Yeah."

He sighed and sipped some pale broth. "So, hit me."

"Sorry?"

"Please. You know you want to."

She gave him a small smile. "I actually don't."

"Do too! So go ahead, rip into the stupid rich guy who takes his money for granted and has no idea what minimum wage is or the cost of a new phone or how not to fall in the canal."

"There's no point." She'd finished her *caprese*—yay, room service!—and was sipping a heavily sugared and creamed cup of coffee. "You just did it for me. You were way harder on yourself than I would've been. Piling it on is mean *and* redundant."

He had to smile. "Blake always said that. Said if I could laugh at myself, no one else could laugh at me." He paused, thinking. "I might have taken that one too much to heart."

"Yeah, maybe. Listen, we could probably get you a cheap used one on eBay for about two hundred."

"Yes! The lady takes pity on me at last."

"I think you mean 'again.'"

"Whatever."

"You know you're Lillith's hero, right?" Delaney asked out of roughly nowhere.

"She should get out and meet more people." He finished

the last cracker, chased it with sparkling water, looked up, saw her frown. "Oh. You were being serious. Sorry, I suck at picking up on that sometimes."

"Hadn't noticed" was her dry reply. "She does, though."

"Well. She's great. Glad I could help. DNA test back yet?"

"Not yet."

"Okay, well, regardless of the results, I need a phone. If I'm her dad—poor kid!—I'll have to start figuring stuff out, not least of which is figuring out where we go from here. And not just geographically. If I'm not, I still have to track my dough and get back home."

"You're welcome to help us with more baskets."

"I'm betting that didn't sound threatening in your head at all."

"Yep. But you can take breaks to barf."

"Wow! Best boss ever!"

She laughed. "I'm probably your first boss ever."

"Since I quit mowing Mr. Nessen's lawn in eighth grade, yeah. You're so much better and in every respect. You don't have any hair growing out of your ears, for starters."

"Oh God," she said, leaning back. "Here comes another story about your odd childhood."

"Nuh-uh! Well, maybe. I'm just saying you're a way better boss than Mr. Nessen. You don't yell, you don't clomp out on your porch to watch me work while furtively picking your nose, you don't have any hair growing out of your ears, you haven't tried to hit me with several issues of AARP magazine, and you're not a racist. I'm pretty sure." He raised his voice over her giggles and continued. "Annnnnd now you're mocking me."

"But there's so much to mock! It's almost entrapment."

Jesus. She looks incredible when she laughs. Not that it's on the table, but if I was going to hook up with anyone here, it'd be Delaney.

Whoa. Where'd that come from? He'd never wanted to get laid less in his entire life. He wanted to earn his money and get his phone and see if he could make Delaney laugh some more and yell at Blake and get his money back and then buy something really really nice for Delaney.

What the hell?

Not something silly and shiny, like her own CVS franchise. Something charitable and selfless, like her own YMCA.

WHAT THE HELL, RAKE?

Talking! Talking would drown out his inner Blake voice. "So besides Easter, what else do you do? For charity, I mean."

The greedy shrew was flaunting her lack of poverty by devouring crème brûlée *right in front of him.* The way she was licking that spoon was definitely bordering on the criminal. Damn, that mouth. That wide, pretty mouth that he definitely wasn't picturing stretched around his—

"Rake?"

"Eh?"

"I've been saying your name for the last ten seconds." She'd paused in mid-lick. "Maybe this is all I do."

"Nope. You're in it deep, Delaney, you're a Good Samaritan down to your bones, and you're hooked on the hard stuff. Most people would be okay with volunteering a couple of times a year, but not you: You need it allll the time."

Her tongue flicked as she licked her spoon again and shook her head. "How have you made charity work sound like a meth addiction? I've talked to actual meth addicts who don't make meth sound like meth."

"So you admit you have a problem. Ha! I should have been a lawyer; you just crumbled under my cross-ex."

"Yes, that's not what happened." She saw him shiver; lately he'd been either too hot or too cold, often within moments of each other. "Want another blanket?"

"No, but a cell phone and access to funds would be great."

She sighed. "I could float you a loan for a—"

"I'm fine." In the Tarbell lexicon, "borrowing" was a sin slightly less dire than theft. "And even if I wasn't, all my money is going toward a phone. I don't care if I get pneumonia, getting yelled at by my brother is my first priority. And I'm not letting you distract me, either. So who do you help when it's not Easter?"

Hmm, what other charities were there? His mother and Blake had set up some tax shelters, he knew, and mailed him gobs of paperwork every three months or so that he never read (what were they even trying to prove with all the paper?). And hadn't the NFL figured out how to profit off at least one charity? But which— Ah! He'd bought an ex a pink Tom Brady sweatshirt a few years ago. He'd picked her up at Faneuil Hall and the expression "rabid fan" did not begin to apply. She'd been fun, and cute, and not shy about semipublic sex

(wait, do I have a thing for al fresco *banging? how have I not realized this about myself?)*

and toward the end he hadn't really minded that she kept calling him Tom and had bitten him so hard on the throat that it hurt to swallow for two days. "Breast cancer awareness, right?"

This prompted an epic eye roll; for a second he worried she was having a ministroke. "Breast cancer awareness? Give me a break."

"Oooookay."

She snapped her head up to glare at him. "Who doesn't know breast cancer is a thing? Anyone? In the last ten years,

who has ever said 'Thank goodness for breast cancer awareness, because I've been alive for twenty years and never knew
it was a thing'?"

"Nobody?" he guessed.

"Nobody."

"But—"

She cut him off, and a good thing, because he had no idea
what followed "but." "The money needs to go to research, not
awareness. But nobody bothers to check. No one looks up
stats. They buy something pink and think they've done their
part. And if I *ever* get my hands on Lance Armstrong, I will
break his fucking neck. Even before the scandal, Livestrong
hadn't accepted new research applications for *years*. And you
know what really pisses me off?"

"No," he replied, and he definitely wasn't terrified.

"People who do charity work Christmas week and don't
give a shit about us the rest of the year."

Whoa. Give a shit about us?

"When you put it like that, it makes me realize I definitely
should stop donating to charity. After this week, I mean."

His lame joke caught her off guard and she snorted in
spite of herself. "Not where I was going with that, you dick."
She cleared her throat. "Sorry. I know you were just asking to
be nice. It's—it's kind of a trigger for me."

"Noted." *Who, Delaney? Who doesn't give a shit about you or
Sofia or Teresa the rest of the year?*

"We work smaller," she said, calming. She was stacking
things on the room service tray, possibly so she didn't have to
look at him while she explained. He did nothing to impede
her. "Not one or two big charities a year, but lots of little
ones. Easter baskets and school clothes and food shelters, and
we're working on a private—never mind, it's not important.

But whatever we do, it depends on the donations we get. And don't get," she added under her breath.

"It's nice you keep busy." He kept his tone mild, and wondered if he dared ask the question. "Me, I collect recipes. It's not just a superfun hobby, it helps with my weekly menu planning!"

"Sure it does." She moved the tray to the desk, went to the closet, and brought him another blanket. "You should probably sleep some more."

"Never! I'm guessing I don't get paid sick time."

"Good guess." But she smiled, and he mentally swore he would fill several baskets tomorrow. At least a dozen. Two dozen!

Twenty-one

I'd never hurt her. I'd never hurt any woman. I've hurt men who have tried to hurt women and never regretted it, not once; black eyes get better and broken noses can be reset. I knew that by the time I was thirteen.

But this is hard. Literally, this is very, very hard. Dear Abby: I'm sharing a room with my (kind of) boss who's supercute and I haven't masturbated in ninety-six hours (that I know of—the Lake Como sojourn is still a total blank) and she has lovely soft, strong hands and I might be getting Stockholm syndrome, because I'm looking forward to working with her tomorrow even though I'm terrified of Peeps. How skeevy is it if, while being very, very quiet, I just lie here and take care of my—

No point even finishing the question. He knew it was unacceptable levels of skeevy. He sighed and flopped over on his back.

After more ginger ale, followed by nap chasers, he'd felt very, very close to human. Lillith still fretted and hovered and practically guarded him—it was equal parts intimidating and comforting—and finally she'd gotten so tired, she'd curled up on the floor beside his bed and fallen asleep. Teresa had scooped her up and put her to bed; he'd fallen back asleep, then woke up hard as a spike.

Which was too damned bad.

Just don't think about it. Of course! Don't think about it! Why didn't I think about not thinking about it?

No, really. Don't think about it. Don't think about Delaney just a few feet away, warm and fragrant in her bed. Don't wonder what her mouth tastes like, and the spot behind her ear, and her lovely long throat. Definitely don't wonder what it'd be like to gently rub your cheek over her stiffening nipples. What she'd sound like if you slipped a hand between her legs and gently stroked her open. Nope. Don't think about any of it. Easy-peasy. And definitely don't grab yourself. A lot.

Delaney sat up, like Frankenstein in the lab after the lighting hit. Rake almost shrieked. *Oh God, she's a telepath and knows I'm a perv! My lustful thoughts were so loud, they woke her up! Let death come quickly!* "What?" he shrilled from the sofa bed. "What is it? Not the face, okay?"

She didn't answer. Just abruptly swung her legs over the side of the bed, stood, and went straight to the biggest window in the room, squashing Peeps and grinding chocolate eggs into the carpet but not stopping. Not even slowing. She got to the window and stood and looked and said nothing and did nothing.

He cleared his throat. "Are you okay?" *Please don't kick me out. You can't help being hot, and I can't help finding you hot, but I'd never act on it. Never, unless you made it clear you wanted me in your bed. And maybe not even then, because although you're hot, I'm a little scared of you.*

Nothing.

She was still, so still. He'd never seen her like that, like a statue in the dark. "Delaney?"

She turned to look at him and he felt a chill; her gaze wasn't on him, not really. It was like she couldn't see him, was looking past him, or through him. "I don't . . ." she began in a low, halting voice unlike any she'd used before.

He pushed his blankets off and went to stand beside her, relieved that when she'd clomped toward the window like a cute Frankenstein, his penis, Mr. Roboto, had turned back into *Flaccido Domingo*. "Are you all right?"

"I don't know where I am," she whispered, sounding young and lost. And damned if she didn't *look* young in the barely lit glow by the window.

She reached out as if she was going to touch the glass, then let her hand drift back to her side. The woman who'd laughed when he'd barfed and yelled when he'd bitched and called him on his entitled douchebaggery was afraid to touch a window, or raise her voice, or make eye contact.

"It's always different, you know," she murmured. "I don't know where I am."

"You're in Venice," he said, and now *he* was whispering. "It's—it's okay. I mean, you're safe and everything. I'd never— No one's going to hurt you."

And God, the way her face lit up. That smile. Jesus. "Really?"

"Yeah. Really."

"No one will come in? Unless I let them?"

"No one," he promised through numb lips. *Fuck. A nightmare that she's sleepwalking in? Or sleepwalking during a nightmare? What is this?* "It's okay. You're safe. You—you can go back to bed. If you want."

"Bed?" And she flinched. Claire Fucking Delaney flinched.

"Well, you don't have to. You don't have to do anything you don't want to."

The smile again. The relief. "Really?"

"Really."

"Okay," she said, and *beamed* at him. Then she turned around and walked back to her bed and climbed under the covers and flopped over on her side and twenty seconds later she was dead asleep again. He watched her for a while to make sure she was really out. Now he had a whole new thing to wonder about. Did that make him a good man, or just easily distracted? Both? Neither? And was he wondering about that so he wouldn't think about how scary she had been, and sad, and afraid?

What the hell was that?

He waited until they were enjoying the modestly priced continental breakfast in one of the common rooms, the others, including Lillith, taking up the table across from them. They'd saved the last table for Delaney, and the two of them had it to themselves for the moment. It had been almost a celebration, his first day back on solids and out of the room. Certainly Delaney's family had seemed happy he was mostly mended.

But the minute breakfast was over, he knew they were all going back to work and if he didn't carpe the diem now, who knew when he'd get another chance?

"So." *Easy. Nice and casual. Nothing weird is going to come out of your mouth.* "Do you remember last night?"

She looked up from her oatmeal, into which she'd ladled a mound of brown sugar and an astonishing amount of cream. She'd brought the laptop with her, of course. She never left it in the room, though there was a perfectly good safe in the closet. It was always within arm's reach; she'd brought it to dinner, too. Maybe she was a paranoid screenplay writer, and sold scripts to fund her charity work? If it was strictly to keep track of the charitable donations, she wouldn't need the secrecy. Twenty-two letters in a password representing something she didn't have to think about. Hmm. And the safe combo. Something else quick and easy. "Delaney? Remember?"

"Mostly, I remember your relentless whining about the cost of cell phones in this day and age," she replied, grinning.

"Tim Cook and his corporate thugs should be ashamed of themselves. But I meant after that. Dammit! I mean I don't whine. And after. In your sleep. You—"

She was waiting for him to finish, and hadn't realized there was jam in the corner of her mouth that he definitely didn't want to kiss away. She wasn't tense, or embarrassed. Just patiently curious. Curiously patient? "I what, Rake?"

You walked and talked in your sleep. You were afraid. You didn't know where you were, and when I said you were free to come and go, you were so happy. And who didn't help you when it wasn't Christmas, Delaney? Why do you hate careless, maybe twice-a-year charitable donations? What's in the spreadsheets you won't let anyone see?

"You— It's no big deal." He hadn't thought of this, and he should have. He'd expected heated denial or embarrassment, not amnesia. "You talked in your sleep is all."

"Oh yeah?" Still totally unconcerned. "What'd I say?"

"'Go, Packers.'"

She laughed. "Now I know you're lying. I don't like football, but if I did, I'd never root for the Packers. That's practically a violation of state law."

Christ, she has no idea.

"Well, you mumbled something, I didn't quite catch it, I was supertired because you're such a goddamned slave driver." He wasn't sure why he wasn't telling her everything. He didn't want to embarrass her, that was part of it, but he also had the uneasy feeling that the Delaney who walked in her sleep wasn't *this* Delaney, the confident young woman who walked right up to a dripping, livid man who'd just been fished out of the canal, who'd tossed a kid into his life, ruthlessly put him to work to earn a cell phone, frequently told him to shut up already, stole the last piece of toast off his plate, and laughed when he complained.

"Sorry if I disturbed you."

"You didn't." Lie. "It was no biggie." Lie.

"All righty." She'd finished her oatmeal, waved at a couple of the others, gathered her stuff. "Ready to get back to it?"

"Not at all. Not even a little bit. I'd rather be doing almost anything else."

"We can get your new phone tomorrow."

"Bring me every Easter basket in this building!" he cried, jumping to his feet. "And then stand back, ladies, because you'll see a basket-stuffing fool."

"Or just a fool," Teresa piped up.

"Silence, peon!"

That got Elena and Teresa and the others laughing, and he smiled at their gentle teasing, and that was good; it was always good when people were laughing because their guards went down and no one ever seemed to notice that while they laughed, he was figuring them out.

Delaney left the table and he was about to follow, when . . .

"She was sleepwalking, wasn't she?"

"Gah! Jesus, Lillith. How do you do that? Only get noticed when you want to?"

"Mama taught me. She was, right?"

"Yeah."

"Because she didn't know what foster home she was in."

". . . Yeah."

"It's okay. I was surprised the first time, too. Just say nice things to her and she'll go back to sleep."

"Yeah." It was low, but his options were limited. He already knew that asking Delaney for details was futile. Time to pump a kid. (*Argh. Phrasing.*) "So I get the feeling she had a rough childhood."

"Yes."

"Like your mother."

"Yes."

"And Sofia and Teresa and Elena."

Lillith nodded.

"There's a bigger picture here, isn't there? It's not just about finding your dad."

She beamed. "I knew you were going to get it. Y'know, eventually. They've been saving for the Big Pipe Dream for years. That's why they need us."

"Wait, 'need'? Us? How do—"

"C'mon, Rake and Lillith." Delaney was standing in the front of the restaurant, beckoning them forward. "And the rest of you lazy bums, too. Back at it."

"*Fanculo questo,*" Eleana replied cheerfully.

Exactly. *Fanculo questo.* Times ten.

Twenty-two

His Stockholm syndrome was coming along nicely. After lunch (still mindful of the toxins swimming in his system, Rake stuck to bruschetta with most of the tomatoes scraped off—so, stale bread), he and Delaney and Lillith got into a plush Peep free-for-all and at one point he was dodging several bright yellow marshmallowy missiles. Her speed was scary, her aim devastating. And Delaney wasn't bad, either. "Not the face, *not the face!*"

Elena, Teresa, and Sofia came back to the room to find them whipping small foil-wrapped eggs at one another, and Elena let loose with a burst of Italian that even Rake had trouble following.

Delaney and Lillith stopped at once, a costly mistake. *Sorry, ladies, Rake didn't get that memo! Ha! Ya like that, cutie? And another! Ha! And—*

"Ow!" He whined and rubbed his cheek. "You could have put out my eye, you rotten bitch."

"You've got a spare," Delaney replied with a smug smile.

"Exactly what I was saying to you!" Elena was about five

eight, pleasantly round in all the right places, with deep brown hair, latte-colored skin, and loads of freckles from forehead to chin. She told Rake she was in her twenties, but only spiritually. "Stop that! Stop wasting the candy."

"She's right," he replied, humbled. "Wasting is the one thing you never want to do with candy. That and boiling it. I really have only this to say and then we can drop it: Delaney started it. She is responsible for everything."

"Ah, yes, Rake Tarbell's go-to excuse for everything: 'Hey, it wasn't *my* fault.'" Which would have been a great point, except she lost the moral high ground when she stuck her tongue out at him.

"The good news is we're done for the day." Sofia was so cheerful she could make the return of the plague sound like a positive ("If I'm sick now, I won't have to worry about being sick later!"), but anyone could make that news sound good.

"Great! We're done!"

"Baskets are done. Not you, pal. We've got other stuff lined up for tomorrow."

He muttered something under his breath that might have been "Well, fuck." "Whatever tomorrow's job is, it won't be worse than what I've already had to deal with. That was not a dare!" he added when Delaney opened her mouth. "Seriously, please don't set right out to prove I'm full of shit again. Always happy to be selfless and also earn more money for steaks and cherry tomatoes and a phone and eventually money to ransom my way to freedom."

Delaney smiled, but it wasn't her usual "Go to hell if you can't take a joke" smirk. This one was sad, and a little . . . bitter? "I don't think I've met anyone who has more freedom than you do. Even now."

Hmmm. Wonder if that's got anything to do with your "eventful childhood" leading to your "eventful adulthood." But he let it go. It wasn't the time (he was hungry and pooped), it wasn't the place (he didn't want to get into it in front of the others, especially Lillith), and, again, it wasn't the place (he was pretty sure he had Peep dust in his hair; he *definitely* had some on his face).

"Did you tell them?" Lillith asked Delaney.

"We're going to pick up Rake's phone tomorrow," Delaney replied. Poverty was making him paranoid, because that almost sounded like a warning. Certainly the others didn't hang around long after that.

"Why'd you tell them?" He didn't mind, but couldn't help being curious. "And why were they in such a hurry to take off after you did?" He'd barely had time to blink before the three of them were on the other side of the door.

"Oh. They—they're curious about you is all."

"I can't be the only American they've worked with."

"True, but you're one of a kind, Tarbell." She shook off whatever odd mood she was in and found another smile, a real one, the pretty one that made him want to kiss her on the nose and collect a giggle. "You want some grub?"

"God, you're so cute and you sound like some kind of cowboy/city slicker hybrid." He'd said it without thinking—it certainly wasn't a criticism; he liked that she had very different moods at very different times. But once it was out of his mouth, he thought about it and realized that sometimes she seemed almost schizophrenic. Big-city sophistication one minute

("The best sushi I've ever had was in Chicago, along with the best pizza and the best pumpkin pie. Isn't that a weird trifecta of best?")

and country cowgirl the next.

("I'm *not* crazy. If you ever tried milk fresh from the cow, you'd love it. It's warm and foamy and rich, it's like drinking dessert. Stop making gagging noises!")

But when he'd asked about it, he'd gotten the patented Delaney shrug and a casual "I lived all over as a kid."

Yeah, I'll bet. Were you happy anywhere as a kid? Or was it all "eventful," all the time? Where'd you come from? What happened between your birth and watching me pitch my wallet into the lake? And where do the others fit in? Especially Donna?

"Take two ladies to supper?"

"No, but I'll take you guys. Don't you make a face at me, Claire Delaney. If you open the door like that, you can't be mad when I walk through it."

"Shut up," she said kindly, and he did. For a while.

Twenty-three

"Hey, there's good news for you, Delaney." He passed the paper over. He couldn't remember the last time he'd read a newspaper made of paper. Some poor sap hadn't grabbed his change out of the vending machine and so the *Cerca News* was his because you snooze you lose, sucker! Was this how hunters felt when they bagged a lion or something? Triumphant and a tiny bit ashamed?

"What's that supposed to mean? Why good news for me?" She took in his startled expression and leaned back, rubbing her eyes. "Sorry. Didn't mean to snap. I'm tired."

No doubt. She'd sleepwalked again last night (sleptwalked?). And though it had been a few days, she hadn't brought up the DNA test again.

To be fair, neither had he. The day they met, he'd been all about reclaiming his life and his money, not even in that order. But then things got weird(er). And now there was Lillith. The truth was, if he found out he wasn't Lillith's dad, the adventure was over. Delaney and her family and Lillith would be out of his life. Forever.

Definitely Stockholm syndrome.

Speaking of Lillith, she hadn't had much to say lately, either. And the man who'd tried to snatch her hadn't been seen since. Neither had his partner, whom they referred to as "the Other Jerk" for the sake of convenience. It should have been good news. But since there was far more going on than Rake had been told, it just made him uneasy.

To hide this, he insulted his host again. "You spend too much time crunching numbers. You're always hunched over your laptop. You're gonna look like the witch when she gave Snow White the apple."

"It's what I have to do," she said shortly. "And I've got better posture than you do. One of my foster mothers was a fanatic about that stuff."

Well. That took the wind out of his sails. Jeez, how many homes was she bounced around in? "Uh, sorry."

She shrugged it off and squinted at the paper. "What's the good news for me?"

"Says right here."

She let out a long-suffering sigh. "Rake, you've got a gift, no question. The girls say you speak Italian like a native, which is a good trick for someone who's never lived here. You're fluent in French, Spanish, Russian, and German, too, right?"

He blushed at the compliment and groaned in embarrassment, two things he had never done at the same time. "Was there anything I didn't tell you that night? The time I threw up on the girl I had a crush on in fourth grade? Where I lost my virginity and got pinkeye the same night?"

"In the parking lot of the MGM grand!" Delaney couldn't even get to the end of the sentence without cracking up.

"Ha! Wrong!" He jabbed a finger at her face in triumph.

"That's where Blake jettisoned *his* virginity. He wouldn't go near the Restaurant Guy Savoy parking lot because they only had two Michelin stars."

That just made her laugh harder. "I'm starting to think you're on to something with that whole 'Blake's the worst' thing."

"Right?" Never had he been fonder of someone he hadn't slept with. The woman was genius-level perceptive! "Anyway, I lost mine to Tammy Terrin in my mom's walk-in closet." *Vermouth must be avoided at all costs; among other things I reminisce about my twin losing his virginity. Not Freudian or weird AT ALL.* "How about you?"

"It's boring," she warned.

"Doubt it."

"I was twenty-two—"

"What?"

"—and it was in a hotel room with an actual bed and everything. Very vanilla. Lights off. Missionary. Wham-bam-etc."

"Perv! Sickest thing I ever heard."

"There weren't any good parking lots around," she said with a straight face. "So we had to make do with a Days Inn."

"But Delaney, you're supercute, I bet lots of boys would have loved to have been your first. Why'd you wait so long?"

Her smile, which had broadened at "supercute," became fixed, and in an instant, the fun was done. It was as if all the muscles in her face froze at once. "Oh, you know," she said with a vague gesture. "A few times I almost did, when I was younger. It—it wasn't exactly my idea, those times. To lose my virginity. I learned how to keep them off me, but—"

"You don't have to finish," he said quickly. "I'm sorry to

be asking. It's none of my business." He realized his hands had locked into fists and made a conscious effort to unclench. *Names, I need names, goddammit. Also addresses. Blood types, too, maybe. They'll all need hospitals.*

"There's nothing to tell—I told you they *tried,* not that they succeeded." She actually patted his hand, because they lived in a fucked-up universe where she'd endured a brutal childhood and now was trying to make *him* feel better. "And to be honest I was kind of scared to lose it—to find out what all the fuss was about. What was it about sex that could make people so completely, dangerously irrational? To take risks they'd never, ever take in their right mind? Something not to be fucked with, no pun intended. So I put it off for a while."

"Okay. I can see that." Dangerous and irrational, yes. Of course. But tender and exciting and wonderful and sweet and sweaty and amazing, all those things, too. And it was even better when you were in love with the person, or so he'd been told. "Makes sense."

"And then I finally met someone nice and we did the deed after his graduation at U of M. And it was . . . you know." She smiled. "Fast. Which was fine with me."

I don't know where I am.

Oh God. Oh my God. Is that what she was talking about? Trying to walk away from? Is that why she feels trapped? For a long moment Rake thought he was going to faint. No, manly men don't faint, he'd pass out, he wouldn't faint and oh fuck, who did it and where could he find them and would Delaney lend him money for a baseball bat? And some body bags?

No one will come in? Unless I let them?

"I'm sorry." It sounded beyond inadequate. "Delaney, I'm so sorry that you were scared to—that you felt you needed to put it off. But good for you. I mean, it was your choice at the Days Inn, right? You had sex on your terms. That's— Some people don't even get that, you know?"

A shrug. He'd never known anyone who could be so eloquent with her shoulders. "It was a long time ago."

A long time ago? She wasn't thirty yet.

"Does this go back to that whole eventful childhood thing?"

Her gray gaze was on him, watching his face for—pity? Wondering if he'd crack a joke? *God, please, please don't let her think I would joke about this.* "Yeah," she said eventually. "It was." She shook her head. "I can't believe I told you that. I mean—I really can't believe it. You're an entitled pain in my ass, Tarbell, but you're sure easy to talk to. It must be the oh my God you're blushing."

"I am not!"

"You're blushing even harder now!" she cried, delighted.

As annoying as that was, it was pretty great that his lack of control over the blood vessels in his face had cheered her up. "Yeah, well," he mumbled. "It happens sometimes."

"It's sooooo cute."

"Please shut up now."

"Downright adorable, in fact."

"I hate you and everything you stand for."

That made her laugh. "That's probably true. But getting back to my point—" She gestured at the newspaper. "My point is, I can barely order a meal in Italian."

"Yeah, I've been meaning to talk to you about that. You *think* you're ordering milk, but you're actually ordering coffee and milk. Which is why they keep bringing you coffee and milk. Then you force it down and glare through the rest of dinner."

"That's because it's not so much Minnesota Nice as it's Minnesota Passive-Aggressive. I'll roll right up on a CEO who changes his mind about a charity pledge, but I've never sent a restaurant meal back in my life, and I've had some stinkers. And for the last time, whatever is in the paper you want to show me, just tell me already."

"Here. Right here." He pointed to the headline below the fold. "That jewelry/handbag shop near the Rialto Bridge. It says they had pledged a donation and then reneged, and then reneged on their reneging." He thought of what Delaney would do to anyone who promised charity and then didn't deliver, and shivered. Decapitation, probably. Followed by one hell of a long shouting match. "This is just the kind of thing you hate, right?"

"Yep." She reached out and touched the paper, looking puzzled. "That made the news?"

"Guess it was a big deal. The owner had made a show of how profits weren't letting him keep up his end, called a press conference and everything. So I guess it was big news when he did another one-eighty not even a week later." He waited, but Delaney just sat there.

Huh. Where was a delighted smile? Not that he'd been trying for one. Just trying to keep Delaney up on current events. With a *paper* newspaper no less.

"Isn't it great that they found the money after all?" he prodded.

"Yes, it's great that they promised money they'd never miss, broke their word, then changed their mind about breaking their word."

"I know you've heard this before—"

"Then don't, for cripe's sake."

"—but anything sounds bad when you say it like that."

"You can stop reading the newspaper now."

Much later, when he found out exactly what Delaney was doing to people who renounced their pledges, he thought decapitation would have been kinder.

Twenty-four

At last, at last they were going to pick up his new phone! He'd check on his accounts to see if the snafu had been fixed and, worst case, would call Blake and beg for a wire, maybe thirty or forty grand to tide him over for the rest of the month. Then: shopping. Clothes, a new wallet, more clothes, and dinner with Delaney in the most expensive place in town, and he'd leave the waiter a *huge* tip, because he was a giver.

"You've been a good sport." Delaney, amused as usual by his antics, was walking very close to him in the narrow alley. Which was just excellent. "And a big help."

"'Good' might be overstating," Lillith said, then squealed and hopped aside as he poked her. "I said *might*!"

"I've been a whiny bitch," he corrected Delaney cheerfully, "and a most reluctant helper, and you know it. But I've learned to count my blessings, like every character at the end of every TV show ever. Could've been worse, you could have worked for the Red Cross. I'd have died of anemia by now."

"That's not how the Red Cross works."

"I know, I was just kidding. I've donated before."

Delaney stumbled on a loose flagstone—nope, she stumbled out of shock. He didn't mind, because he got to put out an arm to steady her, and after that it was easy to hold her hand. Sort of a "just in case you trip again I can keep you safe" thing. Not that he was into that. Besides, he was using his other hand to hold Lillith's hand. Because he was all about safety. "You've donated blood? Willingly?"

"You bet! I'm chock-full of O-positive goodness."

"You liked it?" Her astonishment was a little ego-deflating, but at least she was too surprised to shake her hand free.

"What's not to like? The finger stick is the worst of it and that takes, what? Half a second? Then you get to lie there for a few minutes and nurses fuss and say nice things to you and if you're cold, you get a blanket, and then—cookies! And a sticker. That's my favorite. Do you know how easy it is to talk to a woman you don't know when you're sporting a bright red 'I donated blood today!' sticker and have cookie breath?"

"Gross." From Lillith.

"No idea."

"Supereasy. It's just so easy."

"Yeah, shoulda known. Leave it to you to . . . nope. I won't finish that, I'll just let you have that one. Good for you."

Cookies and blankets and stickers were reason enough, but Delaney's delight was better than a hundred stickers. A thousand!

As they got farther into the street, it got more crowded, forcing them

(yay!)

to walk shoulder-to-shoulder. More people, too, and he had a minute to be glad, for a change, that he wasn't carrying any cash, when Delaney reached back without looking and, spooky-quick, snatched at something. Rake looked and realized she'd caught a kid in the middle of trying to lift her wallet.

"Terrible," she said, looking down at the wide-eyed budding crime lord, and the weird thing was, she didn't sound mad, or even irritated. She sounded almost . . . fond? "You should have come up on my blind side, especially at this time of the day—your shadow was here before you were. Stop that." The latter because the kid was wriggling like an eel on a hook. A lovely gray-eyed hook with fingers like pincers.

"You okay?" Rake asked, stunned. She had captured a thief! With her bare hands! Without looking! Like it was no biggie! An everyday thing! "He didn't hurt you?"

"Course not, how could he? He's the size of a bag of dog chow." She blew off Rake's concern and kept her focus on the teeny thief. "Knock it off, kid, you're going nowhere 'til we're done."

"*Fermalo! Lasciami andare, bitch!*"

"Yeah, yeah, tell me something I've never heard." Far from being pissed, Delaney looked—well, it was hard to say. Her expression was a little strange. Not mad, but not happy. Not resigned, but not anxious.

Lillith, meanwhile, chose that moment to speak up. "Don't be scared," she told the wriggling child. "She's nice."

Delaney stepped to the side, bringing the boy with her, and Rake and Lillith followed. He watched her slide her fingers up under her shirt, deeply, deeply envied those fingers, then stared when she unzipped her hideous belly pack

("Hot-pink, Delaney? Really?"

"Shut up, please."

"I saw it the other night but was too polite to laugh and laugh and laugh at it."

"Shut *up*.")

and extracted a twenty-euro note, stuck it in her teeth, tore it, and handed half to the kid, who was so surprised, he stopped trying to flee. Zipped up the belly pack again, pulled down her shirt. Easy-peasy, and the whole thing took maybe three seconds.

And what was her expression? It was starting to make him a little nuts.

"Rake, my Italian is shit. Will you translate?"

"Sure." This should be good. Delaney made things interesting almost as often as Rake himself did, and usually for better reasons. And her Italian was hardly shit; she spoke it about as well as someone who'd studied it for a couple of years. If she lived here, she'd be fluent in about a year. But she didn't have a year, and whatever she was going to tell the kid, she wanted to be very, very clear.

Lillith said something else to the kid, speaking in such a low voice that Rake couldn't catch it.

"You can have the other half in less than two minutes," she told the kid. She loosened her grip but didn't let go, then squatted so she could look him in the face. "How long have you been pulling?"

The boy maybe wasn't fluent, but he understood enough English to follow her question; Rake chalked up the quick answer to the boy's surprise. He'd either never been caught before, had been caught but was always able to get free before, or the person who caught him had zero interest in talking to him, just wanted to dump him on a cop.

"Due anni, signora."

"Two years," Rake told her. And wasn't that just fucking sad? The boy was maybe nine. Ten at the most, and all elbows and eyes and unkempt hair and astonished expression. He was dressed pretty well considering his day job—the jeans and orange-and-red long-sleeved T-shirt were worn but not tattered; his hands and face were clean; his shoes looked worn but "This is how the cool kids do it" worn. He was a cutie, too, with long dark hair to his shoulders and almond-shaped dark eyes.

"You pulling for anybody special?" Delaney asked. "Or pooling?"

Rake translated the rapid-fire answer: "His older sister. She's head of the group. Parents are dead."

"Uh-huh. How's business today?"

"Great . . . two cruise ships so far." Rake laughed. "Lots of stupid—" He started to say "Americans" but changed it to "tourists."

Delaney grinned. "You didn't have to rephrase. We're the worst."

Rake started to translate, only to be interrupted by the boy. "What's wrong with you? I understand English."

"Some English. And you're pretty mouthy for a crook who weighs less than a bag of Purina," he snapped.

"Both of you shush," she said, exasperated. Then, to the kid: "Okay, so. I won't ask your name, or call the police, or try to take you to them. I won't try to take you anywhere. I'm not being nice to trick you and I'm not giving you money to make you do something you don't want to do. I'm not a cop and I'm not CPS. I'm not a mandated reporter, d'you understand?"

Christ. She's nailing all the reasons someone might grab him, a Good Samaritan or a scumbag pimp. And it's working! He'd probably follow her anywhere, but not to rob her.

"Okay, *signorina*. I know this now."

"But what story do you tell?" Lillith put in.

"*Che cosa?*"

"Lillith, I can handle this." He turned to the kid. "When

you get caught. When a cop busts you, or a well-meaning tourist tries to turn you in. What do you tell them?"

What followed in a terrible flood of words were some of the worst things Rake had ever heard out of a child's mouth. And it wasn't just that what he was saying was so horrible—though it was—it's that he was so calm and *not superpissed* about it. Like it was NBD. Like most fourth graders lived that way.

He talked about how he almost never got caught anymore. When he did, he could usually wriggle free. When that didn't work, he made up stories about shelters just for kids and they always had plenty of beds and food. Or he had run away, but he missed his mom and dad and would go home now and stay out of trouble, cross his heart and hope to die.

Sometimes they weren't so well-meaning. Sometimes they grabbed him to hurt him, to . . . make him do things. But his sister had runners all over, so the locals knew better than to try that shit anymore, and the tourists who tried it usually went back to their hotel with his—his—his something sticking out of one eye.

"Sorry, your what?" Rake asked.

The boy showed them what he'd had his hand on the entire time; sunlight bounced off of the thing, making it shine. "Oh," he replied weakly. "I did hear you correctly. You really said your 'lucky corkscrew.' How silly of me." And ye *gods*, he'd never be able to look at a corkscrew again without picturing it in somebody's eye. "Is there a reason it's not an unlucky corkscrew? Don't answer that!"

"Wow" was Lillith's comment. "You keep it really shiny."

"Why not a switchblade or something?" Rake asked.

A scornful look—from him *and* Delaney: "This is *Italy*."

"Right, right. Sorry."

"Nobody thinks twice about corkscrews here, *idiota*."

"O-*kay*, I get it."

Delaney had been listening to the entire exchange, head down, and at last she looked up. "Okay, that's pretty good. But next time you have to shake a grab, tell them you volunteer at Sorella Teresa's. Tell them they're always looking for volunteers and they can give you a safe place to sleep for a couple of days. A cop might let you go—depends on the cop. But a well-meaning tourist will almost certainly let you go."

"*Perché dire che?*"

"Because it could be the truth. My friends and I are making it come true. A real shelter, but one that isn't constrained by tiresome bureaucracy, one that doesn't have to account for every penny and isn't—never mind. If you go to this place now, they'll give you a safe place to sleep. And they'll keep the lectures to a minimum. Number's on the back of my card, okay?"

She stood, and tried to let the kid go, but Rake saw that the kid was now holding *her* hand. She gave him the rest of the euro bill and the card. "*Buona fortuna.*"

"*Grazie.*"

"That card works for your friends, too, and your sister. Anytime. I know summer's coming, but it's still pretty chilly at night. I'm not disrespecting your sister," she added as the boy opened his mouth. "I'm sure she's working very hard for you, like you are for her. But you've got other safe options for sleeping. And living. You—you do. They're out there, you can find them. It doesn't have to be one or the other." Rake didn't translate; the kid seemed to know exactly what she was saying.

"*Tutto okay*, I get it. It's fine, I'm okay!" That last was shouted, and Rake realized the kid had spotted someone at the mouth of the alley. He turned to look and saw another dark-haired street kid, only this one looked familiar.

"Hey, I think I know that guy."

"*Ciao du Nuovo!*" Lillith called, waving. "*Grazie per il telefono!*"

Rake snapped his fingers. "Got it! That's the boy Lillith talked into letting me borrow his phone a thousand years ago." At Delaney's snort, he added, "What? It's been a busy week." Meanwhile, the kid Delaney had reeled in like a trout had joined his friend and they both took off for parts unknown, doubtless to clip wallets elsewhere.

"Well, that was interesting."

Delaney snickered. "Don't worry, I would have protected you from his corkscrew."

"Jesus! You knew he had his hand on that thing the whole time?"

"Sure." This in a tone of "Of course the ground gets wet when it rains."

"Because that's what you do. Protect."

Another snort. "Don't romanticize it."

I had an eventful childhood.

Yeah, Rake thought, and not for the first time. *I'll bet you did.*

"Hey, can I have one of those?" He'd known about her belly purse, of course, but his mother hadn't raised thieves, just snoops. He'd left the thing alone, and not just because of the color. But now he knew she kept cash, credit cards, *and* business cards in it. "D'you mind?"

"My card?" she said, surprised. Her fingers dipped into the awful pink pouch and she pulled one out for him. "What in the world do you want that for?"

"I like them," he said simply. "If I had cards, they'd be just like this. Well, maybe with bloodred lettering."

"When I grow up, I'm using a hologram for a business card," Lillith predicted. "Everyone will!"

"Makes sense." He tucked her card away. Twenty-two letters. Charity. I. C. Delaney. And he still hadn't asked her about the results of the DNA test. And she still hadn't volunteered them. He knew why he was waiting, but why was she?

And, hours later, when he couldn't sleep after the frightening texts from his brother, Rake was able to put a name to the expression on her face when she snatched the would-be nimble-fingered felon.

Nostalgia.

Twenty-five

"So you buy boatloads of chocolate and stuff and deliver Easter baskets, and don't run marathons, but do take in strays—children and stranded millionaires at least—anything else?"

"No."

"Bullshit!" He was delighted and didn't care who knew it. Every damned day with Delaney was interesting—fun, even! "So you help kids get off the streets? Well, duh, obviously . . . I mean, do you do that all over, or just in Italy?"

"No, I don't get them off the streets," she answered with peculiar emphasis, like that'd be the *last* thing she'd do, like he was an idiot for even thinking it, much less asking. "They get themselves off the streets. Sometimes I can help. That's it. That's all it is."

"Why do you always downplay?" Lillith asked, doing her best eight-going-on-thirty impersonation. "Mama did the same thing. Like helping people was a secret no one should ever find out."

Well, sunshine, given that your mom's idea of helping people was thievery followed by blackmail, it's no wonder she didn't like talking about it.

"It probably goes back to their eventful childhoods," Rake explained to Lillith.

"Boy, that phrase really stuck with you, huh?"

"Oh yeah. Mostly because I thought Blake and I had eventful childhoods. Comparably speaking, ours was a walk in the park."

"Yes. Even when you were poor, you had more than I ever did." As soon as the words were out of her mouth, Delaney looked shocked. "I— Jeez. I can't believe I said that."

"I'm not offended," he rushed to assure her. "Really. It's fine."

"Thanks, but I was more alarmed about being indiscreet than offending you. You should've been a bartender—I always tell you more than I mean to."

He found that incredibly touching. Top Five Compliments Of All Time touching. Praise of any sort, he was discovering, meant a lot coming from Delaney. It could even be argued that she was a steadying, mature influence on him.

Naw.

"Come on, you impoverished jackass, your phone's in here."

There we go.

"Nice try," he said, taking Lillith's hand again and following Delaney off the sidewalk and up the steps to the FedEx service station, "but I can't be distracted that easily."

"I'll buy you some gelato on the way back to the hotel."

"Cantaloupe, please! Two scoops. No, wait . . . chocolate. No—hazelnut with a strawberry chaser."

"I can pay," Lillith piped up.

"I've got it," Delaney said reassuringly.

"Dammit! Don't distract me, either of you, I want to talk about the cool thing that just happened. So you and Donna helped kids, but only sometimes, and you don't want it romanticized even one time."

"No. Donna didn't—she left us years ago, when she found out she was pregnant. We only saw her a couple of times after that."

"Oh."

At the short silence, Delaney elaborated. "Nothing against your mom. She just wanted a different life; she wanted *you* to be different. No shame in that, and we respected her wishes. Though there were some pretty bitchy email chains before the end of it all. . . ."

"She told me she had to run to stop running." Lillith shook her head. "I didn't get it. I still don't."

"The point," Delaney continued kindly, "is that she loved you even before you were born, and wanted you to have a wonderful life. And she needed to make that happen on her own. But she always knew how to reach us. I think she thought of us as an emergency escape hatch. Only . . ."

"Only it didn't work, because she's"—Rake glanced down at Lillith—"gone."

"Don't do that," Lillith said sharply, pulling her hand out of Rake's grasp. "She's not at the store. She's dead. She's not coming back. Ever. It's not an *errand*."

"Sorry. You're right, of course." Rake figured it might be time to shift a bit. "So, Delaney, what about the others? Teresa and Elena and Sofia? Do they help you with this side of it, too? Not just baskets at Easter and stockings at Christmas?"

Delaney looked at him and sighed, doubtless seeing his

firm resolve, how he would be unmoving in the face of this latest mystery, how he was unwavering and—

"You're just gonna bug me and bug me until I answer, arentcha?"

"For *hours*."

"Fine. The others help me when they can. We've all got our own side projects."

"Sorella Teresa's!" he nearly shouted. "That's your Teresa. She runs a shelter for kids like the pickpocket." *For kids like you used to be, but I won't press you on that. Yet.* "No wonder she's so bossy. Like nun-at-a-Catholic-school bossy. My mother bossy. My grandmother bossy."

"It's an off-the-books shelter. But it's not much of one."

"'Off-the—'"

"Less paperwork that way, and they don't have to answer to city regs or explain where they get their money, and there's not a shake-up every time there's an election. When I'm in town, we get together and handle what needs to be handled. But it's way too small and way too underfunded and there's only one of them and we'd like several around the world. Which takes—well, a lot."

Rake could imagine. Not just money, though that was important. But time and research and commitment and any number of things causing any number of complications. It was a dream they'd had since they were kids stuck in what probably seemed like an impersonal and uncaring system. Their dream. A Big Pipe Dream, in fact.

"You have this cool-yet-irritating way of answering questions that just raise more questions. 'Handle what needs to be handled,' are you *trying* to be sexily mysterious?"

"No."

Her matter-of-fact response made him laugh. "Well, you

are. So you and Teresa work together, but what about the others? They've all got day jobs, right?"

"Yes."

Argh. Like pulling teeth. "Like . . ."

"That's their business, Rake" came the firm reply, "not yours. You want their secrets, you ask them yourself."

"Here's something weird about you—something else weird, I mean—asking what someone does for a living or where they live isn't me on a hunt for all the deep dark secrets of your heart. It's asking what you do. It's small talk at parties."

"Not the ones we go to," she retorted. "D'you want your phone or not?"

"FedEx doesn't sell phones. In fact, what are we even doing here? Why am I only realizing this now? Is this a trick? Are you having me shipped somewhere?"

"Ha! Like it'd be that easy." Which made Lillith, who was still irritated with him, look up and laugh.

He glanced around the busy shipping area, marveling that some things—warehouses, loading docks, cafeterias—looked exactly the same no matter where you were. "Are you going to rent-slash-steal one of their trucks to deliver eighteen thousand Christmas stockings in eight months?"

"No, you chatty idiot."

"Please," he said, offended. "I prefer 'gabby dumbass.'"

They'd gotten in line and Rake saw she had a call slip in her hand. "This is where your phone was shipped, dope," she said, clearly not tired of insulting him.

"No one ever gets tired of insulting me," he lamented out loud. Then her words sank in. "Wait, it is? Why didn't they ship it to the hotel?"

"I thought you'd want it ASAP. It wouldn't have shown up at the hotel for a few more hours."

"Oh. Thanks." He was touched, he'd admit it. "So, while we're waiting in line—"

She closed her eyes, rubbed them. "Oh God."

"—we can get to know each other a little better!"

"I already know everything about you I will ever, ever need to know."

"Pshaw! Not even close. There's loads of great stuff about me you don't have a clue about. Lillith, you can stop giggling anytime now. Anyway, so the others—they help you with your charity work, and—"

"God, you're tenacious. I wasn't expecting that."

"Why would you?" The line was moving steadily, which was ironic. On the one hand: phone, phone! On the other, Delaney was stuck in this line with him, and (kind of) answering all his questions. Some of his questions. "So you kind of live all over, and you do charity work, except when you don't, and the girls help you, except when they don't."

That surprised a giggle out of her. "Yes, you've nailed it. My life in its entirety."

"You know who I should be asking?" he added, thinking out loud. "Sofia! She doesn't treat small talk like it's a police interrogation."

"You wouldn't say that if you'd ever been arrested."

"Ha! Shows what you know, Delaney, I *have* been arrested! Disturbing the peace, public drunkenness, assault—but Blake actually started that one, not that anyone ever believed me except my grandma. I always lawyered up before any interrogation could really get going. That pissed my mom off something awful when we were still broke. What? Stop giggling. I'm sharing intimate portraits of my hardscrabble upbringing."

"I wasn't laughing," she managed, then cracked up again.

"Hardscrabble! The local gourmet shop ran out of your favorite pâté?"

"I fucking hate pâté. Uh. Sorry, Lillith."

"What's pâté?"

"It's when a bunch of sick idiots cram geese full of food, kill them, then grind up the body organ that makes bile so people can spend way too much money on it so they can spread it on their toast."

"Nooooo." Lillith looked equal parts fascinated and revolted. "Really?"

"I swear to God, kiddo, somebody lost a bet. That's the only reason they tried it." His voice was rising; he didn't care. People were turning to look; he gave not a shit. "Then they were too embarrassed to admit it tasted exactly like a ground organ that makes puke would taste, and hundreds of years later, people are still pretending it's not the worst thing in the world."

"That's it." Delaney was smiling, the nice smile, not the smirk. "That's it exactly. You've nailed it."

Heh, she said "nail"—focus! "We were talking about how you don't like to talk. Not about important things, I mean."

An eye roll. "That's pretty good, coming from you."

"Touché, jerk. I meant what I said, though, about talking to Sofia. She at least likes to talk about things besides nothing. A master—mistress?—of small talk. In fact, she . . ." He trailed off, remembering what *had* passed for small talk between the two of them.

Her work is my work.

Holy shit.

I would never take her money. She has given me everything.

"Holy shit!" he cried, then waved at the heads that snapped around. "*Scusa, scusa.*" And in a lower voice: "You scooped Sofia off the streets just like you did that kid!"

"No." Delaney's solemn expression cracked and she giggled. "She was better than the kid. She actually got my wallet and was halfway up the street before I caught her."

He was too delighted to speak. Claire Delaney: Pickpocket Bounty Hunter. And then they were at the window and Claire was presenting her FedEx slip and Lillith asked if she could use the ladies' room and he said yes and they both watched her as she went in and then Delaney was handing him a box, which he hugged to his chest and then cradled like the most precious infant ever conceived, and Lillith came back out no harm no foul and everything was right and good in the world, probably.

His last happy moment, in fact, before the nightmare *really* kicked into gear.

Twenty-six

Loathsome brother,
*   I am being held hostage in our mother's hometown and*
cannot escape the observation that this is ALL YOUR
FAULT. She controls the keys to the kingdom, the money,
and the nuclear option. Take a moment and think about
*what that means.**

"Oh my *God*." They'd taken a vaporetto back to the hotel, which was awesome because nothing kicked more ass than a vaporetto. Any water bus instantly put any land bus to shame; it was the rule. Lillith, a sensible and wise child, backed him immediately. Then Delaney talked him down from where he'd perched, arms spread and yodeling, "I'm king of the worrrrrrrllllddd!" by promising he could use her laptop to charge his phone. And, even better, hop on iTunes and copy everything over to the new phone.

---

* Again, the sordid details can be found in *Danger, Sweetheart*.

He'd been slobberingly grateful, which he expressed at the top of his lungs once he'd climbed down. She'd then sensibly/ruthlessly pointed out that he could have had a phone much sooner if he'd just opted for a cheap burner, and he'd retorted that even the poverty-stricken liked iPhones, and two days of manual labor and two of sporadic vomiting wasn't the end of the world, and was she going to criticize how he spent all his money, or just when he used his money for phones?

Then the three of them sulked for a few minutes. (He had no idea why Lillith was sulking, but couldn't ask because it meant breaking his own sulk.)

Back in the room, he'd plugged it in—how much joy the little things brought!—and Delaney watched like a hawk while he used her laptop. "What have you got on here, launch codes? Jesus, I can actually feel your hot breath on the back of my neck. That wasn't a criticism!" he added as she backed off.

Then, as the thing slowly charged, it began to wake up . . .

("It's aliiiiiive!"

"You have no filter, do you? If it pops into your brain, it pops out of your mouth.")

. . . and began rattling and chiming like it was trying to self-destruct.

"So many texts," Delaney commented with a smirk. "The ladies must be missing you."

He flushed, then was annoyed he flushed. He owed Delaney exactly zero explanations for his lifestyle. Besides, it wasn't like he was some careless lothario—that's what Blake called him, right, lothario?—who only cared about hooking up.

Oh, wait. I am *some careless lothario who only cares about hooking up. Though I never mind if they stay for breakfast. Or want to come back after lunch. Oh, fuck it.* "Well, if the ladies are missing me, Ms. Snoopy Pants, it's no concern of yours.

Also I need to download my 'forever *unclean!*' ringtone from *The League*."

"It's odd. I understand the words, but none of the context. How can you be fluent in six languages besides your own?"

"You and my brother would hit it right off," he snapped back, even as the thought came to him.

(Blake's hands, which looked like his but weren't, on her ass; Blake's mouth, which looked like his but wasn't, on her lips, Blake's dick no no no make it staaaawwwpppp!)

He shook himself, but, luckily, Delaney was used to it by now; it didn't even muster a smirk. And God, when did he last get laid, anyway? Not once while he was in Italy, but definitely in—London? Near London? Somewhere that reminded him of London?

No. Paris. Three days before the flight to Milan, Carol Kennedy had met him in the lobby of Le Bristol, and they'd gorged on strawberries and truffles and ice-cold champagne (he didn't like champagne or strawberries, but it's what the babes like, and Rake Tarbell goes along with what the babes like), and they'd started in the impossibly long tub (strawberry seeds got in the weirdest places), and finished by bending her over the glass-topped desk in the other room. She'd been getting over a cold and kept sneezing at, um, inopportune times. Then she'd dressed, polished off the last of the fruit, waved

(waved?)

and disappeared into the mysterious Parisian spring night, which, in this case, had been Serge Lutens at twelve-thirty in the afternoon.

That . . . that wasn't good.

That *really* wasn't good. Because standing in line at a FedEx hub, fully clothed and having a sex-free chat with Delaney while Lillith darted off to use the loo had been more fun than rich-guy banging at the Bristol with a former Miss New York who loved doing mouth *and* butt stuff.

Butt stuff, Rake? Really?

Shut up. I just need to get laid. I need to get ahold of Blake, get my money, do something nice for Delaney, and then get laid. I'll feel better then. I'll be back to myself then.

Yes, but is getting back to yourself what you—

"Shut up!"

"Are you yelling at your inner voice again?"

"No," he grumped.

"Your pants are on fire, you liar liar." And God, it sounded affectionate. Like when a normal woman would say "You're so cute!" Wait, did he want a normal woman? No, he wanted Delaney. Wait, what? Wait.

What?

And now, in the midst of many weird feelings, Blake was sending him the mother of all texts. And/or had lost his mind.

You'll recall we felt the best way to assist Mom would be to pay off the bank holding all the paper. This solved the immediate problem, but as a long-term tactic it was brought to my attention that it will prove to be a disaster. And so, though we are equally culpable in our mother's perceived crimes against Sweetheart, I am the only one exiled. Because you are terrible.

Wait, what? Crimes against whose sweetheart? Paying off what banks? Was that why there was a money mix-up? Did Blake and/or Mom send the wrong money from the wrong account somewhere it wasn't supposed to go? And why the hell had Blake brought up the nuclear option? They had a deal: Rake could joke about everything *except* the nuclear option, and Blake could bring up any topic *except* the nuclear option. Okay, not really a deal. A general understanding they usually stuck to while not acknowledging that's what they were doing.

"Trouble?" Delaney sounded tense but was sitting like she always did: straight, shoulders back, comfortably alert. Like she could scope Cracked.com's *Five Villains Who Went Out of Their Way to Screw Their Own Plan*, or leap out of the chair and stuff a hundred Easter baskets in under twenty, or nail an intruder in the 'nads. "Everything okay?"

"I don't know." He scrubbed his fingers through his clean but unadorned hair—soon he'd be able to buy product! Not that he used it. He just loved knowing he had the option of buying it. *Lord, let me never be bald.* "I haven't talked to Blake in—uh, what month is it?"

"May." This with barely veiled amusement.

"Don't you give me that look," he ordered. "People forget what month it is all the time."

"They don't, though."

"*Anyway*, Ms. Asks a Question Then Changes the Subject, it's been several weeks. See, our mom . . ." He trailed off. "Aw, you don't want to hear it."

She'd closed her laptop by now, the one with the absurdly long password that was at least twenty characters, including *I* and *H* and *Y*, and was giving him her full attention. She even scooted the desk chair closer to him. "I do, though."

Damned if she didn't seem sincere. "It's rich-people stuff," he warned.

She took a deep breath and leveled her steady gray gaze at him. "I can take it."

He snorted. "Okay, the thing is, my mom's been on her own longer than I've been alive. But a few weeks ago, she heard from her hometown, Sweetheart, North Dakota. And . . ."

Twenty-seven

She knew part of the story, of course, from her employer. But she was dismayed to find that Rake didn't know much more. How could he be raised by such a determined woman and not know anything about where he came from? Wasn't he curious? Didn't he want to know everything about those who came before him, *made* him?

Wow, maybe take it easy on the projecting? What's important to you doesn't have to be important to him.

Yes. Maybe.

Probably.

Fine, fine, probably. As a child of the American foster care program, Delaney had known for more than a decade all she would ever know about those who came before her. She had been named for her grandmother, Claire Maybell Snyder. Her mother had died when she was two. Father: unknown. For years she'd thought her father's name had been Unk.

The entirety of her family was dead or unk. That wasn't true for Rake, though. She reminded herself, again, that what was important to her didn't have to be important to him. She had the feeling she'd have to do that a lot.

"... right? I mean, who *does* that? Cuts a kid out of their life because they want to move to the big city? Mom wasn't even pregnant! Not then, anyway. So she left it all behind, thank God, and moved to Vegas, and she and my dad—she was his waitress, and he was some rando rich asshole—did the drunken pelvis two-step . . ."

And then she thought she should stop reminding herself. It was good to be annoyed with Rake, good to feel irritation and even dismay over his choices. Disliking him was much, much safer than liking him.

And she liked the entitled rich whiner.

A lot. Which had never, ever been part of the plan.

Why'd he have to try to rescue me? And why didn't I meet him when I was a kid? I could have shown him . . . trained him. We could be doing hits together. Instead, he met Donna and set the current disaster in motion, and poor Lillith will have to pay for it. Literally.

"... so off she went to Sweetheart, and off I went to Gstaad, and then London, and Paris, and Lake Como, and now here, except I'm pretty sure the last leg of my trip was against my will, and off Blake went to wherever he goes when he's not being reprogrammed by his robot overlords. And look!" Rake brandished his (new) phone at her. "Look at this text that goes on forever and won't die! Just like Blake!"

The terms of my atonement are as follow: 1. No more selling people's homes/farms to the bank. 2. The remaining farm, scheduled for closing next week, is off the market. 3. Said farm must be made profitable within six months. 4. By me.

5. Without my fortune, which she has pulled off the table. (You'll recall that though she allowed access to our inheritance on our eighteenth birthday, we are not legally entitled to it until we are thirty, which is twenty-three months and seventeen days from today.) 6. I cannot terminate anyone or sell anything. 7. Resistance is futile. 8. If condition #7 is ignored, she'll activate the nuclear option.

"What," Delaney asked, terrified and trying to hide it, "is the nuclear option?"

"Never ask me about the nuclear option." Rake stared at her, unblinking. "Not ever."

"Okay."

"Not *ever*."

"O-*kay*!"

"We shouldn't even be talking about not talking about the nuclear option. Thank God Lillith's bunking with Sofia again."

"Your brother knows when you'll both turn thirty to the *day*?"

"See? This is what I've been dealing with. For just under thirty years, apparently."

"And . . . your mom took away his money?"

"Naw. She'd never. He's exaggerating. Blake's always been the golden douche."

"It doesn't sound like it. It sounds like he's"—*in as much trouble as you are*, she thought but didn't say—"being serious. Like she really did cut him off from his funds."

"Impossible."

Sound nigh impossible? I quite agree, but our mother does not.

For this, in addition to many other crimes you have perpetuated upon me since our birth, you will be made to pay and pay. I warn you only as a courtesy, as dictated by the bonds of family.

Good night.

"Wow."

"Right?"

"He sounds like he could be a handful."

"A handful of priggish hypocritical crap. I can't believe it, I can't *believe* it." Rake was slashing his fingers through his longish dark blond strands; he was borderline shaggy and deliciously rumpled. "I was really looking forward to getting my phone, and the first thing that hits is a ton of Blake."

"Which you weren't expecting."

"No!"

Why do I want to keep warning him? I'm not supposed to warn him. "Yes, well, the thing is, he sounds like he's in tr—"

"I mean, look at this thing! Look at it!" He flailed his phone at her. "Who texts like this? This isn't a text, this is a goddamned thesis!" He shook the thing like it was the author of his misery—maybe in his eyes, it was—and seamlessly continued the rant. "All this to tell me he's nuts! Or playing the lamest practical joke ever! What is happening to my family, who were always weird but are now weirder?"

"Okay, okay." She made soothing noises at him, plucked the phone from his hand, tossed it on the bed, then grabbed his hands and walked him backward until he was sitting on the bed beside her.

"I like your hands." He sighed out of nowhere.

"Great. Now calm down. Let's think about this. So, you think it's a joke? In poor taste, but for some reason he's—what? Lying about everything he's doing in—what was it, Honey?"

Rake blinked at her. "Uh, no. Sweetheart." He cut his keen blue gaze away. "Sorry, for a second I thought you were calling me honey."

"Oh."

"It was dumb."

"No, it's—" She shook off the distraction. She was dim enough to start falling for the carelessly casual idiot, but she'd never *ever* be dim enough to make the mistake of telling him. Not to mention that her employer's fury would be dreadful to behold. "Okay, so your mom went to Sweetheart to help— what? Save the town?" At his glum nod, she continued. "And your brother sold a bunch of farms to the bank, thinking it'd help her, but for whatever reason it made the problem worse? Okay. And then she cut off his funds."

"Well, yeah, that's apparently the deal, but—that *can't* be true. He either got it wrong or it's his sad-ass idea of a joke. My mom wouldn't do that. Not to him."

Oh you poor idiot. "Or you just don't want it to be true," she suggested quietly. "Because if Blake doesn't have money, he can't help you. If Blake doesn't have money, it would explain why *you* don't have money. Not because of a screwup, or an online mishap. You'd really be broke. You'd really be stuck here indefinitely."

He just looked at her.

"And if he disobeys . . . the nuclear option?"

Rake shuddered so hard, the bed shook. *Interesting,* she thought. *Even the thought of imminent, permanent poverty didn't make him shake like that.*

"This is going to sound like I'm being a smart-ass," he said at last, looking at her with that blue, blue, blue gaze, "but will you please hold me?"

"Oh." She swallowed. *No. Absolutely not. Don't be ridicu-*

lous. Once you have sex with some random bim, you'll feel better.

"Sure."

He slowly leaned over until his head was resting on her shoulder and, bit by bit, he relaxed, until he was pressed to her side like a sexy lamprey. She eased them back and put her arm around his shoulders, and they lay on her bed hip-to-hip and stared at the ceiling. It should have been awkward.

It wasn't.

Which was bad.

Really very, very bad.

Twenty-eight

Okay, so. Blake had gone insane, which was bad. Very, very bad. But he was in bed with Delaney, which was the polar opposite of bad. Sure, they weren't having sex. They weren't even naked, or breathing hard. And she was a little stiff—even in a bed! Did she have excellent posture 24/7?—and her long, bony arm was slung across his shoulders in a way that was actually a little uncomfortable.

And it was fucking glorious.

"Thanks," he said after another long minute where they both hoped the other would say something.

A small sigh. "S'okay."

"It's awkward, isn't it? It's okay to say."

"No, no."

"Delaney."

"It's awkward." She giggled; he *loved* when she did that. How someone so tall and competent and no-bullshit and not giggly could make that sound was an awesome, endless mystery. "It's a little awkward. But I don't mind if you don't."

"I absolutely do not mind even a little tiny bit," he said, and didn't think he'd ever been more serious about anything.

"Okay, then. And listen, you'll—huh."

Rake groaned. His phone was rattling again. He'd gone from not being able to wait for a new phone to never wanting to see it again. He eased out of Delaney's awkward half embrace and scooped the thing up.

"More long yet cryptic texts from your twin?"

"'Long yet cryptic' is the perfect description and I'm stealing it and using it to refer to Blake forever." He scanned the thing and showed her, and she frowned at the sight of it.

The deepest darkest depths of Hell await you, little brommmmmmmmmmmmmmmmmmmmmmmmmmmmmmmm Text sent 7:45 P.M.

"Huh. Did he break the thing?"

"Never. Blake doesn't break things. He doesn't even drop them. His question, when I dropped my first phone and it broke, was, 'Why did you drop it? How could you not anticipate it would break?' Like I did it on purpose. Like it was a conscious decision. That's what a tight-ass he is."

She didn't say anything, but her expression was eloquent. Time to set her straight. "Hey, I get it. I'm self-aware, kind of. I drink too much and party too much, and have just the right amount of sex"—he ignored her snort—"and am awful in all the right ways—"

"Oh my *God*."

"—but I don't deliberately drop phones. I've adored and respected all my phones. Until today."

Delaney sat up and handed it back. "Damn. If I'd thought

your getting texts would be *this* interesting, I'd have floated you a loan the day you got to Venice."

"Sure you would have," he sneered. "Ha! You'd never renounce your slave-driving ways."

"You're right." She gave him a long look, then leaned in. Why? What was she doing? Who could she be leaning toward? If it was any other woman, he'd assume she was going for a kiss and he'd be delighted or freaked, depending. But this wasn't any other woman. He probably had pink Easter grass in his hair or something, and she was getting close to brush it away. "Listen, Rake, I'm sure things with your brother will resolve themselves. Y'know, one way or the other. But in the meantime—"

"What is *this* now?" His phone had buzzed again, but a picture this time, not a text. He stared. And stared more. Then handed the phone to her. She took one look and started to laugh.

"What is it?"

"Oh my God. I gotta meet this guy."

"Don't even joke about that. You two must never lay eyes on each other. It looks like—but . . . no. No, right? Right." Pause. "Is it?"

"It is," she gurgled through giggles. "For whatever reason, your big-city brother—trapped on a North Dakota farm—has taken a picture of a pile of horse shit and texted it to you."

"So *that's* why they call them 'horse apples.'"

"That's why they call them horse apples."

He collapsed back on the bed. "For this I worked my ass off. For this I stuffed baskets until the fake Easter grass wore my fingers to the bone! Knock it off! None of this is funny!" But he was giggling, too. Christ, what a day! What a week! Well, not quite a week. But "What a six days!" sounded dumb.

"Trust me," Delaney was saying, "that's what it is."

"Yeah, you worked on a dairy farm when you were a kid, right?"

"Yeah." Her giggles tapered off and she was looking at him in a new way, one he found he liked—a lot. It was scrutiny, which he was used to, but it was *good* scrutiny, like she'd expected to see something she didn't like but was pleasantly surprised. "Yeah, it was one of the best times I ever had. You were paying attention, huh?"

"Sure," he said, and didn't elaborate. The truth—that he paid attention to everything she said, that, if anything, he wished she'd talk *more* about her "eventful childhood"— would sound fake. Or, worse, creepy. "It's why you keep trying to score milk at dinner."

"They have cows here!" she almost shouted. "It's not an unreasonable request!"

"All right, take it easy. There's no Italian dairy conspiracy, okay? If I had my money, you could have milk with every meal and twice before bedtime. And room service would bring you milk every hour if you wanted. And I'd—I'd buy you your own dairy farm and they'd ship the good stuff to you wherever you were in the world that week."

"That's . . . sweet," she said, and he decided to ignore the surprise in her tone.

"Because when you're not in Italy, you're elsewhere, and you liked living in Boston except when you were living in the country. You're, what's the word? *Enigmatic?*"

"Or I'm pathologically unable to settle down in one place."

"Oh, baby," he said, reaching out and linking their pinkies. "We're kindred spirits."

Another giggle. "You sound creepy when you leer and call me 'baby.'"

"Shut up and pretend to be wooed by my sexy voice—"

"You do have a sexy voice," she interrupted, and then blushed for some reason. "Sometimes I wish you didn't."

"No need to lie," he said grandly. "Listen, I flew however many miles between Vegas and Paris and Montreal and New York and Vegas again and Majorca and Tokyo—"

"That's about thirty thousand miles."

"Jeez, that's amazing! How'd you do that?"

"You're not the only world traveler in this bed. Also, math."

Oh, crap. Why'd she have to put it like that? Not about math. The other thing, and now he was thinking about all the world travelers in bed together. Specifically Delaney and him. Together. In the same bed. Together. Touching pinkies! Which sadly was not a sexual euphemism.

"I've been traveling since I was a kid—mostly just in the States—and when I was old enough, I did my work—the charity—all over. But the thing about milk." She was sitting up straight again, gesturing as she got into the story. A *good* story, judging from her expression. "Once when I was thirteen, it was just me and two other girls on this big farm outside St. Cloud—that's in Minnesota. They had dairy cows and chickens, and we had to feed them. I thought they'd just eat grass all day, but it's not like it is on TV."

"Is anything? Stupid misleading television programming."

She grinned. "Yeah. Point. Anyway, the first couple of days sucked, but the food made up for it. Mrs. Hardy was a great cook and everything was from scratch—I didn't know people could bake a cake without a box of cake mix before I stayed with her. And there was a pool, and we could jump in once our chores were done. So we'd get all hot and sweaty and we could just jump in the pool, we didn't even have to take our clothes off! Good thing, too, because we didn't have swimsuits.

"Anyway, by the third day we had the routine down and it was work, y'know, but it wasn't difficult and it didn't take more than two hours. And it was kind of fun. The animals were nice, they never tried to hurt us. Okay, once a cow ran Crystal down, but it was kind of her fault—she got between the cow and the feed."

"Never get between a cow and the feed?"

"Never get between a cow and the feed. Besides, there was so much cow shit, Crystal wasn't hurt. She just sort of got pressed into all the muck and had the breath knocked out of her. And when I yanked her out, there was this awesome *splooch!* as the muck slowly gave her up."

"This is a wonderful story."

"Isn't it? And then all the food and plenty of time for homework after supper and after that we could do whatever we wanted. And Mr. Hardy was gone most of the time, so I didn't have to worry—I mean, the girls and me and Mrs. Hardy had the farm to ourselves mostly. It was really great. It was one of the best times ever."

He forced a smile. "It sounds great." Sure. Backbreaking work where she was paid in food. Oh, and not having to worry about being raped behind the barn. Access to a pool, but it never occurred to anyone that the foster kids might need, or even like, swimsuits. Nothing positive about Mrs. Hardy except she fed them, which, apparently, made her aces in Delaney's book.

One of the best times ever. Jesus Christ.

"It also explains why you're such a huge dairy snob. Which is *very* unattractive, by the way." Lie. Nothing about Delaney was unattractive. Why he hadn't noticed this the day they met was a mystery, or just proof he was a blind jackass when he wanted to be. And sometimes when he didn't want to be.

He got a pinch in the ribs for his pain, and couldn't hold back the yelp. "Easy! You don't want to hurt your fingers trying to pinch through all the muscle."

"Oh, *this* muscle?"

"Yeow! Those are—my—rock-hard—abs!" He was gasping around each word, because Delaney's long, skinny fingers were relentless, like evil, sentient bread sticks.

"I can't believe I told you that," she was saying, never letting up on the tickling for a second. "I always tell you things I mean to keep to myself. Forget a dairy, buy a bar, you'll be great at it and no one will care that you refuse to serve vermouth."

"It's the devil's—agh! Quit! You—agh! Don't make me— agh! My abs! My rock-hard abs! All right, that's—huh." He'd used his superior weight and height to tumble them over and off the bed, but somehow she'd twisted in midair and landed on top, her knees pinning his hands flat to the carpet while the tickling somehow intensified. He tried to flop like a fish on the dock, but Delaney had him cold.

"Jesus Christ," he yelped, "the first boss I've had in over a decade is a dairy-loving American ninja with an Easter fetish!" He tried to buck her off, but Delaney rode him easily, and he really wished she hadn't, because now he was thinking about another situation in which she might ride him easily, and it wasn't exactly his fault; she was exceptionally yummy and he hadn't had sex in days, and he tried again to buck her off and it worked just as well as it had the first time.

"Ha! Give up?"

"Uh." *Please don't notice I'm hard please don't pleasedon't-noticeI'mhard.* "Yes. Sure. Um, listen, I don't suppose you'd be interested in—"

He cut himself off, since someone was fumbling with a key card, and then the door was thrown open and Sofia and Lillith were there, and spotted them on the floor, which, for some reason, didn't phase them even a little. She immediately rattled off a bunch of Italian, and they both frowned, Delaney because she couldn't understand, and Rake because he could. (Lillith seemed neutral.)

"Wait, so the church you didn't think you could go to you *can* go to?" he said for Delaney's benefit, and then, to Sofia: "*Ho ricevuto questo diritto?*"

"Yes."

"I just came for my toothbrush," Lillith said, and disappeared into the bathroom. Sofia barely noticed; she seemed a little frazzled, but the good kind. Her carroty hair was standing out in some kind of orange nimbus, and she was wearing purple—again! Her outfits made her look like a mobile migraine. "But we must be quick, Delaney." And she actually hopped in place, like a frazzled, giddy rabbit.

"What?" Delaney stood straight up from Rake's tickled body without using her hands. Just popped right up, like a sexy jack-in-the-box. "But that's great! We didn't think we were going to get in there for a month, at the earliest." Then she looked down at Rake and bit her lip.

Ohhhh, he wished she hadn't done that. Her glossy dark hair fell forward to frame her face, her full lower lip swelled when she nibbled it, and she'd just been riding him a few seconds earlier, so he barely had to use his imagination to picture what she'd look like during his second-favorite sex position. Even better, what she'd look like during sex with *him* in his second-favorite sex position.

Please don't notice I'm hard please don't please don't pleasedon'tnoticeI'mhard.

Then Sofia said something perfectly innocuous

"*Ci può aiutare*—we need the help."

and Delaney just went off. "No! We can't. Absolutely not. No."

Even if Sofia hadn't understood English fairly well—and she did—Delaney's tone alone would have been sufficient translation. But she stuck with it. "*Perchè no?*"

"Because it's our work. He and Lillith need to keep out of it. Especially Lillith—you know Donna would never want this for her."

"*Tale merda! Abbiamo bisogno di lui.*"

"You get that *no* means the same in English and Italian, right?" Delaney asked, exasperated.

"Hey." To his relief, his hard-on was fading. Thank God, because here was a conversation he wanted to be part of. "Hey, it's fine."

"No."

He decided it was good that Sofia had interrupted them. If she hadn't, he would have made a bigger fool of himself than usual. Nothing like putting the moves on a woman you knew (a) you weren't worthy of, (b) had no interest in you, and (c) might be skittish about sex in general through no fault of her own. And since the blood had left his dick and gone back to his brain, he could think (pretty) clearly.

"What, no? Listen, my phone hasn't fixed all my problems yet." In response to their stares, he elaborated. "I mean, it will, give it time, but I've only had the thing for an hour and Blake's gone crazy, my money's still missing, we still can't call the cops, I still have to crash with Delaney at least one more night"—Yaaaaay!—"and pay for breakfast in the morning. I'd be glad for the chance to earn some more money."

Wow. What was happening to him and yet another charitable impulse? It definitely wasn't a niggling fear that Blake had been telling the truth about everything. It definitely wasn't a way to postpone finding that out one way or the other. And it wasn't a way to keep hanging out with Delaney and Lillith without making it look like he wanted to keep hanging out with Delaney and Lillith. It was all altruism, all the time: his new motto. He made a mental note to have shirts made. And maybe bumper stickers.

For some reason, Delaney was shaking her head even as Sofia nodded so hard, she probably made herself dizzy. "*Grazie,* Rake! We need you."

"We *don't,*" came the sharp reply. "Sofia, we can't let him—"

"Whoa, 'let me'? Delaney, how'd you like it if some man came along and tried to tell you what to do? Exactly," he added before she could reply, "you'd drown him in milk or set cows on him or push him into traffic or tickle him until he barfed. I want to help." (Somewhere, Blake was laughing his ass off.) "I demand you let me help." (Laughing so hard he choked. Rake hoped he *did* choke.) "And we still don't know what those two hoseheads are up to. We haven't seen them lately, but they did follow us, and one of them tried to grab Lillith. We should all be sticking together."

"*Abbiamo bisogno di lui,*" Sofia said quietly.

"That's right," he added. "You do need me."

Delaney was rubbing her temples in that "Rake is giving me a migraine" way he often observed in others trapped in close quarters with him. "Aw, man. Bad idea. Really terrible. But you're both right." She looked right at him with her narrow gray gaze. He pretended it didn't make his knees weak. "Okay. You can help and we'll stick together. Let's hope you don't regret it. That *we* don't."

"That's the spirit!"

"Yay!" From Lillith, now reemerged and clutching her toothbrush in a small fist. Then: "What are we doing, exactly? I missed that part."

"It will be as Rake suggested," Sofia added, pointing to him. "I will tell the others."

"We'll need supplies," Delaney replied. "Um, furniture? Supplies? Right?"

Sofia and Rake both laughed. *"Forniture,"* Sofia corrected. "How many years have we worked together? Your Italian is shit."

"Hey, that's my girl you're impugning," Rake protested. He'd finally judged it safe to stand—nothing worse than an erection tenting your shorts to prove you're a hound with one thing on your mind—and did so just in time to sling an arm around Delaney's shoulders. "Sorry, *woman* you're impugning. She's doing the best she can with her shitty Italian. Don't judge." He held his breath; he had no idea if she'd let him keep his arm there or would drive an elbow (and then maybe a fist, followed by a foot) into his solar plexus.

"Non avrei mai giudicare il mio amico. È molto più difficile su se stessa di quanto potessi mai."*

And even though Delaney raised her eyebrows in a clear question, Sofia didn't translate, and seemed satisfied when Rake didn't, either. Lillith, meanwhile, just watched like it was a riveting tennis match. She probably knew more about what was going on than Rake did. Scratch *probably*, now that he thought about it. The kiddo didn't miss much.

---

* "I would never judge my friend. She is far harder on herself than I could ever be."

"So what are we doing? More baskets? Deliveries? Meals on Wheels?"

"*We* won't be doing any of that." Sofia had left the room as rapidly as she'd burst into it, probably in search of a good hairdresser, with Lillith on her heels. "It's all you, baby." Then she blushed—again! Twice in the last ten minutes. "Rake, I mean."

"You can call me 'baby,'" he said, trying not to fall all over himself with how rapidly he put that out there. *You can call me anything you like. Baby, sweetie, darling, pet, yummypants, porkmeister, jackhammer, studmuffin, Stan the Rammin' Man . . . sky's the limit!*

"Oh, sure." She found a smile—odd how her mood had shifted so radically with Sofia's announcement. "Let's talk tomorrow, see how you feel."

As it turned out, her fears were more than justified. But the church disaster wasn't even the most interesting thing to happen that day. The most interesting thing happened before the sun had even come up.

Twenty-nine

It was scary, really, how quickly he adapted to the sofa bed, now on night four—five?—of trying to cripple him. He barely noticed the bar pressing across his shoulders, and was idly on his phone, updating his Amazon wish list

(No, I already read How to Be a Super Villain Without Even Trying.* Fewer books, but more—good Lord, Amazon sells lube by the gallon? How have I not known this?†)*

when it happened again: Delaney went from deep, motionless sleep to moving-around sleep. She sat up and, like last time, went straight to the window.

This time he was right behind her. "Hey, it's okay. You're safe."

"Really?" God, the hope in her tone! Like she wanted to believe but was afraid to.

"Yeah. No question."

---

* This is a real book.
† It's true! They sell it by the gallon.

She pulled her gaze from the window and looked through him. "I can leave anytime?"

"Anytime you want. And you can go anywhere you want, too," he added firmly. "Nobody can stop you. You're not trapped here." *With me.*

"Oh." She smiled at him in the dark. "That's a relief. I don't like it when I can't leave. Sometimes they won't let me."

"Not anymore." *Don't touch her. Don't hug her. Don't wake her up.* All of these, he figured, would be bad. Wasn't there an old wives' tale about how waking someone up while they were sleepwalking makes them go crazy? Blake would know. He could use some of Blake's healthy skepticism right about now. "You'll never be trapped again. And—" Inspiration hit. "And neither will the kids you're helping. Sofia's not trapped, either. You saved her from that." *Saved yourself from that.* "Okay?"

"I can go back to bed? Nobody will . . . do anything?"

Why was it so fucking dusty in here? It was a nice hotel, but the dust was making his eyes water. Time to talk to housekeeping; this was unacceptable.

"Course not," he soothed, steering her back to bed without actually touching her. It worked! (He had no idea how.)

"Okay, then." She went, docile as he'd never seen her, climbed in knees-first, like a little kid, and then flopped over on her back. He pulled the blankets up

(don't kiss her)

(God I want to kiss her)

to her chin and in the dim glow from the ambient light, he could see her blinking up at him. Her eyes were already going half-lidded as she started to slip back under.

"There! Now you can go back to sleep. For as long as you want. This is *your* room. The only people in here are the ones *you* say can be here."

"Rake can stay here," she said, startling the holy hell out of him. "He's nice. When he wants. You know?"

"Yeah, he's not a total asshole one hundred percent of the time, it's true," he agreed. This, then, was what people meant when they talked about damning with faint praise. "Sweet dreams, Delaney. I mean that literally: only good dreams for you. Okay?"

"Okay," she said, and closed her eyes.

He'd never wanted to crawl into bed with someone so badly in his life, and that included the night he'd watched a *Jaws* marathon when he was ten. Blake's comfort

("For God's sake, we live in a desert! *Carcharodon carcharias* would have to escape from the ocean, find an airport, fly into McCarron International, and then take a cab to our apartment before consuming you!")

somehow didn't get the job done. His mom didn't yell, or laugh, though. Just scooted over to make room, and read with the light on until he fell asleep.

But this. This thing with Delaney. This was something else. He'd never wanted to comfort and snuggle with someone like this. He never minded when the one-night stands spent the night, but he felt no actual connection with them, and he was fine when they left, which, naturally, they all did at one point, even when the one-night stand took six months.

You're getting it bad, Rake.

Yup.

When you get your money back, you can hire a platoon of private investigators and track some of these assholes down.

Definitely.

Thirty

It was hard to remember how much he wanted to sleep with Delaney when she woke him up

("It's so early I don't know what time it is."

"It's four-forty-five A.M., ya big baby."

"I've only been up this early when I haven't gone to bed yet."

"Shut up.")

and shooed him from his uncomfortable sofa bed to work at San Basso, which once was a church but was deconsecrated and turned into, respectively, (a) a haunted house, (b) a post office, and now (c) a charity. Why Sofia and Delaney thought he would find this at all interesting at any time, never mind the wee hours, was a mystery.

And Lillith was a morning person. Ye *gods*.

"So, what?" he asked, yawning. He made noises of gratitude when Elena handed him a cup of coffee, Lillith a cup of hot chocolate (at least he hoped it was), then hiked up her navy blue skirt (the hem was a prudent two inches below her knee; Elena scolded and dressed like a fifties housewife) and climbed into the van's driver's seat. "Meals on Wheels? What? And the reason we couldn't start at noon is . . ."

"*Colomba di Pasqua,*" Delaney replied, "and lots of it."

"Dunno what that is."

"And we do not start at noon because we are not lazy Americans," came Teresa's pert reply.

"Whoa! Too early for generalizing!"

Delaney ignored that, all of it, his yelp and Teresa's cruelty. "While you're doing that—"

"Doing *what*?"

"—Elena and I will work on inventory and then have a meeting with the chairman." Sofia, he had been told on the drive over, had spent the night at Teresa's shelter and was keeping an eye on the kids, as she often did. She was the youngest of Delaney's little group, and Rake had assumed her days on the street weren't as far behind her as the others' were. Teresa's third in command had also been plucked from the streets, and helped run the place. If he'd known babysitting might have let him sleep in, he would have—no. Not if it meant doing charity without Delaney. And Lillith assured him between slurps of cocoa that she'd help him do whatever it was. "Okay?"

"'Kay. Thanks for letting me finish charging my phone. When we get back tonight, I'll try to reach out to Blake again."

"Great!"

"That sounded suspiciously cheerful. So eager to get rid of me?" he teased. *Please don't say yes.*

"No. I sort of can't wait to see what Blake sends you next," she admitted with a guilty smile.

"That makes one of us." Rake drank more coffee and groaned. "He'd better be sane this time, that's all I have to say about it. Um, Teresa, not to look a gift barista in the mouth, but why are there five tablespoons of sugar in my cappuccino?"

"Whoa," from Lillith, who now had a tiny chocolate mustache, which was so friggin' adorable, he wasn't going to tell her.

"Aw, man." Delaney shook her head.

Elena turned around to scold Teresa, finishing with "You will succumb to diabetes!" which, for some reason, Teresa found hilarious.

"Sono fiducioso di morte violenta sarà la mia fine. Diabete? Ha!"

Rake said nothing; he had noticed that Europeans tended to (rightly) assume most tourists weren't fluent. Even though the other women knew he could speak Italian, they kept forgetting. And so he didn't comment when Teresa explained that she knew she'd die a violent death, something sudden, violent, and unrelated to diabetes. Given how the others (except Delaney, who was bent over her laptop, and Lillith, who didn't comment) agreed, he assumed they all shared the same outlook.

She drove the van right up to the former church, which, like every other building in Venice, looked like it had been built in the eleventh century, remodeled in the fifteenth, then benignly neglected ever since. It was near the St. Mark's clock tower which, when it wasn't so early, he appreciated as a beautiful sight. The area was mostly deserted, because Venetians were a clever and resourceful people who understood that 5:00 A.M. is still bedtime. And the tourists didn't have a clue about anything, so they were still in bed, too. (Lucky bastards.)

He walked past three pillars to the entrance, Delaney and

the others leading the way, and then they led him straight to the depths of hell: the kitchen of San Basso.

Colomba di Pasqua was a terrible fruitcakesque confection people were forced to eat at Easter. Not only that: It was tradition to *give* them at Easter. What kind of deep loathing does someone harbor to give a loved one a dense terrible cake studded with orange peel?

"It's the garbage of the orange!" he cried, then had a coughing fit when he accidentally inhaled some flour. "It's not a gift, it's a prank! Something you do to someone you don't like, every single year. *It is not dessert!*"

He was floured from eyebrows to knees, despite the apron Delaney had insisted on tying on him. Which was fine. He was a manly man and not threatened by any apron, however frilly, and better yet *oh my God Delaney'd had her arms around him while she tied it in back!* Their faces had been mere inches apart! And when her pretty wide mouth opened, he wondered, *Oh God what is she going to saaaay?*

"Try not to hurt yourself. There's a lot of sharp things in here."

"Right," he replied, because honest to God, it was all he could think of. "Thanks for the tip. No picking up knives with my mouth." This made Lillith laugh so hard, she almost fell off her stool.

"Just don't be a dumbass," she said, already on her way to the meeting. "You'll be fine."

"Hey! I don't wake you up in the wee hours and give you impossible tasks and then demand you change your entire personality!" he shouted after her.

"Shut up, please," she said in a tone he was starting to love. From Delaney, that was almost "Kiss me, you fool."

Man, do I wish she'd kiss this fool.

Then she callously abandoned him—them—to their fate, and for the first time in his life, he regretted learning Italian. It meant he was reading the recipe right. He really did have to peel dozens of oranges. He really did have to scoop up cup after cup after cup of disgusting dried fruit. He really did need a buttload of almonds, the most disgusting of all nuts, and tube after tube of almond paste, the most disgusting of all pastes. He'd cracked so many eggs, his fingers were numb as well as stained orange. He was sticky and he stank and flour was fucking everywhere and he'd been at it for *hours*.

"It's been forty-five minutes." From Lillith, who looked adorable in her giant apron, and who was as flour-splashed and orange-stained as he was.

"Don't you hate this? Why aren't you sulking because you can't stare at a screen? Any screen?"

"I like you" was the simple reply. "And if you're my dad, we have to get to know each other."

That gave him pause. "Right," he replied carefully. "But if I'm not—"

"Then I'm no worse off than I was before."

"If you don't mind my asking—"

"Uh-oh."

"—how did your mom die?"

"Hit-and-run. And nobody figured out who did it."

"Oh." But Donna had made arrangements of a sort—she must have; otherwise, Delaney wouldn't have learned of her estranged friend's death.

As if reading his mind, she added, "My friend Jim's family took care of me until Delaney came. We used to play at each other's houses all the time, before. His mom said we were practically siblings anyway."

"Yeah?" He kneaded more disgusting dough, hoping that a lack of eye contact would keep her talking. "Did you mind? Being an only child?"

". . . No."

"Because I kind of envy you."

"You shouldn't."

"So it was just you and your mom? The whole time?"

"Sure."

"Did she ever talk about me?"

"Sure."

"She did?" He stopped with the dough and looked up. "Really?"

"Mm-hmm." Lillith was working on her own smaller pile of disgusting dough, but now she looked up and smiled. "She said meeting you changed everything."

He hadn't expected to feel pleased. "Really?"

"Sure! She said when she found out she was pregnant, she knew she couldn't waste any more time scamming pretty boys, she had to grow up and be a responsible human being."

"Oh."

"You were responsible for her one-eighty. She always gave you credit for that."

"Great."

"Why haven't you asked about the DNA test?"

"Uh." *Wasn't expecting that from the kiddo. Delaney, yes. Not Lillith.* "I'm not sure that's something we should—"

"We're friends, remember?"

He nodded. "Yes, that's right. And friends don't lie, so I'll tell you the truth—I haven't asked because I'm not sure what's going on. And I'm curious. Because I thought all I wanted was my money and my life back, but . . . I just don't want to walk out of the theater until I know how the movie ends. And . . ."

"And you're wondering why Delaney hasn't brought it up, either."

"Yeah." He surrendered, reminding himself he was in the presence of a mind quicker and less cluttered than his.

"It's limbo, kind of. The in-between. No one's in a rush to get to the next stage of—of whatever this is."

He nodded.

"Which is curious." She was fixing him with that dark gaze again. "Don't you think? I mean, I know why *I'm* in no rush. And you know why you are. But what's motivating Delaney?"

"You're . . ." He tried to think of the word. Settled for a poor substitute. "Extraordinary."

"No. Just smart." But she smiled down at her dough, and edged a bit closer to him.

"Break time!"

"Thank God," he groaned as Delaney and Elena came back to the kitchen.

"For the child, *idiota*."

"Oh, please, not another one of those 'Working children fourteen hours a day is cruel' softies." But he was already helping Lillith clean up, handing her a damp kitchen cloth to destickify her hands. When he moved to brush the flour off her shirt she jerked back so quickly, she nearly fell. "Whoa! Careful, hon."

"Sorry. Ticklish."

"Come along, my sticky tickly sweetheart."

"Please don't talk to me like I'm three."

"You would prefer if I talked to you like you're forty?" Elena asked.

As he and Delaney watched them leave, he grinned to hear Lillith's "Come to think of it, yes."

"How's it going?" Delaney asked in the tone of someone who didn't actually care how it was going.

"Well, I'll tell you." He shook his head so hard, flour flew and, fuck, it was in his hair now? How was that possible? What was the apron even doing? Because it wasn't keeping flour out of his hair, that was for sure. "I'd pay someone a thousand bucks to get out of this."

"Be glad I let you skip the hairnet."

"Oh my *God*," he replied, appalled. "I'm not vain, but that would be a crime against nature." He clawed his fingers through his hair, then realized how the flour had gotten there. "When it's clean, I've got great hair, and a hairnet—it'd be like drawing a mustache on the *Mona Lisa*."

"But you're not vain," she teased.

"Not even a little."

"See? Count your blessings. However terrible things are, they can always get worse."

"Thanks for the pep talk." He took a break from kneading awful dough to glare at her. "I love it when you drop by."

"We're almost done here. But seriously. Rake. Things can get worse." She *sounded* serious, like she was actively warning him, as opposed to rattling off a cliché.

"This isn't really a church anymore, right?"

"Right."

"Good. Because this *fucking* sucks. And I'm gonna blaspheme the shit out of the place, because making awful bread takes forever."

"Again: forty-five minutes."

"*Fucking* sucks."

Delaney was, as usual, unmoved by his pain. Heartless, gorgeous wench! "If you worked while you bitched, you'd be half done already."

"Why are you talking like that's some kind of incentive? D'you even know what Easter is about?"

"Nope." She leaned against the opposite counter, crossed her ankles, crossed her arms, and watched him. "CPS has a hard enough time taking care of kids' physical well-being, never mind the spiritual."

He admired the way she said it: like one of her flat facts ("Cantaloupe gelato is the best gelato, no others are worth discussing"), not something to elicit sympathy, or attention. He had the feeling that anyone who pulled the "There, there, poor darling, I'll take care of you" crap with Delaney went home with a black eye.

"Okay, so, not much church. Got it." He held his hands up, placating, and coughed when he stirred up more flour dust. "I'll lay it out for you."

"Goody."

"Easter's about shiny fake grass and crappy-ass chocolate and scary-ass Peeps and coloring eggs that no one eats and getting a bellyache from eating too much crappy-ass chocolate. That's what it's about. Not"—he gestured to the messy kitchen, his floured body, the piles of orange peel, the tubes of almond paste, the utter nightmare surrounding him—"this!"

"That was beautiful." She smirked. "You should write greeting card verses in your spare time."

"I know you're being sarcastic, but thank you."

"Y'know . . ." She gestured at the piles of garbage destined to go into the next batch of dough. "It's pretty good."

He could feel his temper unraveling. "It's not! Not even a little."

"You've been to Italy before, have you even tried a piece?"

"Yes! Once, when I was trying to bang a baker. She made it for me and I had to eat the whole thing and it sucked!"

"You know you're screaming, right?"

"I'm aware!" Worse yet: screaming his sexual résumé. The baker had been way too fixated on using food during sex. Chocolate he didn't mind. Dough, though?

That grin again. Any other woman would be pissed, or backing off, or yelling back. Claire Delaney just looked like a stranded millionaire shouting at her in a deconsecrated church kitchen was a present she got to open early.

"Look on the bright side," she suggested, "now I know what to get you for your birthday. And thanks to Blake, I know exactly when it is."

"I! Hate! Everything!" Each word was punctuated by his fist slamming on the countertop, raising a cloud of flour. Then he ruined his rage roars by sneezing.

"You seem tense. Maybe you should suck on a tube of almond paste until you calm down."

"Oh my God, you are a horrible bitch," he groaned.

"Yes." The smirk was gone to wherever her smirks went when she wasn't smirking. *Hmm. Might not have gotten enough sleep last night.* "It's good you know that, Rake. It's a good thing to always keep in mind."

He shook his head and stepped away from the counter, which had the doubly pleasing effect of distancing him from piles of orange peel and getting him closer to Delaney.

She had her dark waves pulled back into a ponytail, which rippled whenever she turned her head, and ignoring the urge to touch it and press it to his lips was taking not a little self-control. She was wearing faded jeans and a black BOSTON EST. 1680 sweatshirt

(Somewhere else she lived? Or just passing through? Does she belong anywhere? Did she ever?)

and on anyone else it would look like she was getting ready to paint, or move

(odd clothes for a meeting at church)

but on her it was exactly right, perfect for supervising an entitled millionaire when not scooping pickpocketing children off the streets and keeping half an eye on a brilliant child who might be his.

"I can't touch you," he said, and why was he hoarse? The hour? The screaming? "I'll get flour on you."

"It's a risk I'm willing to assume for the greater good" was the solemn response, which made no sense and was ruined by a giggle.

He touched her anyway; he couldn't help it. He cupped the nape of her neck in his hand and tasted her mouth, her ripe, sweet mouth. She tasted like hot chocolate (Delaney was not a fan of coffee) and smelled like clean cotton, and her hands came up to press against his chest. He started to pull back, thinking she wanted him off of her, but she tightened her grip and he couldn't move, and never was being held in place so glorious. He traced the seam of her lips with his tongue and she opened for him; her tongue touched his and she nipped at his lip.

He pulled back and groaned, then ran a thumb over her full lower lip. "That's so good, Delaney, my God, your *mouth*." And then he had to have it again, had to taste it, taste her, and it took several seconds to find the discipline to stop.

He sucked in a deep breath and shut his eyes, his lips still on hers, but now barely touching. "If you're going to retaliate, could you just knee me in the 'nads or something?"

"Not the face," she said into his mouth. "Got it." And then kissed him *back*.

Thirty-one

This is stupid. You are stupid, Claire Delaney. You are making something already complicated and dangerous even more complicated and dangerous, and for what? To kiss a pretty boy? To find out he tastes like oranges and sugar?

It'll be so much worse later. You're making it so much worse right now.

She didn't care. Rake was a wonder, bigger and stronger, but he kissed like he wasn't; he kissed like she could leave off anytime. He had one big hand on the nape of her neck, holding her skull like an eggshell, and the other was on her lower back, pressing her into him. She didn't feel overwhelmed, or trapped.

Just safe.

She was safe. Tough to worry about anything when she was safe. Not that she needed Rake Tarbell to feel safe. Or anyone.

Then: *What are you* doing? *Of course you have to worry; it doesn't matter that he's got a doctorate in locking lips.*

True, but where would you even go to school to get that kind of doc—

You have to leave! Bad enough you let him get mixed up in this, but lingering after a hack isn't smart. You knew better than this when you were fourteen.

She pulled back and Rake groaned again, a deep rumble she felt all over, but he let her go. "Should I be preparing for a beating?" he asked. "It's fine, you know. I just want to know what to expect."

"Don't be an idiot. It was as much my idea as yours." She'd been working up the courage to go over to him and kiss the flour off his nose, when he'd crossed the room and kissed her. Like it was easy. Like it wasn't a terrible idea.

And then, because she was a stupid, stupid woman and had to know: "There've been some positive things, right? Being trapped here, um, with me . . . it hasn't been all bad?"

He smiled. "It's been pretty much all positive since I stopped compulsively barfing."

Pathetic how much that meant to her. But at least now she could get back to business. "We have to go. The volunteers will finish."

"Really?" He made no effort to hide his delight. "We're done? No more orange peeling? No more paste squeezing? We're finished?"

"You are." *And why aren't you asking about the DNA results, Rake? Because I don't dare bring them up until you do.*

Operation: Make Rake Embrace Responsibility aside, she'd have to follow up to see if that selfish pig of a chairman was going to see reason or if she'd have to use the hack, but that wasn't Rake's concern. She almost hoped he wouldn't see reason, so she could put out the hit. That was happening more and more often these days. . . . "I might have to come back."

"Charity's never done, huh?" he said, and for a wonder he wasn't teasing.

Charity. Revenge. They were often the same, she'd found out. At least the way her family did things. "C'mon. I'll lend you twenty bucks for a small coffee. You like tons of whipped cream and syrup in your coffee, right?"

"Who doesn't?" He was whipping off the apron and swiping halfheartedly at the messy counter. "We're really leaving it messy like this?"

"Like I said, the volunteers"—the *real* volunteers—"will take care of it."

"Excellent." Then he gallantly held out a (floured) elbow. "Shall we?"

Enjoy this. He won't be speaking to you soon enough.

"We shall," she replied, and found a smile from somewhere.

Thirty-two

Rake made it back to their room with every intention of texting Blake, but when the adrenaline rush of the kiss wore off, he realized it wasn't even 8:00 A.M. He could actually get in a nap and wake up closer to an hour that wasn't quite so horrific. Besides, Delaney was only a few minutes behind them— she'd lingered with the others to tell them about her meeting at the church. Maybe they'd kiss more. Maybe they'd kiss a *lot* more. And she seemed pretty interested in his texts from Blake; maybe there'd be more pictures of animal shit to show her. (Wow. That was a sentence he'd never thought before.)

So he got comfortable on the hide-a-bed to wait, and the funny thing was, he wasn't even tired. He should be; between playing with his phone and then thinking about Delaney's sleepwalking, he'd gotten about two hours before she yanked him out of (sofa) bed. Should he tell her? Would she freak? Hard to imagine Delaney losing her cool; it was more likely she'd be embarrassed. Self-assured people didn't like it when other people saw their vulnerabilities. He'd grown up with two of the most self-assured people he'd ever met (helloooo,

Mom and Blake!); he knew all about how they didn't like looking vulnerable.

Well, he'd think about it while he waited for the gray-eyed whirl of sarcasm/slave driving that was Claire Delaney—and what was happening? Why was she looming over him? And shaking him?

"Rake? You okay?"

"Course." He yawned, glanced at the clock— Oh. "Huh. Ten o'clock? Really?"

"Did you— How'd it go?" Delaney was actually nibbling on her lower lip, which was distracting as all hell, because it made *him* want to nibble on her lower lip. "Are you okay?"

He was warmed by her concern and caught the small hand shaking his shoulder. He squeezed it, then reluctantly let go. "I haven't tried to call him. Thought I'd wait for you first."

"Why?" Delaney's eyes were narrow with suspicion, because he could never figure her out. To be fair, they'd only known each other for a few days. "Why would you do that?"

He didn't even have to think about it. "Because I like being around you guys. What, that's so hard to believe?"

"Yes. Very. You didn't think you were going to get laid, did you?"

"No! I swear!" Truth! At best, he'd thought . . . "I wouldn't have said no to another kiss, though. You're the best kisser." He saw the unwilling smile bloom. "You are! You fiend, you knew it all along."

"I did not!"

"You're always walking around with your lips hanging out, flaunting them, being all oh my God please don't tickle me again."

She'd been reaching for his ribs but pulled up short when he begged. "Hmph."

He grinned up at her and squashed the urge to sit up, grab her, and pull her down onto the bed into a full-bodied hug. "Your 'hmph' isn't fooling me, look at you! You were worried and everything. What, you thought I'd have such an infuriating conversation I'd pass out in a rage?"

"Kind of," she admitted.

"You're sweet!"

"Shut up."

"'She said sweetly.'"

"Stop it. Look, will you please call him? Don't you want to get this over with?"

"All *right*, jeez, such a nag. A nag with good advice, actually." He got up, unplugged his phone from Delaney's charger, then reread Blake's doctoral thesis of a text. He sat back on the bed and got right to it.

Christ Blake I thought my phone was going to blow up what's going on with you I mean jeez?

Ahhhh, felt so good. He didn't have the vocabulary to express how good it felt to be texting again. And this was just the sort of text that would aggravate the bejeezus out of his brother: profane, a run-on sentence, no punctuation. Heh.

A few seconds went by, and then:

Did you lose another phone, idiot?

Nice. All his bro knew was that Rake hadn't been returning his texts. Was it because he'd been kidnapped? Hurt?

Gored by a bull? Run over by a train? Bobbing facedown in the Grand Canal? Any of those things could have been true. (One of them was maybe true, and the third one almost happened.) But noooo, it must be because Rake lost another cell phone. God, lose five in two years and everyone rushed to judgment.

No! I know right where it is, it's still at the bottom of the canal so now who's the idiot?

Canal? Never mind. Thank you for eventually acknowl-edging my dozens of communiqués.

Ugh. Blake texted just like he talked: like no one from this century.

Only YOUR phone autocorrects communications. See? Mine didn't. Where are you?

If you'd listened to any of your voice mails, you'd know.

Rake snorted.

And if you had a Facebook page like a real live boy, I'd also know. Where?

The fifth circle of Hell.

He reread the text, troubled. Blake didn't just say things; there was always a double or triple meaning. If he was comparing something to Hell, that meant he was in the middle of something truly awful. Shit. Blake was supposed to help *him*, not the other way around.

So let's see, since Blake loved to be literal, where was Hell? Or, more important, where did Blake *think* was Hell?

You're back in Vegas?

No. The real Hell. Actual Hell.

Even more puzzling! But at least that narrowed it down a little.

What are you doing in L.A.?

Having an incredibly irritating text chat with my twin.

Ha! That was more like it. For a second, he'd been worried. He glanced up and saw Delaney watching with a tense expression. "It's okay," he told her, "he's okay." Supersweet of her to worry, though. Maybe he should be milking this. He affected a scowl as he texted.

Because I'm terrible? People have told me you think I'm terrible. Personally I don't see it.

"That'll get him," he chortled to Delaney, who managed a small smile. "Hey. Are you okay? You seem kind of— Ha!" He showed her the phone, which had started chiming. "Blake hates talking to me on the phone. *Hates* it. Whatever's he's up to, it's gotta be bugging the shit out of him, or he'd never call after a tiny text war like that."

"I'm sure you're right." She looked away as he got ready to answer.

Would it be crass to ask her out before he got his money

back, or a few hours from now, when he'd be rich again? Because even though he'd soon be back to being able to afford any hotel in the city, he had no intention of just disappearing from her life. Though, in fairness, it'd be more like she'd disappear from his. And, worse, Lillith would. He'd never in his life met people more rootless (root-free? sans roots?) than himself.

It was exhilarating, and a little disconcerting. One thing was for sure, though: Pretty soon his troubles would be over.

Thirty-three

"Dude! Do you know what time it is here?"

"No," came Blake's answer, and it was always weird to hear his own voice on the other end. They were nothing alike, except in looks, mannerisms, voice, and love for their mom.

Time to tease. "Damn. Was hoping you did, because I'd kinda like to know. I can't tell if the new phone is right, and when I use the hotel phone, the guy on the other end won't speak English."

An exasperated sigh from Blake's end; Rake grinned. "I cannot help you. And you're a grown man who's nearly thirty, stop using *dude*. Where are you?"

"Venice."

"But you loathe California."

"No, the other one." Rake wasn't quite the careless playboy Blake assumed, but it was fun, sometimes, pretending he was, and so he stuck it to him a little. "I'm pretty sure."

"Pretty sure? Even for you, that's odd."

Annnnd now to really jam it. "Venice is the one with canals instead of streets, right? And people speak Italian? And the Italian food is really good? And there's gelato all over the place?"

A frustrated sound, like a swallowed groan, came through the line. "Yes, you dolt! Italy is seven hours ahead of the central time zone, so that should help you narrow it down." Rake could hear Blake moving around on the other end, probably getting ready for the day, and was that—it was: He distinctly heard the sound of a toaster being turned on. "You are in Venice."

"That's a relief," Rake teased. "It sucked, not knowing where I was. Why are you making toast at oh-God-thirty?"

"Never mind." A pause, then: "Wait, you weren't making another tiresome joke? You just *woke up* in Venice?"

Well, *finally*. "See? You're not the only person having a weird month. Not to belittle your woos or anything—"

"Woes," his brother snapped back.

"—but I'm neck-deep in my own shit, I promise." And he was. But talking to Blake was having the usual effect: He was annoyed, but he also knew Blake would fix it. Why had he postponed this conversation? Just to see if Delaney would give him another kiss?

"Your shit is not as all-encompassing as my shit, I assure you."

Hmm. A challenge? Foolish mortal. "Wanna bet? I'm stranded on the other side of the planet with no money in a country where I don't speak the language—" He loved, *loved* that Blake got *polymath* and *polyglot* mixed up. "And I don't know where my pants are. Doesn't that make you feel better?"

"It does," Blake admitted. "What's her name?"

Oh no he didn't! Delaney and Lillith were *his* secret. Nothing about them, including their names, was any of Blake's business. "There are five of them, I think." Right? In ascending order of weirdness: Elena, Teresa, Sofia, Lillith, Delaney.

"Good God." Ah, this was more like it: Blake sounded appropriately appalled.

"Now I just have to figure out which one is responsible for my being here." Not really. He'd apparently gotten so drunk, he'd been able to con someone into giving him a ride from Lake Como to Venice. And that was the *least* interesting thing that had happened all week. Even cooler: He barely minded. If he hadn't pitched his wallet and drowned his phone, he would never have met Delaney or Lillith. "And what I have to do in order to get the hell out of here and get back home."

"Rake, I know exactly how you feel." Sorry, *what*? Was that actual, honest-to-God sympathy from Blake "Tightass" Tarbell? Meanwhile, his brother was still pontificating: "Wait. You said you're stranded with no money. You didn't return my call to find out what trouble I'm in, you called for a loan so I could get you out of the trouble *you're* in."

Busted. "Anything sounds bad when you put it like that."

"You are terrible," Blake hissed. "And it gives me genuine joy to tell you I have no money, either."

"What? Oh hell, you can't be serious. What am I saying? Of course you're serious, you're constantly, tiresomely, relentlessly serious. Fuck and double fuck! Fuckity fuck!"

Blake, always courteous, let him finish with the potty mouth. When he took a breath to swear more, he could hear running water—ugh. "Like me," he said while Rake paused for breath, "you've brought this on yourself."

"You know I hate listening to you spit." Was there anything more disgusting than watching someone brush their teeth? No. There was not.

"There are far worse places to be stranded," Always Pontificating Blake said, "than Venice."

"This is true." Rake could feel himself perking up in spite of everything. But it wasn't being stuck in Venice. It was being stuck with Delaney and Lillith. "So your messages said you're in Mom's hometown? And you're working on a farm?"

"Are you asking me? If that's what my messages said? Because you're using an upward inflection at the end of your sentences? Denoting a question?"

"God, I hate you . . . *Yes.* I'm asking if it's true."

"I am incarcerated in Sweetheart."

"Ha!"

"And I am working on a farm. Not one our mother inherited."

Rake had to puzzle that one over for a few seconds. Their mother had inherited a number of farms, but Blake . . . *wasn't* working on one? Just some random other farm? "Uh, that's good, I guess?" But why? No. He wouldn't give him the satisfaction. "Not really sure what you're wanting to hear from me on this one. . . ."

"Our great-great-grandfather built it."

Okay, weirder and weirder. "He did?" Rake could count the number of times their mother had talked about her family on one hand. Their great-great-grandfather could have been a Hoboken butcher, for all he knew.

"Or was it our great-grandfather?" Blake mused, like they had time for *that.*

"Are you serious with this shit?"

"Completely." Then, compounding the weird: "My toast is ready."

"Did you just say your toast is ready?"

"Is it a bad connection, or are you tracking more poorly

than usual?" Ah, there was the nasal nastiness Rake had come to expect. "Yes. My toast beckons. And after that I might have time to steal some bacon if I can somehow lure Gary from the table. Then I must feed my pony, the terrible Margaret of Anjou, and foil whatever plan B Garrett Hobbes may be putting into motion so his fertilizing company goes under and he's free to open a chain of strip clubs in Hollywood. Or possibly design toilet paper."

Jesus Christ. Rake, for one of the few times in his life, couldn't think of a thing to say. It sounded like his twin was losing his shit. Or his mind. Or both. Yes, both. "You use the word *terrible* a lot." Then, because out of all the nonsense, that was the part Rake found most intriguing: "They gave you a horse?"

"They cursed me," Blake corrected, "with Margaret of Anjou, the foulest, cruelest, most vile pony in the history of equines. And perhaps she isn't terrible."

Annnnd it was official, Blake was drunk. "Sorry, did you say it *wasn't* terrible?"

His twin let out a sigh/groan hybrid. "*She* is just one more problem I can't solve on a list of problems I can't solve. If you're drowning, you don't especially care if someone pours a bucket of water over your head."

"You need to get laid," Rake said, his go-to answer for every problem Blake discussed with him. "Clear your pipes."

"Vulgar," he sniffed.

"And effective! Tell the truth, you haven't gotten any farm tail, have you?"

A growl. "You are terrible."

"Old news, big brother, and answer the question."

There was a long, telling pause

Knew it! He's not getting any!

and then: "I don't deny having infrequent intercourse of late."

"Knew it! That's always Blakese for 'major dry spell.'"

"By choice!" his so-horny-it-had-driven-him-clinically-insane brother protested. "I've been trapped on the desolate prairie, and the opportunities for intercourse have been rare."

Brrrr. Where to even start with this? "Okay, first thing, maybe you'd have more frequent intercourse if you stopped referring to it as intercourse."

"It's accurate."

"Hmmm."

"Stop that."

Got it. It's not that he hasn't been laid. It's that he wants to get laid by someone in particular, and she's not into it. "There's a girl, isn't there?"

"Of course not."

Rake made a face. "Ugh, fine, a woman, there's a woman stuck on the prairie with you."

"There are"—ah, the familiar sound of Blake evading—"several. Of course I'm not interested in all of them, just Natalie Lane."

Got him! "You're sooooo easy," Rake chortled. Delaney had noticed in a day and a half that people told him things they meant to keep to themselves. Blake had known that for decades but still made that same mistake. "So talk about Natalie Lame."

"Lane, you imbecile," Blake hissed. "And she's wonderful. Smart and driven and fierce."

That gave him pause. He'd never heard Blake use those three words in any sentence ever, much less in any sentence describing a potential romantic partner. Could it be? Was his big brother falling in love?

That . . . would be so cool. Like, the best thing ever. Teasing Blake about dying alone was one thing, but Rake had never actually wanted him to, y'know, *die alone*. But better not let him figure that out. Not yet, anyway. "Uh-huh, and what's the body situation? Is it wonderful to watch her arrive, or watch her leave? Or is it more about the face?"

"You are a pig."

Rake waited.

"And she has a lovely face. She's Irish and Native American"—a goofy sigh while Rake tried to build a mental Etch A Sketch of this Natalie Lame person—"and has wonderful blue eyes and gorgeous cheekbones."

"Nice." Speaking of wonderful eyes, Delaney had a pair! But he wouldn't discuss that now. Delaney was *his* sigh-inducing lady, thanks very much; Blake could stick with what's-her-face with the cheekbones.

"She's kind," Blake agreed, "but she doesn't think she's kind. And she loathes me, of course."

Rake, who had been scrunching into the pillows to get more comfortable, sat up so fast, he nearly tumbled off the edge. "What, 'of course'?" Not this shit again! Blake was the worst, but that didn't mean he was actually *the worst*. "She hasn't known you enough to loathe you, so where's she get off? Hey, if she doesn't get what a great catch a history-obsessed, technology-loathing, glum, slutty stick-in-the-mud like you is, screw her."

"Thank you." Rake could actually hear his twin smiling into the phone. "She sees me as an apathetic interloper who has contempt for her way of life, and she's not entirely wrong."

Fuck that. Fuck that *twice*. And with extreme prejudice. "You're too hard on yourself." Then, lest Blake think he was going soft, he added, "That's *my* job, you apathetic, interloping jagoff. Ask her out!"

"To what end? She won't leave Sweetheart under her own power, and I won't stay."

This again. His brother, who had once taken on three bikers and an elementary school teacher at a Vegas indoor BBQ, was terrified to put himself out there when it came to anything beyond getting laid. "Um, I dunno, because you like her?" Dumbass? "And she'd like you if you unclenched long enough?" Dumbass. "And it'll make your prairie sentence go a little faster?" Dumbass! Then, lest he scare the guy away from it: "You don't have to marry her, for God's sake."

A sigh. "Thank you for the advice. I'll consider what you've said."

Rake didn't bother holding back his snort. "Uh-huh, Blakese for 'You're full of shit, but I'm way too classy to tell you.'"

A laugh. "Yes."

"So let's talk about something we *can* agree on—namely, how we can get back control of our money."

"Excellent question." Blake's tone brightened at once. "And it's fortunate you chose this week to acknowledge my messages—"

Rake ground his teeth. "I *woke up* in another *country*! Without pants!"

"—because you need to understand: I have employed the nuclear option."

Ha ha ha very funny Blake it almost sounded like you said oh my God so dizzy so very dizzy ow . . .

Thirty-four

"You have to tell him, or authorize me to tell him." Delaney was on the phone in Teresa's room, speaking in a low voice. Pure force of habit; Rake couldn't have heard her if she'd stood on the bed and shouted.

A murmur from the other end.

"I don't care. Step up, or I will." A pause while she listened. "Yeah? Well, he's talking to his brother right now. He's about to find out all of the bad but none of the good and then you'll be toast. Listen: He's a good guy. Annoying and entitled as shit, but decent, and I'm sure if you— Ouch." The snarl of static not only cut her off; it made her ears ring.

(Huh. I thought that was just an old saying.)

"No, I'm not telling you your job." Not anymore, that was for sure. Cripes. She reminded herself that the Big Pipe Dream was going to be the Big Thing That Never Happened if she didn't hold up her end.

"Listen. Please. You gotta authorize my follow-through. He needs to know what's going on, not just part of what's going on, and they're— What?" She listened, then said,

"No, I haven't seen them around. Pretty sure they've decided they're on the wrong track—which is what we both wanted, right? Now. I need to be able to go back into our room and— Of course, 'our' room. I didn't think that when you took his money you *actually* wanted him to sleep in the park." She listened, her unease rising every second. That was fine; it could keep her nausea company. "No, of course not. He sleeps in the hide-a-bed, and— Nuh-uh. No. That's not what you're paying me for." Unfortunately. "The hell's the matter with you? I'm going to have to— You will? Right away?" Huh. Unexpected. And it would make everything worse and then maybe—maaaaybe she'd be off the hook and everyone could go back to their Rake-free lives.

Their lives is what she meant.

Or maybe her employer would just show up and slaughter everyone. That could be okay, too.

Thirty-five

For a moment, Rake thought he'd honest-to-God faint, just swoon like a heroine in a black-and-white movie. Bad enough he'd fallen off the bed; now passing out seemed imminent. He'd been gripping his phone so hard that his fingers ached, but finally he managed to whisper, "Don't even joke about that."

"I would never, because I agree," Blake said, also subdued. "It's not a thing to joke about."

"You didn't. Right?" Rake heard the pleading tone but was helpless to stop it. "Blake? Come on, man, you're winding me up. You didn't really do that. Right? Blake? You didn't, right?"

"Rake, our mother left me with few alternatives."

He slapped his hand over his eyes. It was, unfortunately, the hand holding the phone. "Ow! Oh *God*." His mother had cut Blake off—that alone was difficult to wrap his brain around. But she had threatened Blake with the nuclear option if he didn't obey. So Blake . . . deployed the nuclear option? It made no sense! It was like using a tank to go grocery shopping: total overkill. The guy was drunk. Or nuts. Or suffering from a high fever.

"And if nothing else," Blake was blah-blah-blahing, "it will be a way to get some answers out of Shannah Banana."

"Who? Listen, tell the truth. I won't be mad. It's a good joke." Rake managed to croak a fake laugh into the phone. That sounded natural, right? Not even a little like a duck being slowly strangled. "Really good, but you didn't really do it, right? The nuclear option? You've eloped with Natalie Lame instead—"

"*Lane.*"

"—and this is just—" What? What other explanation could there be? "—just a weird way for you to break it to me gently." An odd, shitty way. "It's fine. I'm not mad. You really got me on that one, bro, good one."

"I did, Rake." Uh-oh. That was his brother's determined "This is serious, you incompetent moron" tone. He never used it when he was joking. The man barely joked at all. "This is not a drill. I called her last night. She's coming."

"You arrogant ass," he breathed. "You've killed us all!"

"The line," Blake said, because he was just so fucking awful, "is 'You arrogant ass, you've killed *us*.'* And, in fact, Tupelev's arrogance did doom his crew, although technically the explosion when the torpedo impacted the hull killed them, and if not that, then the water pressure, or they drowned. Whatever the official cause of death, it was, in fact, his arrogance that doomed them all."

Rake missed phone cords. He could be halfway to unconsciousness right now if he'd started wrapping as soon as his brother mentioned the nuclear option.

"Seek help, Blake. Not just for being stupid and crazy

---

* *The Hunt for Red October* by Tom Clancy.

enough to call Nonna Tarbell . . ." Although that was incredibly stupid. And extremely crazy. "But just in general. You're completely nuts."

"Could be." Blake was almost eerily calm, which was finally a mood Rake understood. Sometimes when you've pulled the switch, the relief is incredible: You've done the worst thing. You'll live or die, but either way, things will change. No more suspense and dread. "But watch yourself, little brother. It's probably genetic."

"Great. Just keep my name out of *everything*. I'll figure out my own mess on this side of the world, and you and Nonna stay over there on your side, and we'll meet up in the middle during Christmas or something and, I dunno, shake hands or hug or something, and that'll be fine until our birthday." Rake shivered. "Assuming you even survive."

"Yes, there's every chance this will get me killed, and that's only if I'm not dying at the bottom of a canyon."

Huh? "Blake. Seriously. Call someone. You've lost it, dude."

"Don't call me 'dude.' *Godere Venezia.*"

Rake managed a smile, which was progress. Anything was better than free-floating dread. Messing with Blake was just a plus. "Sorry, what?"

A sigh. "It's 'Enjoy Venice' in Italian."

Sometimes he wondered if Blake was only pretending to forget Rake was octolingual. "Oh, shut up. Fucking show-off." He heard a chuckle, and then Blake was gone.

He sat up and looked for Delaney, then realized she was gone, too. And in a hurry—she'd left her laptop.

Hmmm.

Thirty-six

She was reaching for the door handle to their room

(My room, dammit!)

when it opened and Rake filled the doorway. And boy, did he . . . those *shoulders*.

(Oh, Christ, stop drooling like a besotted teenager, please!)

"Come for a walk?" he said by way of greeting.

"Uh . . ." She looked at him the way she'd watched adults when she was a kid. You could keep an eye on them without them tumbling to what you were doing; peripheral vision was about 150 degrees. "Okay. How'd—how'd it go?"

"He wasn't kidding about being cut off by our mother, and he's tattling on her by activating the nuclear option." When she didn't say anything, he added, "He's calling our grandma."

"That's bad," she guessed. (Knew.)

"Atlantis disappearing into the sea bad," he confirmed. "Come on."

She fell into step beside him, irrationally glad to see him wearing the tacky sweatshirt she'd gotten him yesterday.

("I can't afford it!"

"Yes you can, it's unbelievably cheap. Don't wear it near an open flame."

"I hate the color!"

"I know. Shut up and put it on, it gets chilly at night.")

"So, the other girls—women—they're off doing whatever it is they do when they're not helping you be mysterious?"

"Uh. Yes." She was trying to put a name to his mood, and failing. He didn't seem angry, or sad, or afraid. Just quiet.

Yes. *That* was what was creeping her out: He was being calm and thoughtful and quiet. It was more alarming than if he'd burst into flames.

"And Lillith?"

"She's with Elena. What's wrong?" she asked, knowing exactly what the problem was and, even now, too chickenshit to say anything.

He still doesn't know everything.

So tell him, idiot!

I can't. I gave my word.

And to that, her inner voice said what it always did: not a goddamned thing. Because when she was nothing and had nothing, that was the one thing that had value: her word. If she said she would do something, or wouldn't, she'd stick to it. Every time. She'd gone to sleep with a black eye more than once, and her favorite consolation was always the same: *I told them if they tried anything, I'd make them pay. And I did.*

"Rake? What's the matter?"

"Oh, everything. I still can't believe she cut him off like that. Me, I could understand—my mom loves me but essentially thinks I'm useless. But Blake? The golden child? Cutting him off is just odd."

"So"—she paused, increasing her stride to match his—"you really don't have any money?" *You know he doesn't. Could you sound more insipid?* "Blake can't help you?" *Jesus Christ. What are you doing?*

"Blake can't help me," he agreed, and it still seemed like a brisk stroll between friends, but it wasn't.

"And he thinks your grandma . . ." The nuclear option. Because things weren't bad enough. Another lesson from her childhood: *Surprise! Everything's worse.*

"I think Blake isn't thinking straight. He might even be sick, or at least exhausted from working too hard.* I don't think he's thought it through. Because there's very little chance our mom orchestrated this without Nonna Tarbell's approval. They respect the hell out of each other. Always have."

"You never talk about them. Just Blake."

"You mean during the course of our long, affectionate friendship?"

She said nothing, and he shrugged.

"Yeah, well. It's annoying, having a genetic double who's your evil opposite. So he comes up a lot in my conversations. Though Blake would tell you I'm *his* evil opposite." They were through the lobby now, stepping out into the Venice sunshine. Lunchtime and, for once, not a lot of tourists.

"Do they spend much time together? Your mom and grandma?" She never got tired of hacks, hits, or stories about other people's loving families. In that order, which was proof, if any were needed, that there was something wrong with her.

He laughed, a short, humorless bark. "God no. They almost never see each other. Which suits my mom. And Blake

---

* Blake is, in fact, running a high fever and is in a world of hurt of his own, per *Danger, Sweetheart.*

and me, of course. We never even met her until we were teen-agers, when our dad died. Christ, that was a day."

"Will you tell me?" *Please tell me. I like hearing about your family. Okay, anyone's family. But especially yours.*

"Why not?" And he still hadn't shaken that odd, quiet mood. But perhaps reminiscing would put him in a better frame of mind.

Thirty-seven

"Dead?" Oh, what the holy hell? He and Blake had just gotten home—no detention for once, and better than that, he'd sprinted past Blake and gotten to the door first—and there was Mom, home between two of her three jobs, and some strange old lady who was looking at them with a hopeful smile.

"Our father's dead?" Blake asked, sounding as numb as Rake felt. It was like walking in the door and getting whapped with a pillow full of popcorn. Not painful, but disorienting.

"I'm afraid so, boy." Mom let go of the back of the kitchen chair and gestured to the old lady. "This is your grandmother, Ruth Tarbell. Ruth, this is—"

"My son's seed!"

Rake flinched. "Oh, man. Please don't call us that." Before he could ask her not to call us anything, really, the old woman had moved

(like a basketball forward! quick, with fast hands)

and pulled him

(ack!)

and Blake

(ack!)

into a hug that smelled like lemon tea.

"Thank God," she was babbling, and her lipstick was perfect, which was kind of amazing. "Oh thank God. Look at you, so handsome. I haven't seen you since you were babies, when I made your idiot father— When I was at the wedding."

Blake was gently trying to get free of her lemony embrace. "It's nice to meet you."

"I'm missing b-ball practice for this," Rake reminded everyone.

After a decade, their fuzzy

(what's that sweater made of? wool? very soft steel wool?)

grandmother let them go, observing, "You're surprised."

"People aren't usually this happy to meet us," Blake said. Rake rolled his eyes, because he knew what was coming. "Rake is terrible."

He flipped him off, low and quick, so the other two wouldn't see. "Blow it out your butt sideways, Blake. Um, Mom, are you . . ." Then he took another look and went over and put his arm around her. "Um, I know you guys were technically married, and it's okay to be sad. And it's okay not to be sad. Right, Blake? That's okay?" Blake was way better with the whole "this is socially acceptable, that is not" thing.

"Of course."

"See, Mom? Blake's all 'it's cool.' So if you're sad—"

"I am fine, Rake." Then to their—this would take some getting used to—grandmother: "Thank you. Mrs. Tarbell—"

"Ruth, darling."

"—was telling me about your father's will. It seems . . ." She paused, took a breath. Let it out slowly. "It seems he left us some money."

"Oh." Blake looked cautiously hopeful, and it wasn't hard to figure out why: Blake balanced the family checkbook, and they both knew any amount of money would be great. Their mom not only worked hard; she wouldn't let either of them get jobs to help. If their newly dead old man left them a few hundred bucks, that was great. More? That'd be more great.

"Look, you don't expect us to cry or anything, right?" Rake said to his, err, grandma. He stuck to his mom's side like a sweaty barnacle. "I mean, we get how you'd be upset, but we're kind of not." *Okay, maybe that's a little heartless. Try again.* "Because he never visited. We didn't know him. I mean, we're sorry for you, Mrs. Tar—"

"Please don't call me that," she interrupted. She didn't sound mad or anything, which was good. "Ruth, if you like. Nonna, if you want to know my preference."

"Italian for grandmother," Blake spoke up. Rake instantly decided to learn Italian so that stupid Blake couldn't show him up in front of his new grandma again.

Nonna Tarbell gave Blake a great big smile. "Clever, clever boy."

Rake managed not to roll his eyes. "Oh, gross."

"God, you're both his very image." Then—No!—Nonna's eyes got brighter. Or just wetter. Please let it be allergies! No tears! No little old ladies crying in their kitchen! Luckily, she recovered, which is when Rake started to like her. She never lost her smile, either; it seemed she really was happy to meet them. Rake was old enough to know that not everyone had a positive reaction to the news that they had bastard grandchildren. "I'm told you have your mother's brains." Pause. Her smile got even bigger. "Thank the Lord."

"Yep, praise Jesus and all that . . ." Grandmas were usually religious, right? Ugh, she wasn't going to insist they go to church while she was in town, was she? Their mother would shit. "So what'd he leave us?"

Their mother gave him a look. "Rake." *Ulp.* Time to hand off the rest of the chitchat to Blake.

Then (amazing! miraculous! a dead dad, a live grandmother, outracing Blake, Blake sticking up for him—what a day!) Blake actually took his side.

"It's a fair question, Mom. Nonna wouldn't have come all this way for no good reason."

"Everything" was the stunned response. "He left you everything."

Thirty-eight

"And that was the end of our money problems," Rake finished, still musing in that calm, quiet tone. "But my mom and Nonna think it was the start of all our other problems. We're not married."

"What?" As if his tone wasn't unnerving enough, Rake was kind of all over the place with his storytelling. Odd to feel chilled in the Venice sunshine, while happy tourists drifted around them, hailing gondolas and vaporettos to hurry off somewhere else. Delaney, who usually liked Italy, wanted very much to be hurrying off somewhere else.

"We're confirmed bachelors. And if we were women, people would say we're sluts. My mom has a huge problem with it, and the nuclear option does, too. Which is asinine."

"It is?" *Wow, you're definitely holding up your end, conversationwise! Double thumbs-up!*

"Mom never wanted to marry; Grandma did but hated her husband. And yet the solution to all our problems is to shackle some poor woman to our rich yet empty lives." Rake sighed. "That's what I used to think. I never found anyone I wanted to pull into my orbit, be with, forever. Until . . ." Then he stopped, verbally and physically, ignoring the tourists he'd inadvertently forced to swerve around him, and looked right at her.

"Until . . ." she managed. It wasn't what she was thinking/hoping. It wasn't. The end of his sentence wasn't "I met you." And the follow-up wasn't "Will you marry me, darling?" This wasn't a romcom, or even a romantic suspense. This was real life: brutal and dirty, sometimes, and sad, and stuffed with people you didn't want to need but did.

"The clues were all there," he said, like that was an answer. "I was happy to ignore them. I couldn't *wait* to ignore them. Isn't that ridiculous? But I really am broke, Blake and me both. Blake can't see Nonna's hand in this, but it's there. They really did take our money, they're really grounding us like we're still teenagers. Lillith really might be mine, Donna really might have been murdered, strange men have really been following us, and you really knew all about it."

He put his hands on her shoulders and turned her so she was facing back the way they'd come. He kept talking, only now it was so much worse—now she couldn't see his face.

"I'm not a genius," he told the back of her head, and she shivered, "but I'm not a moron, either, as even Blake would agree. I ignored the evidence that I was in real trouble because I didn't want to face what that meant. Not just being broke—that's a pain in the ass, but it's survivable. I won't like it, but I know how to live without money. Millions get by every day. That wasn't the biggest problem. No, I didn't want to face what your complicity meant. Did you *ever* like me? Or was it just a job? An errand to run in between stuffing Easter baskets?"

"Rake—"

"I didn't get a burner, even though I could have gotten one a lot quicker than an iPhone, one you so obligingly ordered for me. I could have followed up with Blake's increasingly alarming texts right away, but I didn't."

"You couldn't have kno—"

"I didn't ask you about the DNA tests, though they've probably been in your safe for forty-eight hours. And the very next day, when I had the perfect opportunity to reach out to Blake and get some answers, I decided to hold off and hope you were going to kiss me again. Then I took a nap. These are not the actions of a smart person. They're what someone who wants to stay blind does."

"Rake . . ." What? What could she say? That without his money and at her mercy, he was vulnerable in a way he'd never been in his life, and there was no shame in being afraid to face that? That yes, she was complicit, but never for spite, and she never would have let any harm come to him—as his two would-be muggers could attest? That there was nothing she wouldn't do to keep Lillith safe and make the Big Pipe Dream happen?

Was there even a way to say *Hey, Rake, don't beat yourself up* without sounding stupid and condescending?

"How do I get it back, Delaney? What's the trick I have to perform to get back in my mother's and grandmother's good graces? Keep working for you? Giving back? Making cakes and stuffing baskets and driving for Meals on Wheels, until the nuclear option is satisfied I'm going to be a Good Boy? Adopting Lillith so she's mine whether or not she's mine? So you don't have to take care of her until she's an adult?"

Christ, she wasn't ready for this conversation. She hadn't taken the job expecting to even be conflicted, never mind falling for him. She'd thought having the moral high ground would be empowering. Instead, it made her feel small, and mean.

She shook herself free of his grasp and turned. She grabbed one of his hands, took a step back toward the hotel, and tugged. He didn't budge, and she wouldn't hurt him to make him follow. She could only ask. "Rake, come back with me, it's getting chilly." It wasn't. She was so upset and nervous and embarrassed and confused, she was sweating. And he was in that silly sweatshirt she'd bought him; he wasn't cold, either. Now she wished she'd bought him ten shitty sweatshirts. A dozen. Told her employer to fuck off twice. Never promised anything. Saved him from the muggers and then given him everything in her wallet. Showed him the DNA results instead of walking that particular tightrope. Kept Lillith away from this, from them. *Donna was right. It's a Lost Boys lifestyle; it's no way for actual adults to live. She was right to be done with us.* "C'mon, okay?"

He shook his head. "No, thank you."

That cool courtesy: the worst. "Please?" God, he just looked so sad and calm; she was amazed to find she couldn't bear it. "C'mon back with me, come in and—and we'll order room service, you love that—"

"I do love that," he said thoughtfully.

"—and we'll get a bite and some sleep and you'll—it'll be better. In the morning."

"Sorry" was the polite reply. "I haven't earned the money for a bite and some sleep." The worst of it was, he didn't sound particularly biting or nasty. Just tired. "In fact, if I'm going to be your charitable dray horse, I need to find much cheaper accommodations. And you haven't answered me: How long does this go on? When will I be considered an adult who can handle his big-boy checkbook?"

"It's not—it's not like that." Once, sure. Now? No. She was ready to give him all of *her* money at this point, the money she'd earned and the money still owed her, the money she had to take when people thought they could promise to help, when they thought their word meant nothing. The money that made her blighted childhood worth something, granting her a skill set she could use to undo all the wrongs of her early life.

For the first time, she got a glimpse of why someone would take something that wasn't theirs and give it to someone else. "You don't have to—come on. Come inside. I'll tell you what I can."

"But not all of it."

"I can't," she said with fierce desperation.

"Because you gave your word."

"Yes. I know that sounds—"

"It sounds fine." And just like that, he let her steer him back toward her

(our, dammit!)

hotel.

"It's fine?" she repeated, not quite believing his 180.

"Yeah. I know there's stuff you have to keep to yourself, because I'm doing the same thing. I've done something I'm not ready to tell you about," he said, but she was so happy they were going back, she didn't give half a shit.

"Okay. That's okay."

"You'll be angry when I do tell you."

"All right. That's—" She took a breath, tried to imagine what he wasn't telling her. Took the coward's way out and decided she didn't want to know. Let out her breath in a whoosh. She felt lighter, which was stupid. Nothing had been resolved. Everything was shitty. He didn't like her anymore, and he would never, ever love her. Lillith was still in limbo. Donna was still dead. "Fair. That's fair. So I won't—I mean, I'd understand. Even if I didn't like what you told me."

"Yes." He looked down and shifted their grip; now she wasn't yanking him down the street; now they were holding hands like any one of the couples around them. "That's a big thing for you, right, Delaney? Maybe the biggest. Fair play."

"Yes."

"That's all right, then," he replied, and even smiled a little.

Thirty-nine

He didn't say another word until they were in the elevator, so when he did speak, it startled her. She'd been thinking, *Just a few more hours and I can tell the rest. Just a few more hours and I'll have kept my word.* "What happened to the San Basso guy?"

"What? Oh." She frowned. For once, she didn't give a shit about the hit. "He's gone. He—he saw you left the kitchen a mess and left town." Her joke fell flat with an almost audible *thud.*

"Yeah, he's gone." Rake wasn't surprised. Why wasn't he surprised? Was it a test? Did she pass? "I checked, you know."

Her reply was cautious. "Okay." She was so glad they were moving away from her complicity (though she would later realize he'd never left the topic), she didn't think to question what he was asking, or why.

"I know why you did what you did, and maybe it was even a good thing." He shook his head. "But you shouldn't have done it."

"How do you even—"

Ding! Never had an elevator chime been more annoying. He popped out and made straight for their

(yes, their, it was theirs)

room. Once inside, she went straight for the room service menu to make good on her word, but he put a hand on her wrist to stop her. "Will you come to bed with me?"

"Do you want bruschetta or— What?"

"I really, really need to have sex with you," he said patiently, like it was an everyday feeling, like she shouldn't be amazed. "Can we?"

She could only gape and thought she must look ridiculous with her big eyes staring and her big mouth hanging open. Every time she thought the conversation couldn't get more surreal, he topped it. "I didn't—I never thought you'd want to. With me."

"I never thought *you'd* want to. With me." He was looking at her with a steady gaze; those baby blues never wavered. "I hoped, but . . . I didn't have the courage to ask until now."

"You know I've been up to—to bad things, and that I'm partially responsible for—for things. . . ." *The mess you're in. The mess I'm in. The mess you didn't deserve. The mess I did deserve.* "And you still want to?"

"Oh, God, yes." The cool reserve slipped and she saw his desire, which fed her own repressed hunger. "Since Friday."

"But today is— Oh. You're teasing."

He smiled. "Maybe a little. I mean, I don't know for *sure* that it's Friday, but I'll take your word."

"You shouldn't," she said earnestly. "About anything. Not anymore. Maybe not ever. Maybe my word is shit, and I've been fooling myself. Maybe building a life around keeping promises and making things fair is juvenile and stupid."

"Hey, hey." He stepped a little closer and she closed her

eyes; he smelled like Venice: complex and rich and wonderful. "Maybe you're just scrupulously, pathologically fair." His thumb was gently stroking along her pulse point, and when she opened her eyes, she saw his smile wasn't wavering.

She took a breath, and slowly let it out. She wanted. Oh, how she wanted. But. "Please not yet," she begged. "Wait twenty-four hours, wait just a little bit longer and after you hear—if you still want me—" Ha! She was clearly swimming in the realm of the inconceivable. "—then I'd—I'd love to go to bed with you. Mine or that awful hide-a-bed you've been sentenced to."

"No" was the gentle response. "It's now or never, Delaney. We're almost done is the thing. This is our one chance, I think. And it's not an ultimatum. I want you—badly. But I'll jump into traffic before pushing you into sex. I just—I want you. So much. Even if it's only for a little while. Even if it's maybe a lie. I want you until we have to go back to our lives."

She saw his point, and it made sense. Whether he was punished for another week or a decade, eventually he'd want to get the hell away—he likely wanted to get the hell away *now*—and he'd put as much distance as he could between them. Eventually he'd go back to what was his and she'd go back to what was hers, and one of them would have had a narrow escape, and the other would have to live the rest of their life knowing they destroyed their own happiness for pride.

She knew, just like he did. No question: This was their only chance. She'd have to live on the memories; she'd have to make that enough.

"Yes," she said, and reached for him.

Forty

She went right into his arms, and it was a revelation, it was the best thing ever, it was all contradiction, and pure Delaney: She was soft and firm and gentle and urgent and sweet and sharp. She had him out of his clothes faster than he believed possible, then pressed her hand against his bare chest and pushed. He fell back on the bed, then propped himself up on his elbows to watch her make short work of her clothes: She yanked the sweatshirt over her head and her lovely apple-size breasts bounced free

(no bra oh my God this might be over the second she touches me)

and she shucked off her jeans and kicked off her shoes and wiggled out of her gray hip-huggers, a panty and color he had never found erotic until this moment. Then she climbed on top of him and he caught her around the waist.

"Wait, socks? You're leaving your socks on?"

"Shut up," she breathed, and kissed him through his giggles. He put his arms around her and then stroked down, cupping the firm globes of her ass and going lower, until . . .

"Hey! That— You're tickling!"

"Purely a side effect," he grunted, getting ahold of her left sock and—nope, lost it—wait, there it—ah! "No fair," he growled as she nibbled and kissed the skin over the pulse in his throat.

"Very fair; I gave consent for sex, not sockless sex." Her hand slid down

(oh God)

and she found his length just as his hand closed over her other ankle. She clasped him and gave him a firm stroke, then used her thumb to swipe across the wetness at his tip; he groaned into her neck and groped blindly for the sock.

"Split the difference?" he managed, and she laughed and jerked her foot out of his grasp.

"One on and one off? You're a filthy, filthy man."

"None of this should be sexy," he observed. "They're god-damned tube socks, the least sexy socks in all of sockdom. And you wear old-lady underwear."

"I wear comfortable underwear, you fucking whiner. Walk around all day with the lace of a G-string up your crack and then tell me how much fun it is."

"No, no! If I gave the impression I was complaining, I'm sorry. Your clothes shouldn't be sexy, but they are. I shouldn't want a tricky bitch like you, but I do. And you shouldn't be with an asshole like me, but you are."

She groaned and her fists bopped his shoulders, lightly. "Are you trying to torpedo the mood?"

"No! It's just happening," he admitted, thinking, *What are you doing? Why are you fucking this up?*

"Shut up," she suggested, "and kiss me back."

So he did. And it wasn't just glorious; it was excellent advice, too. Her mouth bloomed beneath his like a dark flower, and he could feel her nipples tightening against his chest. He was a tit man, always had been, and Delaney's were outfuck-ingstanding, firm and sweet like Anjou pears, with dark pink nipples. She pulled back so he could palm them, and the feel of her tender skin in his hands, and her gray gaze on him, almost made his eyes roll back. She was, in a word, exquisite.

"Condom?"

He nearly shrieked in disappointment. "In my wallet. At the bottom of Lake Como."

She grinned down at him and sat up. "S'okay. I've got a couple in my bag."

"Thank God," he said, possibly the most sincere he had been in twenty-eight years. "Really. Thank . . . *God.*"

She hurried into the bathroom and he had the extraordinary pleasure of watching her go; she was all dark hair

(the waves tumbling about her shoulders, the sweet dark tri-angle of her sex . . . ummmm . . .)

and pale skin studded with freckles. Her hips swelled from a narrow waist; her legs were long and trim.

She came back holding a condom aloft in triumph

"Ta-dah!"

which made him laugh. "Christ, you're gorgeous," he said when she climbed back on top of him. "I mean, you are just top to bottom the whole package."

"Awww. You say the most nonsensical things."

"That wasn't my best," he admitted. "It's getting kind of hard to mink. Think."

"Yes, well." She grasped his prick in her small warm hand and he shuddered and bit back a groan as her hand slid up . . . . and down . . . and back up. Slowly. So goddamned slowly. He wanted her to stop. He wanted her never to stop. He wanted her to . . . Um. Do something. Or nothing. Huh?

"Your brain's lost a lot of blood."

"Buh," he agreed. "Um. Come down here. Might die. If I don't kiss you s'more. 'Kay?"

"I don't want you to die," she whispered, bending and giving him her mouth. "I can't think of anything worse."

He put his arms around that small pretty waist and pulled her in so closely that she gasped for breath, and it still wasn't enough. He rolled until she was on her back and licked the tender spot behind her ear. She stiffened

(careful, careful)

and he pulled back. "Is this okay?"

"Tickles," she said, and shivered when he did it again. "Um. I like that."

"Good. We're only doing the things you like. Yes?"

"Oh, yes. But I'm not made of glass. You don't have to baby me."

"I'm not. I'm cherishing you. I've thought about this a lot in the last few days and I don't want to rush."

"I kind of want to," she confessed, reaching around and lightly scratching his back and then his ass. "I've been thinking about it, too, y'see. And then, when you've rested, we can go again." She bit his earlobe. "As many times as you like. 'Til morning, when we have to . . . be ourselves again."

"Oh my God."

"You should talk, though. A lot. I love your voice. Goddamned verbal velvet, that voice."

"If you're not careful, this will be over before you can get the condom unwrapped," he growled in his goddamned verbal velvet voice. "Possibly if you move your hands another few— Yeow!"

"So firm." She giggled, then pinched his ass again.

His kissed her through her giggles, attacked her neck, tried to hold back

"It's okay. I don't mind a few marks."

and then latched on until a dark love bite was blooming halfway down her throat. He wanted to see it. He wanted other people to see it. This was their only chance, but tomorrow, when he was gone, other people would look and see his mark on her. The thought made his hands shake.

"Rake, it's okay. It's— Oh. *Oh*."

He licked at her nipples like a cat until they were straining and red, then rubbed his stubble over them until she arched and sighed beneath him. He moved lower and nuzzled the tender undersides of her breasts, licking at the sweet curves there, and then lower still, and kissed the soft skin around her navel.

He moved lower, taking his time, and ran his hands up her long, sleek thighs, gently easing her legs apart. He got a whiff of her—soap and musk and warmth—and nuzzled against the dark curls covering her mound. He blew softly, then nuzzled again, and then licked a slow, gentle stripe that parted those plump outer lips. Delaney let out a groan and he shuddered and fought the impulse to spread her wide and lunge and go and go and *go* until he came, until they both came.

He licked and teased and sucked and—gently!—nibbled, while Delaney moaned and squirmed beneath him, her fingers locked in his hair, her legs spreading to allow him more access, and when he slipped two fingers inside, he had to grit his teeth

(God, God, like crushed velvet, like hot crushed velvet, and if it's this good around my fingers, how will it feel around my ah God)

and fight the impulse to be extremely ungentlemanly.

"Keep them there," she said hoarsely, "keep doing that."

Then she brought her own fingers down and while his slid slowly in and out of her, she held herself open with one hand and stroked her clit with the other, legs spread

"Rake, Rake, that's so good, that's perfect, don't stop, don't . . ."

(God oh God oh God oh God oh God)

and squirmed and brought herself to orgasm while he watched, while she showed him exactly what she liked and how she liked it, and he'd never, not ever, seen anything hotter. When her fingers stopped, his did, too, and she gasped for breath. When she relaxed and opened her eyes to look at him, he darted in close and licked at her clit once, twice, and then sucked it into his mouth, and she fell into another orgasm, her thighs clenching around his head

"Rake! Ah, God, ah-ah-ah!"

as she shook through it. Then her thighs relaxed and she seized him by the shoulders and hauled him up.

"You now. You, please, I need to feel you, you have to be inside me, you have to, I want to do that to you, I want you to come as hard as I did, now, Rake, right now."

It took, at rough estimate, a thousand years to get the condom on. But it was, finally, and then he was slipping into her, and thank *God* for the condom, or they would have been done, it would have been over. She was wet and delightfully tight, hot and smooth and luscious exactly where he needed her to be, and her legs came up and locked around his waist

"Harder. Please, Rake—more. More."

and he could have wept in relief. He knew enough about her teenage years to worry about doing the wrong thing at the wrong time, but Delaney goddamn *owned* her sexuality and had no problem telling him what she needed.

So he surged forward, and her moan was like music; he

pulled out and slammed back in, and did it again, and again, and her hips met his every thrust. The headboard was thumping and the DND sign wasn't on the door and he gave not a shit; the Sistine Chapel Choir could have stormed the room and started vocal warm-ups and he couldn't have stopped.

"It's so good," she groaned beneath him. "Rake. That's so good."

"Yes," he managed. "Perfect. You're perfect. God, I adore you."

Her eyes widened. "No. You don't—you can't. It's okay, you— Ah!" She whimpered a little and tightened her grip. "You don't have to say nice things."

"Shut up. I do. You—ah—*God*—" And that was it, he was tumbling over the edge and no turning back. He felt his eyes roll back as his orgasm burned through him, felt her shudder against him as he filled the condom, as she found one last orgasm.

He didn't want to. But it was necessary, and, for the first time, the worst part of the sex act: pulling out, pulling away.

Normally he didn't care. Normally it was a relief: He'd come, she'd come, they'd had a good time, and he could think again. With other partners, this was usually the time he felt affectionate and grateful toward the lady in question. Did she want to stay? Great, they'd watch TV. Did she want to go? Great, he'd help her get dressed and call a cab. Did she want to spend the night? Great, they'd snuggle and snooze.

He wanted Delaney to stay, and not for a *Fargo* marathon. He wanted her to stay forever.

And of course, that was never an option. He knew that before he knew what color her nipples were.

She waited as he got rid of the condom and, when he

climbed back into bed, curled up into his side. His arm went around her at once.

(Thank God! A cuddler!)

"Mmmmm. Normally I don't get off so fast. Been wanting you for days," she mumbled.

"Oh? Uh, me either. I'm not normally that fast. Definitely. Slow and steady wins the race, that's normally my— Ow! God, you fuck like an angel and pinch like a witch."

"Shut up," she said into his bicep, and wriggled closer.

"That was wonderful. You're wonderful. The most—" He stopped himself.

"Words out of my mouth," she murmured, then yawned. "Jeez. Sorry. I'm not usually like this."

Yes, well, having a guilty conscience is probably exhausting. He couldn't say that to her, though, even if it was true. Not now, when she was small and vulnerable and trusting against him. "Go to sleep," he said, and kissed her.

She did.

Forty-one

Where was she?

Was it safe?

The door. Or even a window. If she could look out. If she could see. Then she'd know.

Oh but what if it was the apartment in Manhattan or the farmhouse in Wyoming? What if there were hard hands groping in the dark, yanking her from sleep?

"Delaney. It's okay, honey. You're safe."

She was?

"You can go anywhere. Do anything."

She could?

"You don't have to stay here."

But—she did. That was the problem of the foster care system in its entirety: You had to stay. No matter what. Until you were eighteen. There were rules. So many rules, and so many people who ignored them or, worse, obeyed them. She wished she and her friends could have their own safe place. Not just one, either. But that meant surviving; that meant turning eighteen and then working to make it happen.

But . . . she *was* eighteen. And . . . maybe older?

Wasn't she?

"Of course, you're a grown woman. You don't take shit from anybody. And you go wherever you want, every day."

Could it be true? *Oh, please let it be true.* She wouldn't ask for anything else if she was safe. Being alone wasn't so bad if she was safe. She wasn't greedy. She hated greed. She'd never ask for more than she earned.

"You deserve everything in the world, Delaney, and wanting to be safe *and* happy isn't greedy. Won't you please come back to bed? You're only wearing one sock."

One sock? But that was ridiculous. And these thoughts—these tiresome, constant worries she had—they weren't ridiculous. They were *scary*. They were *real*. If something was ridiculous, it must be a dream.

So this was a dream.

This was a *wonderful* dream.

"Okay," she said, and the ridiculous man who chased away the scary stuff seemed pleased, and that was nice, too. She let out a small giggle, but the ridiculous man didn't mind at all, which was more proof—not that it was needed!—that he was ridiculous.

More proof this was one of the nicest dreams ever.

Almost as good as the ones where she could fly away.

"C'mon, honey. You and your one sock, won't you come back to bed?"

Well, *sure*. Grand idea! One sock! Ridiculous man!

"Okay," she agreed, and felt herself tucked in and kissed, very lightly, on the forehead. A ridiculous spot for a kiss! Which was the point!

Better than the dreams where she could fly. And once she'd decided that, she tumbled back down into sweet dark sleep.

Forty-two

When she woke, it was just getting dark. *Napped the afternoon away. Never get to sleep tonight. Oh, well. I was going to have trouble sleeping anyway.*

She rolled over on her side and saw Rake was awake and looking at her. "There you are," he said, smiling.

"Here I am," she agreed. She stretched, not caring that the sheet was around her knees—she never understood when women got modest about their bodies *after* sex. A classic case of locking the barn door after the horse ran off. And then had the best sex of its life.

Besides, he liked her body and she enjoyed how his gaze dropped to her breasts when she stretched. That was all right; she pretty much thought he had the best body she'd ever seen, too. All long gorgeous lines, broad shoulders, long muscular legs, flat stomach, defined biceps, big hands, big—oofta.

"Hungry? You must be."

"Yes, but it's time to finish our talk. Tomorrow's going to be here way too soon."

Her stomach didn't sink; it plunged. He was talking in

that awful new voice again, only now the calm, sorrowful tone was laced with regret. For what they had done? For what was coming?

"Okay," she said, and pulled the sheets up to her neck. Suddenly it was no good being exposed; she hadn't felt a bit vulnerable when his glorious thick cock was filling her up, and before that his fingers and tongue, *Christ*, good-looking men were almost always shitty in bed, but Rake was the exception—but she sure did now. She didn't want a bedsheet, she wanted a parka.

And all he was doing was holding her hand.

"You know I'm fluent, and not just in Italian."

"Sure." Of course she knew. It was cool, but annoying. Rake was hot enough *without* being able to whisper sweet nothings in French or order blood sausage in German or curse at Peeps in Italian.

(She had no idea what "*Fanculo*, Peeps, *e leccare le mie palle!*" meant, but Sofia's *and* Teresa's eyes went big when Rake let loose, and the two of them had heard everything. His shame-faced apology right afterward just made everything funnier.)

"The thing about languages," he went on, "they're codes. That's all. You just have to figure out what the letters stand for, right?"

"Sure."

"And for some people, that's easy. Me, I'm great at figuring out languages, but I suck at poker and chess."

"Okay." Wary now. Which felt like the appropriate response.

"But the wiring that makes me good at languages but terrible at chess makes me good at crossword puzzles, Sudoku—stuff where the object is filling in the blank."

"Okay . . ."

"And passwords. I'm really good at those. Because those are codes *and* puzzles."

She froze. As far as clichés went, it was pretty accurate: She actually felt everything in her lock up, like she'd been plunked down in the middle of a blizzard.

"You didn't—" No. Impossible. It was long and dumb and had no significance except to her, and the odds that he guessed were billions to—

"I knew your laptop password had twenty-two letters. And now and again I saw which letters you were hitting, though you were careful never to let me see you put the whole thing in. We were

(past tense? yes, of course)

sharing a room, after all. And I didn't have a laptop of my own, or a phone until recently, to distract me, so there wasn't much to do in here except worry about Lillith and listen to you type and think about your password."

Definitely should have tried to seduce him, then. To think I didn't dare!

"I didn't think you'd put in twenty-two numbers—you'd need a password to mean something. So what could be important to you? What does Claire Delaney care about? Not money—you don't give a shit about it . . . unless someone goes back on their word. Baby-sitting random millionaires? I'm pretty sure I'm the only one. The other girls sure seemed to think so— No," he said, seeing her expression. "They didn't rat you out. I'm fun, I'm laid-back, and when I ask questions, it's not at all threatening. And they keep forgetting I'm fluent. Which is just fine."

She sat there, brain empty. Absolutely no idea what to say, or even think.

"So!" he continued briskly. "Twenty-two letters, and some of them were *C* and *H* and *M* and *E* and *I* and *A* and *B*."

"You still couldn't have—" It was actually hard to talk; her lips had gone numb.

"C-H-A-R-I-T-Y-B-E-G-I-N-S-A-T-H-O-M-E-I-C-U." When all she did was gape like a trout, he elaborated: "Charity begins at home. I see you." He shook his head, amused. "You *really* hate when they renege."

"Yes," she managed. Cracked it. Cracked it in two days and never said a word. Cracked it for fun, to pass the time, and never said a word. "Blake's a fool to underestimate you." She managed to look at him and said it, one of the biggest truths of her life: "I was, too."

"Thanks." He seemed pleased, which was a sizable improvement over pissed.

"I can't really tell you every—"

"Hacks and hits. That's what you do. All around the world."

"Yes." His eyes. Oh his blue, blue eyes that held reproach, but not as much as she deserved. "Since before I could vote."

"Which one was I?"

"What?"

"A hack or a hit?"

"No. Oh, no! You're a side project." She bit her lip, hard. "I'm sorry, let me rephrase—sometimes I take on work outside the charities."

"To get money to fund your hacks and hits."

"Yes! And the Big Pipe Dream." Of course she didn't have to explain. He'd already figured it all out. That should have been a relief. (It wasn't.) "That's, um, this thing that we've all been working toward since we weren't much older than Lillith."

"The off-the-books shelter network."

"Yeah."

"So I was a paycheck."

She winced, but he deserved the truth. And this she could answer without breaking her word. "Yes. One I couldn't turn down, one that would pay me in a week what I'd make in years. So we wouldn't have to wait anymore. We *can't* wait anymore. So it was a bit of a now or never situation. Or, at least, now or not for a long, long time."

"Because fair is fair, so the ends justify the means."

"Well, no, but—" She tried to think how that was a case of 'Well, no,' but after a few seconds she had to admit, "Anything sounds bad when you put it like that."

He didn't smile when she used his own words. "It's worth getting caught?" Why, *why* did he look so sad? Just about anything else would be preferable; disappointment would be preferable. Anger. Disdain. Contempt. "Prison?"

"It's worth everything," she said simply. Because in the end, that was nothing but solid fact. "Even if it means tricking a wonderful guy for reasons that sounded great at first, then turned to shit. Even if you're in it just a few days and you realize you're the villain this time."

"Well, you and your boss. Client? Whoever's paying you to fuck with me, anyway."

"It's on me, too," she replied firmly. "That 'I was just doing my job' thing has always been bullshit. Nobody made me do any of it. *I* made me do it." And she had, stuck fast by her own word, and not for the first time, but definitely the worst time. "And there's Lillith to think about."

"Yes. But how does she fit into this?"

"Who do you think the Big Pipe Dream is for? Donna would never forgive me if I let her child fall into the foster system. Lillith would be among the first of our charges. Not just a roof over her—their—head. Private teachers and counseling and scholarships for the older kids, instead of jettisoning them out of the system the second they turn eighteen. That's what happened to Elena. She was barely into her senior year at high school when she turned eighteen. Literally overnight you're expected to find a place to live and feed and clothe yourself, even if you're still in high school. But with the Big— We're getting off track," she realized. "So getting back to Lillith, there was a chance you were her dad, but not a guarantee, and she can't stay in limbo. Her life has been upended quite enough—she deserves stability and a future where she's not afraid to go to sleep. And if you were her dad—are her dad—then we'd still be able to—"

"Your off-the-books shelter would be an excellent plan B if I wasn't up to facing my responsibilities. Because that's also what this has been about, right? Seeing how I interact with a kid who might be mine? You needed to see me up close, you needed me to need *you*, because you wanted to see how I behaved during low points."

"Yes."

"Did I pass?"

"Yes."

He let out a breath, and she was shocked to see his relief. "Okay. Well. That's one problem solved. And while we're talking about Lillith—"

Here we go.

"—when were you going to tell me I was on the short list? The *very* short list."

"Ah. Um. The thing about that—"

"The short list of two: me, and Blake."

OhGodohGodohGodohGodoh—wait. "That . . . wasn't in my computer."

"Nope."

"You cracked the safe, too."

"Sure." At her astonished gape: "Four-two-eight-three. Which on a phone pad corresponds to I-C-U-D. *D* for Delaney, I assume." He shrugged. "Seems to be the way your mind works."

"I'm just gonna sit here and stare and be astonished for a minute, okay?"

"No, you're going to explain to me why the only names on your 'Who Is Lillith's Daddy' list are mine and my twin's."

"You figured out my combinations but not that?" As he waited (calmly, to his credit), she added, "Donna seduced both of you that month. And before you ask, I don't know why—she'd been distancing herself from us for a while. I *swear* I had no idea, Rake. I didn't know about any of it until she met us at Subway, announced her pregnancy, ordered a foot-long club, and disappeared from our lives."

"You remember the lunch order?"

"I don't know if the plan was to get pregnant so she'd have a rich baby daddy or if she was just getting close in order to scam you in a non-baby-related way."

"Huh."

"It's, um, none of my business, but—"

"Of course I wore a condom! We'd *just met.*"

"Right, right. Sorry."

"One she handed me."

"Ah."

Rake was rubbing his eyes. "Jesus Christ. So I'm either Lillith's dad or uncle."

"Yes. And since it's long past time we settled the issue, let's—"

"Nope."

"What?"

He'd plucked a sealed white envelope she instantly recognized from his pocket and waved it at her. "See this?"

"Yes, you're holding it ten inches away from my face."

"Good. Watch." And he tore it in two. "Lillith's my daughter."

"Rake—"

"She's a member of our family and it doesn't matter if it's Blake or me, because she's *my* daughter and I'll take care of her now and that's how it's gonna be. I don't give a shit about the test."

"Well, that was all very dramatic and impressive, except I also got an email from the lab. And a pdf file. And they'll mail me another hard copy if I ask. So it doesn't actually change—"

"I'm. Lillith's. Dad."

"Got it." Not that destroying a paper copy of the test results actually changed anything. But Rake had a point—one way or the other, Lillith was a Tarbell. And as incredible as it sounded, they actually had bigger problems than playing "who's got the Lillith."

"Glad we got that straightened out. And getting back to your weird hobbies—Delaney, they'll catch you." He had leaned forward and taken her hand in his. Gripped it. "Maybe not this week, but it's going to happen. You won't survive prison."

"Whoa! Who said anything about going to prison? I'll be—"

"Do not say 'fine' to me, don't pretend it's okay. You'll fucking hang yourself if they lock you in a room and never let you out." His words were fierce and blunt, but he looked . . . afraid?

"Rake," she began, amazed.

"You'll die in there. Please stop what you're doing. All this. Please."

"I'm a grown woman," she said, squeezing back until her knuckles whitened; he didn't seem to notice. "And these are my choices. You're wonderful to worry . . . it's more than I deserve. But tomorrow you're going to do what you need to do—and I will, too. And either way, Lillith will be safe. And no matter what, I'll never be sorry we met. Just sorry about the manner of it."

"Please stop the hits." He leaned forward and rested his forehead on her shoulder, and she was amazed to feel him shaking.

"I can't." No. That was a lie. "I won't," she clarified. "But I don't think you're giving me enough credit. I've never even come close to getting caught. They can't say anything, you know. They're trapped." *Like I was.*

"You don't do it very often."

"No, I'm not greedy. Two, three times a year, max. Only once last year." Usually they were smart. Usually they gave in. Usually that was enough . . . until the next time.

He nodded. "Okay. I mean—that's not great, but it's something. And maybe you'll change your mind. Maybe you'll retire."

"Maybe," she said, and thought, *Doubt it. But hell, if it'll make you feel better.* Then a thought struck her. "Okay, so you found my spreadsheets and even looked through a couple. You didn't also by any chance—"

"Yeah, I looked at your porn." Finally, a smile. "*Assablanca?* Really?"

"You shut up!" she cried, then burst into giggles. Rake cracked up, too, and she was so relieved she'd made him laugh, she decided just to be mortified, not mortified and furious. "It was a gift from a friend. I swear!"

"Sure it was," he managed, then laughed harder.

"I refuse to apologize for being interested in terrible porn!"

"Which is yet another reason I adore you."

Well. He was sweet to say it, even if it had to be a lie. Then he started tickling her, and then she showed him a thing or two about pressure points and leverage, and before long their giggles had faded and they were hot and panting and needing each other, and soon enough

(too long took too long)

he was inside her again, filling her up with that glorious cock, and she was clutching him to her while her heels dug into his back and he murmured, "You're glorious, God, you're so wonderful," and she very determinedly did *not* think about tomorrow.

Forty-three

She woke up once, reached for him, started to panic.

"Shhh. I'm right here. I had to make a couple of phone calls."

"Oh."

"It's okay. Not going anywhere now 'til morning."

Morning, she thought with despair, and snuggled back up to him.

There was a firm knock at the door, and Delaney extricated her limbs from Rake's—three bouts of sex had done the man in; he was snoring like a lumberjack with a head cold—grabbed the hotel robe out of the closet, and called, "Who is it?"

"It's me."

Oh. *Fuck.* "Rake!" she whispered. "Wake up."

Nope. Too busy snoring.

"Rake!" She kicked the bed. "Rake, you gotta wake up now."

No time to get dressed. No time to think up a plausible—

You know what? Fuck it.

"Hnnn? 'Laney? S'wrong?"

"Everything," she said, and opened the door.

The older woman was impeccably dressed in a yellow tweed suit with a cream-colored blouse, sensible flesh-colored panty hose, and sturdy brown shoes. Her hair was blond and silver and pulled back. Her eyes were Rake's.

They measured each other. "Nice to meet you in person, dear."

"Yeah," she said, but really, it wasn't. *Nice* was the wrong word. She stepped back from the door and turned toward the bed. Rake was on his feet, focused on wrapping the sheet around his waist. The early-morning sunlight gleamed in his chest hair.

Gleamed in his chest hair? Get ahold of yourself, woman.

"Rake, I know this is going to seem impossible, but this is my client. She's—"

"Hi, Nonna Tarbell." Rake, now wrapped like a burrito, crossed the room and pulled the nuclear option into a hug. "What took you so long?"

Thank goodness for the robe, because all the strength went out of Delaney's arms. She'd have dropped a sheet. Or her pants. Rake, however, was in no danger of flashing either of them, more's the pity. "No," she said. "You couldn't have." The password was one thing, but this?

"You *did*," Nonna Tarbell said, beaming. "So smart. Both of my boys. Thank heavens you took after your mother in that department. And—ahem." She cast a pointed look toward their dishabille, and the rumpled bed. "No more hide-a-bed, hmm?"

"That's none of your business," she snapped.

"I can see why you'd think that," the older woman said with an approving nod.

"She's right, Nonna. It's none of your business. Just like what we do with our dad's money is none of your business, and the fact that we aren't married is none of your business, and—"

"I may have overstepped," she began, but Rake cut her off.

"I love you, but I could strangle you. You know Blake's in a mess, too, right? Of course you do. You put him there."

"It was only—"

"Only bullshit." He just looked at her, the old woman with his eyes, the one who had hired Delaney to keep an eye on him, take care of him when he realized he was out of money, steer him toward charitable work, help him become a better man.

You picked the wrong bitch for that job, Delaney thought.

"You were always waiting for us to fail," Rake said simply, and his grandmother went pale. Her eyes filled, but the tears didn't fall. "You keep waiting for our father to come out. But he's dead, Nonna. We're our own men, like it or not. We never even met him, and never will. You're the one haunting us. Not him."

"How'd you even guess?" Delaney asked. She felt sorry for the nuclear option, and decided to pull Rake's focus back on her. The woman was a meddler, but she'd acted out of love and concern, which was more than Claire could say about her own motivation. "The password thing I get—he guessed my password!" she added, unable to keep the admiration out of her tone. "But out of all the people on the planet who could have hired me, how'd you guess it was your grandma?"

He went to the bedside table, picked up his phone, glanced at the time. Odd—were they going somewhere? Did he have an appointment? Then he said, "Can I get dressed? And how about breakfast?" He shot a look at his grandmother that Delaney prayed would never be directed at her. "You're buying."

"Of course, darling. I'd like to hear those answers myself."

Bemused—whatever Delaney had dreaded about the morning, she hadn't expected *this*—Delaney went to find her clothes.

Forty-four

"First off, the friendly lady I met in Lake Como, and again in Venice, just *happened* to have a set of clothes in my size?"

They were seated at the hotel's outdoor café, Rake with a Virgin Mary and Delaney with iced tea. Rake's grandma had hot tea she fussed over (one and a half spoons of sugar, a splash of cream, just a splash, absolutely no lemon, and stir and stir and stir) but didn't drink. If Delaney was right—and she'd been wrong about everything else this week—Rake's grandma was embarrassed. Not about catching them postsex; she seemed positively thrilled about that. About the other. About setting spies on her grandson, then taking all his money.

Rake was shaking his head. "I assumed you'd hooked up with some stud in Italy. I was even a little jealous of your mystery guy."

"I don't do that," Delaney said quietly, looking at her tea.

"No?" he teased.

"Well, okay, but believe it or not, I made an exception for you. *You're* the stud in Italy."

"O, glorious words, music to my ears." He turned back to his grandmother. "Then there was this." He showed them his phone. "This isn't a used one that happens to be in incredible shape from eBay. My grandma knew exactly what kind I had and sent you exactly the right replacement."

"We didn't have to go to FedEx, though," Delaney said quickly. "I really didn't think you should have to wait for it to get to the hotel."

"Sweet," the nuclear option commented. When Delaney leveled her a look, she didn't drop her gaze. "No, really. That was sweet. I knew you were a nice girl under all that bravado."

Delaney snorted.

"And I don't think I ever told you my last name," Rake continued. "Maybe when I was shit-faced in Como—sorry, Nonna—but I don't think so. You knew it, though. And when I called myself a millionaire, you weren't surprised. You didn't even blink. You knew I wasn't an ordinary tourist, when all you were supposed to know was that I was some random idiot who pitched his wallet and woke up stranded in Venice." He took something out of his pocket and looked at it. She realized with a start that it was her business card. He'd kept it? And looked at it quite a lot, judging by how worn it was.

He showed the card to Mrs. Tarbell and turned back to Delaney. "I. C. Delaney. I See Delaney. Not just seeing people. Seeing what they're up to, good *and* bad. I must have seemed like everything you hate: a spoiled rich guy who never gave much thought to anyone who needed help."

"No," she choked out. "No." Then, because it actually hurt to keep the truth from him, she elaborated. "At first. Yeah. But it didn't last long. You couldn't hide your essential wonderfulness." She blinked. Man, falling in love shot her vocabulary to hell. And wasn't it strange? Irony: She could finally tell him everything without breaking her word . . . and didn't want to. Almost didn't dare.

"It's how I found her," Mrs. Tarbell said, giving Rake back Delaney's card. "She's a special kind of private investigator—"

"No. I don't even have a license." Too much paperwork, too wide a trail. Too many questions she couldn't answer.

"—and Teresa couldn't recommend her enough." And when they both stared at her: "Yes, I know Teresa. One of her little charges tried to steal my purse when I was here last summer. Ohhh, the *scolding* she gave that child! I slipped him fifty euros when she wasn't looking."

Delaney smiled, the first real one since the three of them had sat down. "Teresa sees everything, Mrs. Tarbell."

"Those big beseeching dark eyes, I couldn't help it." She stirred her tea more. She hadn't so much as taken a sip, as far as Delaney could tell. "Though he cheered up quick enough when he had my cash." Then she glanced over Rake's shoulder. "And speaking of big dark eyes . . ."

He turned and saw Elena approaching while leading Lillith by the hand. Who promptly lit up and ran the rest of the way to the table. "Hi, Grandma!"

Rake felt the muscles in his jaw give up as his mouth fell open. "Lillith, you know who this is?"

"Sure! Why, do you need an introduction? This is Nonna Tarbell, my paternal great-grandmother." She stepped into the nuclear option's welcoming hug. Then, to Rake: "But I bet you don't know who *this* is."

"Hey, guys, how's it goin'?"

"Elena? Why do you sound like you're from Massachusetts?"

"It's Ellen, actually. And I'm from Andovuh.* Figured we were lettin' all the cats outta all the bags, time to drop the accent. Well. *That* accent, anyways."

"What is happening?" Rake wailed. "Do you all have deep dark secrets and/or multiple identities?"

"Yeah," Delaney admitted.

"Pretty much." Elena—sorry, Ellen—shrugged.

"How do you know my grandmother? Lillith, when did you guys meet?"

"Just a few days ago."

"But it's only *been* a few . . . oh, hell. The Fedex office."

"Well . . ."

---

* Andover, Massachusetts.

Forty-five

Thank goodness, Lillith thought as she entered the ladies' room. She liked Delaney, and Rake seemed nice (if deeply confused), but she hated peeing when she knew people could hear it. Even strangers. *Side effect of being an only child, maybe?*

And speaking of strangers, an old, pretty lady was standing beside the sinks

(not washing her hands, not checking makeup, not on her phone, standing straight, facing the door)

waiting for someone.

She was pale and chubby, with silver-streaked brownish blond hair pulled back and pinned in place. She was wearing light blue pants, a white blouse, black tennis shoes, a black cardigan, and she had a black purse the size of a pillow slung over one shoulder.

When she spoke, her voice was warm and welcoming. "*Buongiorno,* darling."

"*Ciao, signora,*" Lillith replied, smoothing her slightly too-small shirt over her belly and standing straighter. "*Come va?*"

"Just fine."

"*Posso aiutarti con qualcosa?*"

"I'm sorry, dear, but you just heard the extent of my Italian. I'm much better in French."

"Oh. *Puis-je vous aider avec quelque chose?*"

The woman's smile brightened. "You're just full of surprises, aren't you, sweetheart? Did you know that we have a friend in common? Her name's Delaney. I wanted to meet you and asked her to arrange it. I'm so happy to see you."

"Oh." Lillith studied the woman's elegant clothing and nonthreatening mien. "That makes you Rake's mother or grandmother. If you don't mind, when's your birthday?"

The woman blinked, then replied, "Nineteen fifty-seven."

"Grandmother, then." She held out her hand and answered the unspoken question. "You and Rake have the exact same eye shape and color. It's nice to meet you, Mrs. Tarbell."

"Thank you, darling. Lovely to meet you, too. And I can't tell you how happy I am that you've joined our family."

"Have I?"

"Oh yes."

"Then . . . can I tell you something?"

"Anything."

So she did.

Forty-six

"I get that you're a pack of duplicitous sociopaths, but did you have to drag the good people at FedEx into it?"

"Don't whine, Rake dear. It's unbecoming."

"I'll whine anytime I like," he whined. To Lillith: "She's a horrible human being. Never say I didn't warn you."

"You're just mad because you don't know what's going on."

"You're right, Lillith," he admitted. "That's exactly why I'm mad."

The waiter chose that moment to check on them, and Lillith chatted with him in Italian while Mrs. Tarbell visibly puffed up with pride. "Isn't she brilliant? I can't wait for her to meet the rest of the family."

"Take it easy. She's been through a lot."

"Oh, I heard." The nuclear option lowered her voice. "Delaney told me about her mother. Are you any closer to finding out if the car accident was accidental?"

"Yes, which may or may not work out for us." Delaney spread her hands. "It's too soon to tell."

"It's always too soon to tell," Rake pointed out. "That's pretty much the theme of the week."

"Got *that* right," Delaney agreed. "But getting back to how you knew my employer was your grandmother . . ."

"Yeah, I'd like to hear that, too," Ellen said, making herself comfortable and helping herself to Delaney's drink. To Delaney: "We're gonna recruit him, right? Boy's got skills."

"Well, Ellen-not-Elena, I'm flattered and also a smidge terrified. But getting back to my brilliance—shut up, you asked—Delaney not only kept a set of clothes in my size on hand, she also knew how my brother lost his virginity."

From Ellen: "Ew."

"And she knew because my grandma knew."

"Again: ew."

"She only knew because I ratted him out. Which was shitty," Rake acknowledged, "I won't deny it."

"But such a good story," Nonna Tarbell added.

"That was a big one, Delaney."

"You're right," she said, seeing the scope of that particular blunder. At the time, he'd seemed to think he had blurted that out to her in Lake Como. She'd been relieved that he'd given her an out. Now, of course, she realized he'd just filed it away with all the other clues she, forever a fool, had dropped. "I'll say it again: Underestimating you was stupid."

He reached past his glass and took her hand. "That means a lot, coming from you." The gesture wasn't lost on anyone except Lillith (who was trying to coax the waiter into bringing her chocolate milk). "You also said you hadn't been warned I was tenacious. My grandmother would have warned you that I'm kind of a slut—"

A snort from Mrs. Tarbell. "Kind of. Hmm."

"—and careless, and self-deprecating, but tenacious

wouldn't have come up. The worst, though." He let go of her hand. "That was pretending you wanted to hear about the Sweetheart situation, even though you would have known all about it."

"No." She was shaking her head so hard, her face was momentarily obscured by hair. Mrs. Tarbell had opened her mouth, maybe even to defend her, but she raced ahead. "Rake, I promise that isn't true. I'd only heard about *your* part in all of this. At the time, when your grandma hired me, I didn't give a shit about your brother or his predicament. I didn't give a shit about yours, either. But . . ." She looked away, and then back. "That changed. And then I wanted to know more about you. And the people you love. That's why I asked. Your family is so *interesting*. Not just to me, either. I bet a lot of people think you guys—"

"Put the *fun* in dysfunctional?"

At least he said it with a smile. "No. You're good, you're all—I mean, you love each other. Even when you're yelling at each other. You're not afraid to get dirty to help each other. Literally, in Blake's case. He's shoveling horse shit, for God's sake, to help his mom. That's interesting to me. I don't—" She broke off as two men in dark suits approached their table. She didn't recognize either one, which could be good or bad.

"Signore Tarbell?" The shorter, balder one took out his wallet and flashed ID. "*Per favore, vieni con noi.*"

Shit.

"What's this about?" Mrs. Tarbell asked sharply, knuckles whitening as she clutched her gigantic purse. But Rake was already getting to his feet.

"I know what it's about. My sordid past finally caught up with me. Twice in one week," he added with a wry look at Lillith. "Lead the way, gentlemen."

"Rake, you can't just—" Delaney realized Ellen had already done a discreet fade; wise, considering the circumstances. "You can't assume you know what—"

"I'm not assuming I know anything," he replied. "Believe me."

"Don't worry, dear." Nonna Tarbell was already poking her phone while glaring at the men taking Rake into custody. "I'll get my lawyer on the line and meet you at the consulate."

The short one cleared his throat. "You, too, miss."

Now that's interesting. Delaney didn't move while she weighed her options: (1) assume they were government suits and go along quietly, (2) assume they weren't and kick their asses, or (3) stay put. Of course, there was Lillith to think of, so she couldn't just—

A high-pitched yowl shattered her thought process. And possibly glass. *"Don't you take my daddy!"* Lillith shrieked. She'd lunged for Rake and was now sitting on his feet, both arms clamped around his knees, face turning red as she held on with all her strength and kept shrieking. *"I wanna be with Daddy!"*

"Agh, Lillith! You're pinching a bunch of my leg hairs!"

"Don't you take my daddy away!"

"Rumore veeramente inaccettabile," the taller one mumbled. Then, louder: *"Molto bene lei viene."* And when that did nothing to decrease Lillith's impression of an air raid siren: "You may come with us, child!"

Well, then, Delaney thought, getting to her feet. *Decision made.*

Forty-seven

"This isn't the consulate."

Delaney smirked. "No kidding."

One of the more hilarious dilemmas presented by the city of Venice: If you need to take someone(s) into custody, you can't just bundle them into a car and drive them away. You can hop a vaporetto, and in a pinch you can rent a gondola and *pole* your suspects/prisoners away, but it's not especially intimidating.

Instead, Tall and Small had marched them, on foot, for several blocks until they reached . . .

"No. No. Nooooooo!"

. . . the church of San Basso.

"We had to get all the way inside before you knew where you were?"

"I was half-asleep last time!" he yelped. "And we came in by a different door." Rake was looking around the hall as they walked along a narrow corridor leading to the offices. "Jesus, what *is* this?"

"Phones." The short one—Delaney didn't remember the

name from his ID and didn't much care—held out a propri-
etary hand. They'd stopped just short of a closed door and
clearly weren't going farther until the niceties were observed.
Delaney took her time as she carefully pulled it from her
pocket and handed it over. *Passive-aggressive tart,* as Donna
would have pointed out with a smirk. Rake took even more
time, possibly because he had trouble bitching and digging
out his phone simultaneously, which culminated in the tall
one all but snatching the thing out of Rake's hand.

Amateurs. Should have taken them right away.

"You stay put, okay?" Delaney said to Lillith, who had
been with them the entire way, sometimes holding her hand
and sometimes Rake's. The child had obediently taken one of
the chairs outside the office and was idly looking around and
swinging her feet back and forth. Small and Tall were clearly
relieved she'd stopped with the tornado sirenesque yowls,
and they had no interest in damaging the child's equilibrium,
which could result in frightened hysterics or, worse, more
yowling. "You stay out here and we'll be just inside, talking
to his boss and straightening everything out. See? We can all
see you through the windows."

"How do you know what we're going to do?" Small asked,
having the hilarious nerve to look affronted.

"Because you've got no imagination." Delaney opened the
office door and gestured for Rake and Tall to enter. "Not a
single one of you."

"*Non tieni la porta per me,*" Tall grumbled, trailing her
in. "*Ti tengo la porta per te.*" Then, louder: "Mr. Kovac, you
wanted to talk to these people." Then, unnecessarily: "Here
they are."

Kovac nodded and tossed him a small hammer, the kind
with a head you could unscrew and replace with any number

of screwdriver heads; the handle was decorated with small pastel flowers for that extra surreal touch.* Small and Tall took turns destroying Rake's and Delaney's phones and, judging from their grunts of exertion and wide smiles, quite enjoyed themselves. Delaney took a step closer and slightly in front of Rake, in case the hammer was going to be utilized in even less pleasant ways.

"Hey! Knock it off, dickheads!" Rake yelped, because his survival instincts were for shit. "Do you have any idea how hard I had to work for that thing? The debasing tasks I had to perform? I don't even want to think about them, but being here is bringing it all back."

Tall let out a disbelieving snort, which paired nicely with Delaney's eye roll.

"All right," Kovac said with a mild American accent. He was short—Delaney could see that although he was seated, he was like one of those crash-test dummies with no legs—announced his baldness with a bad comb-over, and his eyes blinked slowly behind rimless glasses. He looked like an insurance adjuster, which, she supposed, was valuable in his line of work. "Let's get to this. Where is it?"

"Where's what?" Rake asked.

Kovac sighed. "Jesus. Really? You're gonna make me do the threats and intimidation thing, and then rough you up a little? Can't we just get to the part where you put my mind at ease and we all go back to our lives?"

"No one's *making* you do anything," Delaney said.

"So you're definitely not cops," Rake said, nodding. "Or from the consulate. I'm pretty sure."

---

* This is a real thing!

Delaney smothered a giggle. "What tipped you off first? I told you when they rolled up, you shouldn't have assumed you knew what it was about. They don't care about your al fresco park sex almost a decade ago."

"Why not?" Rake threw up his hands. "Everyone else does! If you knew it wasn't a legit arrest, why are you here?"

"Why *wouldn't* I be here? What, I'm gonna let you and Lillith ride off—well, walk off—into the literal sunset? Besides, you're looking at this all wrong. It's good they're not cops. Better than if they were cops, actually."

"What? Why?"

"They have no lawful authority, for starters."

"Excuse me." From Kovac, in the tone of a man forced to watch a tennis match he didn't care about. "This is my meeting."

"We don't have it," Delaney told him. "We've never had it."

"Bullshit."

"Donna's been dead for months. It would have turned up by now," she pointed out. Then, colder: "I would have paid you a visit by now."

"And again I say bullshit. That dim quim wouldn't have dropped off the grid without giving you what she had."

"Dim . . ."

"Oh boy," Rake muttered.

". . . quim?" Delaney wanted to pace—well, she wanted to break Kovac's nose, blacken his eyes, and then really go to work on him—but time and place, time and place. Unfortunately, there wasn't room to pace; the windowless office was only about six feet by five, and other than the wooden desk and two chairs filched from the kitchen, the only furniture in the room were multiple heavy bookshelves crammed with any number of heavy old tomes. "D'you want to get down to business, or do you have more insults to run through first?"

"I can do both. And I'm not sure you're getting it, sunshine. I have to know what Donna Alvah had and where it was, because I fucking hate prison, and while I don't mind having my guys smack you around a bit, I don't want to kill you."

"Also because you hate prison," Rake guessed.

"You got it," Kovac replied, smiling like Rake was the prize pupil who correctly guessed the capital of Serbia.*

Delaney leaned back against the bookshelves and shook her head. "You're not hearing me. I don't know what she did with the flash drive. Hell, I didn't know what she'd done with her daughter for *way* too long. If it hasn't surfaced yet, you're probably in the clear."

"'Probably' isn't gonna do it for me. 'Probably' means there's still a chance I'll get pinched again. And at my age, I've got no interest in making new friends on my knees."

"Uh, I don't think that's an age thing," Rake began.

Delaney shrugged, cutting him off. "I don't know what to tell you, Kovac. She left me a letter. And that's it. That was always it: two pages, single-spaced."

"A letter."

"Yep."

"In code?"

"No, in English. But it's not the smoking gun, Kovac. And if it was—well. Like I said. You wouldn't have had to spend the last week having your people skulk around. The cops would have knocked on your door, or I would have. Oh—and what happened to the A and B teams?" she added, jerking her thumb toward Tall and Small. "Why are you using subs?"

---

* It's Belgrade! (I had to look it up.)

"I like how you're asking me that, as if you don't know the answer. They were on your boy toy until Lake Como."

"Hey! I'm a *man* toy."

"Then somebody kicked the shit out of them, and they lost him."

"Aw."

"The B team picked him up again outside the hotel that first morning, and then *someone* stole their wallets, led 'em on a merry chase, and called the cops and reported a pickpocket. Who brings their righteous ID along when they know they're gonna be up to some shady shit?" Kovac lamented.

"Right?" Delaney said. "Amateur hour. What I've been saying."

"And whoever this was also planted a dozen *other* wallets on them. Dumbasses are still in jail. I'm sure as shit not bailing them out."

Yes, loading the bad guys with stolen property was slick. Teresa's latest stray, the nimble-fingered teen Lillith and Rake would have recognized as the Roma Gypsy who lent them his phone that first day, was quite the talent. And when the cops get a call from one of the more affluent areas in the tourist quarter, they show up in a hurry. The whole thing had taken less than twenty minutes.

"Wait, that's why you ducked out on Lillith and me? You spotted a tail?" Rake was, to her surprise, getting into fret mode. "Jeez, Delaney, I wish you'd said something."

She spread her hands. "Where would I have even begun?"

"You could've been hurt."

"Oh, please."

"Hello? My meeting, remember? So then I remembered this isn't a goddamned spy-caper movie, so I put guys here at San Basso—I figured you'd have your eye on the place. In a way, the story started here. And on a practical note, your hotel's a quick walk from here." He shrugged. "So."

"So you spotted us again."

"Yeah."

"Which is when you got a little desperate. And a lot stupid."

"Whoa." Kovac put his hands up as if (false hope) he was being arrested. "My guy was just supposed to ask the little girl about the flash drive."

"You were gonna take my kid?" Rake demanded. He'd gone from listening to the exchange with a slightly disbelieving look on his face to taking two steps, slamming his hands palms down on the desk, and glaring straight into Kovac's eyes. "Your grubby brigade of fucksticks was gonna snatch my daughter?"

"I told you, he was only supposed to talk to her." This in the tone of a man mildly inconvenienced by a waiter bringing the wrong order, instead of facing off with six feet three inches and 195 pounds of irked Tarbell. "But you put an end to that quick enough."

"If you *ever* come *near* my—"

"Yeah, yeah, vengeance will be yours. Hell, vengeance *was* yours. The guy you upchucked all over has been sick as fuck ever since."

"Good. When it comes to gastroenteritis, I like to share the wealth." Rake straightened and stepped back from the desk. "And there's plenty more where that came from if you guys get any other moronic ideas."

"It's his superpower!" Delaney said brightly.

"Consider me horrified." Then, to Delaney: "So, sunshine. About this letter—"

"She only *talked* about the flash drive. There weren't any instructions on how to find it or what to do with it."

"So what's the point? Why bother writing anything?" Kovac asked, scowling.

"You *are* a sociopath, aren't you?"

"That's what my therapist says," he admitted.

"I'd try to explain why a letter that doesn't lead to figurative buried treasure is worth writing, but you wouldn't get it."

"Do it anyway."

Forty-eight

Delaney—

So running away didn't work. Which you told me would happen, but since you're insufferable when you're right, that's all I'm gonna say about it.

I wasn't even looking, that's the stupid part. I hadn't for years, ever since I renounced our family "tradition" after my come-to-Jesus moment with Rake Tarbell in fucking Venice, of all places.

And it wasn't too bad, me and Lillith pretending to be citizens. After a while, it didn't feel like we were pretending. But then I smelled a fat rat and it was like when we were kids and we just had to snoop.

I volunteered. That's it. That's why I'm in this mess— except I was always going to be in this mess, it just took me the better part of a decade to fall. There was a major fire at the church and they were running fund-raisers to fix the nave and the meeting house and I was helping out the office gals, all that filing and refiling and asking for new financial statements to replace what they lost, pretty boring shit, and then I thought some of the statements looked . . . off. So I poked. And then I asked. And the church ladies were all "Oh, no worries, Mr. Kovac takes care of that and he's a brilliant investor who's always moving money around and we don't really understand it but he gets results," and I don't have to tell you how many alarm bells that set off in my brain.

Old habits die never, which is why I didn't call a cop. And tell you what, kiddo, you coulda cracked this guy's files with your eyes closed and your thumbs broken. That's how easy it was. He is into a ton of shit and I think he got over-confident. Scratch that—I know he did. This isn't even the first church he scammed—he got his start in Europe. In fact, he's going back to Italy in the next few months.

I didn't squeeze him.

I thought about it, and if I was still living for myself, I probably would have, just for the pure joy of fucking with a scammer, but I'm out of practice and there was Lillith to think of. I put the bomb back in the box and got the hell out of there—how's that for a what do you call it, a metaphor? Except I'm worried snooping sped up the countdown. And that it'll blow before I can get us clear.

So I didn't squeeze him, but I did make copies—like Ellen says, a little CYA goes a long way. Something like that, I dunno, 'cause when Ellen starts with the acronyms, I tune out.

Anyway. We're going. No idea if this guy's got software on his system that'll tell him if someone's been peeking, and I won't take a chance. Not with Lillith to think of. I'm setting up a fail-safe if, God forbid, something happens to me, I've got the drive in a safe space, I've pulled my savings, *which are also in a safe space, and I'm sending you all the info I pulled on the Tarbell family back in the day when the plan was to scam and leave town, not get knocked up with a baby and leave town. My advice, start with the grandmother. She'll be all in once she knows there's a new Tarbell in the mix.*

Lillith doesn't know who her dad is, but she knows who you are. I've told her that if you ever show up, she's to drop everything and go with you straightaway and no questions asked and that you'll explain everything.

She's amazing, Delaney. Brilliant and beautiful and about a thousand times nicer on her worst day than I am on my best. If I mysteriously vanish like in a bad police procedural, I want you to grab her, find out which Tarbell is her dad, and keep them both safe until the shitstorm's passed. After that—well, fuck if I know. Live happily ever after? Y'know what—I'll be happy if you guys just live.

It's a lot to ask, I know. And I hate asking, which you know. I'm sorry we couldn't stay close. I should have kept in touch and I'm paying for that now. Don't make Lillith take the weight of my bad decision(s).

Love my girl. And give my best to the rest.

Better luck next life,
Nedra

Forty-nine

Kovac leaned back in his desk chair, the middle buttons on his shirt straining as he took a deep breath, then let it out while shaking his head. "I don't get it."

"Toldja."

"You did. And regardless of the alleged contents of this so-called letter—"

"Did you go to law school while Delaney was telling her story?"

"—you know I can't take you at your word, right?"

"Yep." Delaney smiled. "And *you* know you'd better have a D team on standby. Right?"

"Oh, come on!" From Rake, sounding equal parts exasperated and pissed. "Really? You two are gonna stand around talking about missing flash drives and allude to beatings? *We don't have it.* So let us go or beat us to death."

"Whoa!" Delaney straightened up from where she was slouched against the bookshelves. "You know there's middle ground between those options, right?"

Kovac opened his mouth, but before he could answer,

or order their deaths, or otherwise incite violence, they all flinched at the horribly familiar shriek from the other side of the door.

"*Papa, ich werde mich übergeben!*"

"The hell was that?" Kovac shook his head. "Jesus, that kid's got some lungs on her."

"*Beeil dich, ich bin krank!*"

"She says she's going to throw up—she's really sick." Rake at once looked like all his systems were screaming threat level red, when the most he mustered for his own peril was threat level puce. "She wants me!"

"So go help her," Delaney said, giving him a helpful shove. To Kovac: "That gastroenteritis is really getting around."

"Oh, Christ." Delaney could almost see Kovac working this out. *Clandestine snatch = good. Private interrogation = good. Screaming kid + vomit in hallway where anyone might come in = not good.* "Don, walk them down to the bathroom. *Just* the bathroom. And stand outside 'til she's done. If the guy tries anything, open up his skull with the hammer."

"Not the face," Rake said, yanking open the door.

"Fine, plant the thing in the base of his skull, what do *I* care?" Then, as the door closed: "Now. What to do about *you*, sunshine?"

Fifty

"Okay, hon, I'll stay here 'til you're done." Rake set Lillith down as the bathroom door wheezed shut behind them. "And listen, don't be scared. Delaney's got this under control." *I'm pretty sure.*

"Uh-huh." Lillith was—wait. Why was she yanking up her T-shirt? And exposing her little belly? And why was she tearing her belly away and handing it to him? And unzipping it? "Here's Mama's phone. Don't worry, it's charged. Call one one two."

"Huh?"

"It's our best bet. Dialing one one three brings the carabinieri, which is overkill—we need help, but not military help. And one one eight is for medical emergencies, which we don't have. Yet. Here."

Dumbfounded, Rake looked down at the pile of bills she'd just slapped into his other hand. "What is this?"

"It's eight thousand, three hundred and twenty-six euros."

He blinked at her. "What?"

"Oh, *scuzi*. I meant nine thousand, six hundred and forty-three American dollars."

Like a cornered cat, he was torn between fight or flight. Within thirty seconds of taking Lillith to the bathroom (he'd scooped her up and sprinted, sure she was going to be sick all over him), he had a phone and ten grand.

"I'd better hang on to this for a while longer, though," she added, showing him a tiny pineapple. Correctly reading his blank stare and rapid blinking, she plucked off the top of the pineapple, exposing a flash drive.

Of all the weird things to happen during this day in this weird week, this is definitely the weirdest.

"Hurry *up*," she hissed. "We still have to text Sophie and Teresa our location. They won't give us privacy forever."

Right. Of course. It was gratifying to be able to rely on such a cool-headed leader in times of crisis. He hit 1-1-2 and in a low voice reported a kidnapping (it wasn't, technically, but it would get the cops moving), unlawful detainment, and threats of felony assault. As he started to elaborate, Lillith chimed in, *"Imi stanno spaventando, penso che abbiano delle pistole! E non riesco a trovare mia madre!"**

"Nice touch," he said admiringly.

"And almost the truth." She took the phone back and began texting. "They're bad, but I don't think they have guns. There are really, *really* unpleasant consequences if you're carrying here, and I doubt any of them has a permit. Which lands them in a ton of trouble. They don't have a Second

---

* They're scaring me! I think they have guns! And I can't find my mother!

Amendment here." She chewed her lip. "At least not about that."

Rake at last shook off his stunned apathy. "This is fucking incredible!" he whisper-shouted. "You've had the—and also the—you've literally had *everything* the whole time? *All week?*" He reached out and tugged the hem of her shirt back down; it was what she'd worn the day they'd met: I'M MY OWN SAFE SPACE!

"Jesus Christ!" he praised/hissed. "The whole time? No wonder you were always offering to buy me gelato!"

"See why turning me down was dumb?"

"I didn't know you had ten grand on you! Wait, *why* did you have ten grand on you?"

Before she could answer, there was a brisk rap on the door. "How's she doing?"

"Oh my God, the diarrhea and vomit are everywhere! Get a mop! Two mops! And the smell! Maybe you should get in here and help!"

"Pass."

"See?" she said smugly. "We make a good team."

"Yes, but that's not news."

"Yes, but I get the feeling you're the type who needs to actually see something up close before you'll believe it. It's why I was glad when you got sick."

"Um. What?"

"So I could take care of you. I know finding out about me was a nasty shock." Before he could protest, she cut him off. "But I thought if I was quiet . . . and helpful . . ." All at once, the preternaturally self-possessed child had trouble looking him in the eye. "If I did that, then maybe you wouldn't think it'd be hard to take care of me. You know. If I tried to take care of you."

His eyes stung. Fucking allergies. Which had only now developed. "That's—that's not your responsibility, hon."

"It's not about responsibility." Then, abruptly: "Did you mean it?"

"Mean what?"

"When you got mad at that man who tried to kidnap me? When you said I was your daughter?"

"You heard that?"

"Well. Thin doors. And you were kinda screaming. Especially when you called them a 'grubby brigade of fucksticks.'"

"Probably shouldn't quote me when I'm throwing around words like *fucksticks,* and yeah, Lillith, I did mean it. Of course I did." He knelt and put his hands on her slender shoulders. "I know I'm a poor substitute for your mom and that you must think I'm a flighty, selfish jackass. . . ."

"I don't think you're flighty."

"But you're mine. Like I'm yours." He hesitated, wondering if now was the time to mention that Blake might actually be her father. He ultimately held off because (1) time and place—they *were* still in the clutches of the bad guys, after all, and speaking of, he really should get back to Delaney, and (2) it didn't fucking *matter* if Blake's sperm got there first. Lillith was his child. End of discussion. "And that's always going to—"

"Doing okay in there? Do you two, uh, need anything?"

"Will you just give me a minute?" he shouted. *Christ. No sense of decorum at all.* "We'll figure it out," he finished. "All of it. Because we're a team now. Which reminds me, another team member has been alone with the bad guys long enough—"

"Exactly long enough," Lillith agreed. "Here." She pressed a slender dark tube into his hand. He blinked down at it, then with a snap of his wrist the telescoping baton tripled in length. "Don't worry. Those are legal here. So's pepper spray, but there wasn't room for that in my belly bag."

"I feel so safe with you," he said with absolute sincerity. "Now keep back. Daddy has to go give the bad guy a concussion."

"I'm not calling you Daddy."

"Noted. Keep out of the way regardless."

Fifty-one

Well, that escalated quickly.

Rake had only been gone a minute before Kovac had calmly instructed Small to "grab her and I'll cut her face—oh, wait, all that 'not the face' stuff is *his* thing. Well, it'll be ironic." To her: "No offense, but it'll be easier to believe you if we hurt you and your story doesn't change."

No offense? Really? Delaney wasted no time hurling a book—not for nothing had she been using the bookcase for back support—straight at Small's face. All she hoped for was a hit, a distraction that would let her follow up with something painful and immediate. To her immense satisfaction, the thing caught him square in the face and everyone heard the raw carrot–snapping sound that heralded a broken nose.

"Are you kidding me?" Kovac cried. The bad news: The idiot had a gun. The good news: He didn't make much use of it, as evidenced by how long it took him to snatch the thing up and fumble with the safety. Delaney had plenty of time to slap his wrist, hard, which sent the barrel pointing at the floor. There was the dull boom of a bullet plowing through the carpet, and Kovac was so startled by the recoil, he almost dropped it. Delaney stuck her finger through the trigger guard, preventing him from firing, and while it hurt like hell as he mashed the trigger in frantic attempts to shoot, it was a lot better than a .38 exploring her lower abdomen. Also . . .

"A thirty-eight? Really?"

Kovac ignored her firearm critique in favor of shouting, "Don, get that kid and Tarbell the fuck back here *now*!"

"I don't think he can hear you." Delaney slapped his other hand away as he tried to smack her, then snapped his pinkie for good measure. The shriek was indecently satisfying.

The office door burst open

(let's hope Tall is as easily incapacitated; three versus one is a little much)

and Tall fell in. He hit facedown, revealing an irritated Rake behind him brandishing—oooh, was that the Guardian twenty-eight inch? *Nice.*

Even nicer to see him smack Small with it, further compounding the damage to his face. "Should've stayed down," Rake growled. Then: "Delaney, is it sexist if I offer to help you beat Kovac to death? And before you answer, please don't think I'm implying you'd need help beating someone to death."

"Thank you. And no, it's not sexist. Or necessary." This because after she'd broken his finger, Kovac was more interested in getting away than escalating.

"This is fucking ridiculous!" he yelped.

"Tell me. Just let go of the gun! That's why you can't get away."

"I'm *trying.*"

"You are truly terrible at this. At all of this. I can't believe you managed to have Donna killed."

"I didn't!" Kovac freed himself with one more yank, staggered, caught his balance with his bad hand, let out another shriek, and fell flat on his ass on the carpet. She could see his eyes watering with tears of pain as she trained the gun-barrel site on his forehead. "But she sure as shit deserved it! She was going to ruin me!"

"No. She. *Wasn't.*" She knew she should hand the gun over; it was getting harder to resist the impulse to empty the rest of the clip into the bridge of his nose. "She wasn't running from you. She was just running. She wasn't going to expose you, she just wanted to keep her kid safe. The flash drive was just to protect herself. It was a reflex, like how it hurts when someone pokes a bruise."

"Wait." Rake was still holding the baton—Delaney could see his knuckles were white—and looked ready to bust more heads, but he paused. Which seemed safe enough; Kovac was whimpering and cradling his bad hand, and Tall and Small were semiconscious at best. "You're saying you didn't have someone run over Donna on purpose?"

"What, you need a narrator? Fuck off."

"So when she disappeared, you assumed she was about to blow up your life, so you acted accordingly." To Delaney: "And you assumed that he killed Donna over the flash drive and acted accordingly. That's all this is? A misunderstanding?"

"An epic, gross, violent misunderstanding," Delaney agreed. And that was the worst part. Donna died running from her past, but not the way Delaney assumed. It was one of those laugh or cry moments, if *laugh* meant succumb to hysterics, and *cry* meant the same.

"Aw, dammit." This from a new voice, and everyone looked. Ellen/Elena was framed in the doorway, and Teresa was behind her, holding Lillith. "How did I know you weren't gonna save any bad guys for us?"

"Wow! How'd you guys get here? I didn't spot a tail."

"Donna texted us. Which was as unsettling as you might imagine." Elena nodded at Lillith. "Well. Donna's phone texted us."

"She— What? Amazing."

Rake shook his head. "That's the least amazing thing she's done in the last ten minutes. The cops are on the way, too, so anyone with a record—not *you*, Kovac—should be vamoosing."

"I'd like an ambulance, please." Kovac groaned.

"Go!" Rake made shooing motions with his baton. "I'll tell the cops what happened. The parts of it I understand, that is. So it'll be a short conversation. But use the delay to get clear."

"I'm staying."

"Delaney—"

"I'm staying, too," Lillith added. "You said it yourself: We make a great team."

"True, but irrelevant. Out!"

"But they'll kick you out of the country!"

He smiled at his daughter. "And you, too."

Fifty-two

"You thought I was going to kill Kovac? You thought I killed all those other people?"

"You were talking about hits and hacks! You were insanely secretive and you lie like you're getting paid." Rake paused and guzzled half his ginger beer. Stress made him thirsty, clearly. "Actually, you *are* getting paid."

"Point," Delaney conceded.

It was hours later; Kovac and the C team had been arrested, lawyers had been summoned, statements had been taken, paperwork had been filed, teeth had been gnashed. Rake had been politely but not really asked to leave the city, the nuclear option vouched for him and promised to put him (and Lillith, and herself) on a plane ASAP, and the others did a fade, then met up with them for supper at Antiche Carampane, a centuries-old restaurant justly famous for its homemade desserts.

And just in time, because they were all starving and had walked past several acceptable restaurants, all vetoed by the nuclear option.

"I'm sorry, darling, but I simply refuse to eat in a restaurant that employs the use of neon lighting to lure customers, specifically makes a point of saying Americans are welcome, or serves chicken tenders."

"This," Rake said. "This is what I had to put up with, you guys. All my life. Oh, and Blake, too. I guess."

"Gift horses, dear. Lillith, you come sit by me. Now: all of you. I'm dying to hear the whole story, beginning to end."

"Come to think of it," Rake said, "so am I." But he smiled as he said it, clearly relaxed for the first time in days.

"But first, we'll order." Then, proudly to the waiter; "My granddaughter will be ordering for me."

So she did, suggesting the carpaccio of raw wild fish

("You like sushi, right, Grandma? Then you'll probably like this.")

spaghetti with spicy sauce, and finishing with several sorbets and *biscottini della casa*.

"She's trilingual!" Mrs. Tarbell announced to the waiter, the table at large, the tables behind them, a third of the kitchen staff, the street outside. Rake caught Delaney's gaze and they both smiled when Lillith didn't correct her.

What the hell, Delaney thought. *Let her keep some secrets. That one at least won't get anyone killed.*

Meanwhile, Ellen was breaking it down for the Tarbells. "To be clear: Hits and hacks don't equal murder. They mean that when someone promises money for the Big Pipe Dream, then reneges, we investigate why. We break in, in every sense of the word. We look at *everything*."

Delaney picked up the narrative. "And if we find out they broke their word for a legitimate reason—unexpected hospital bills if it's a private person, or needing to rebuild after a storm or fire if it's a company, or not pulling in the contributions they anticipated . . . that stuff happens, and it's nobody's fault. Something like that, we let it go and no hard feelings."

Mrs. Tarbell was nodding. "But if, say, somebody wants to buy his mistress a summer home—"

"Right. Then I go to them, and lay out what we were able to dig up, and I tell them, 'Keep your word, or we'll put all your dirty laundry out there. I'll expose you as a liar *and* a cheat and you'll lose a lot more than the donation you promised.'"

It wasn't a calling, exactly. But they'd been doing it forever—since a few months after she'd kicked Elena's bully in the balls back in middle school, in fact.

"Exposure is their worst nightmare," she continued. "Their exposure going viral is too terrifying to even be contemplated. They've always given in."

Elena had gone quiet, and Delaney could guess why. The first person they'd hacked, years ago, had been their mutual foster father, who had a bad habit of "accidentally" walking in on them if they were in the bathroom, or dressing, or undressing. Pretty soon there were dozens of accidental sightings every week. The foster mother refused to take it seriously

("Oh, you girls are so sensitive! Aren't we all one big happy family? Who cares who sees what?")

and the girls knew from experience that CPS was overworked and unlikely to be helpful without proof. So they'd hacked his home office and computer and found the porn, which was gross but not unexpected, and the monthly payments to the seventeen-year-old mistress, which was gross but helpful. Which they discussed with him. At length.

End of "accidents."

"I wish you'd told me what you were really up to," Rake said, having the gall to sound wounded.

"How could I? Your takeaway from Lillith's story was 'Your dead mom was a thief and a blackmailer.' Why the *hell* would any of us confide anything we didn't absolutely have to?"

"I like how she's lumping us in with her," Ellen commented with a grin. "I actually wouldn't have cared if you'd confided."

Rake cleared his throat. "So . . . you guys didn't go to prison together?"

"What? No." Delaney saw what he was getting at and realized she couldn't give him shit for this one, because that's what she had told him earlier in the week: *We did time together.* "We were in the same foster home. Why do you think I didn't care about talking to the cops once we knew exactly how Donna died? I'm the only one in the family who doesn't have a record. And do you know why, Rake?"

"No, but I'll bet it's a great story."

"It's a *wonderful* story," Teresa confided. "We come off as *piuttosto eroico.*"*

"It's not because I was smarter or faster or trickier. It's because they"—pointing at Ellen and Teresa—"took the fall. Each time we got caught—which admittedly wasn't often, and certainly not since we were voting age—they kept me clear of it. We're all dirty, but they help me at least look clean."

"Is that why the Big Pipe Dream is so important? Why it has to be an off-the-books shelter? Because some of you have records?"

"Yes, that's exactly right," Delaney said as the other girls nodded. "It's one more piece of bureaucracy that gums up the

---

* Rather heroic.

works and makes it harder to make kids safe. But, thanks to your grandmother . . ."

Mrs. Tarbell was already nodding. "Oh, yes, dear. You've done your part and then some. I'll be wiring the rest of your funds first thing in the morning."

"You— Really?" From long habit, Delaney had already began mustering arguments. "Just like that?"

"It's not 'just like that,' Delaney. You did everything you promised, even though your life was in danger—"

"Repeatedly," Rake growled.

"—and your friends were at risk, to say nothing of my littlest darling."

"Aw."

"Not *you*, Rake." Lillith giggled.

"It was worth being at risk," Teresa said. "To find out what happened to Donna. To find her girl and make her safe. We would have done such things for nothing."

"Which is not a hint to delay sending funds," Ellen said. "Like, at all."

"I wish I had friends like you guys," Rake said with bald honesty.

Delaney smiled. "Everyone does."

Lillith tugged on his hand. "We agreed, remember? You and I are friends."

Rake smiled down at her. "I remember. Now I just need five more of you."

"Listen, why do you think we paired you and Lillith up as soon as the principals were in place? Who the hell would trust a kid with ten grand?"

Ellen's hand shot up. "I know!"

"Former street kids," Delaney said, ignoring Ellen's hand

waving. "Plus, look at her! Could she appear more disarming and cute?"

Lillith smirked.

"And who would view a notorious carefree playboy with suspicion?"

Rake snorted. "You Bruce Wayned me?"

"Oh, I like that," Ellen said, nodding. "Yep. That's exactly what happened. You're pretty and careless and spend your money doing pretty, careless things. Hell, googling you brings up loads of pics of you with supermodels. And not a little public nudity."

"I went to *one* Victoria's Secret fashion show," he mumbled.

"My point! Who'd ever think you were doing anything but being Rake Tarbell on vacation?"

"We made you guys as safe as we could by putting you together," Delaney added. "But one thing I don't get— Lillith?"

The girl broke off the "I've got no use for a pony, but I would like the latest MacBook Air, please" discussion with Mrs. Tarbell. "Yes?"

"Why didn't you tell me you had the flash drive? Why wait until we were literally under the gun?"

"That's exactly what I waited for. Mama told me it was my spade, and to hold it for six months or until our backs were to the wall, whichever came first." At their uncomprehending looks, the little girl elaborated. "Remember, Mama didn't actually act on the information she hacked. She figured if that awful Mr. Kovac didn't intrude in our lives within six months, he never would. But if he *did* intrude, and things got bad, then I was supposed to give it to *un adulto fidato*."

"Your spade?" Delaney glanced at Ellen, who shrugged.

Rake laughed. "Your ace."

"Oh. Yes, my ace." Lillith shrugged. "I don't play cards."

"But I've been with you the whole time. Ever since I found you at the neighbor's after I got your mom's letter."

"Delaney, I barely knew you. And my *mother* had just *died*. I'm smart, but I don't get it right every time."

"*You* didn't do anything wrong, darling," the nuclear option said, glaring at literally everyone in the restaurant except Lillith.

"Abort," Rake murmured to Delaney. "For the love of God, *abort*."

Delaney surrendered. "Fine. Yes. Excellent point, Lillith. It's not your fault that things got weird in a hurry." She shook her head and laughed. "It wasn't just Murphy's law, it was Murphy's ongoing disaster. First you gave me the slip in Lake Como—"

"I'm still vague on how I got to Venice."

"—and then when I picked up your trail again, you jumped in the canal!"

"Fell, dammit! Do I have to write it on my forehead?"

"I mean—who could plan for that? Then once you were fished out, I clocked the new tail, so I had to leave Lillith and hope you guys would make it to the hotel while I played rodeo clown with the B team."

"Nerve-racking?" Mrs. Tarbell guessed.

"Just a smidge. I was beyond relieved when you guys showed up at the Best Western."

"You may well be the only person ever to be relieved to show up at a Best Western, dear."

Delaney quirked an eyebrow at Mrs. Tarbell. "So when I think we've finally got stuff under control and I'm about to bring the hammer down on Kovac—"

"Under the guise of stuffing Easter baskets. Darling, you *have* had a week."

"—Rake gets sick! Like, violently, flat-on-your-back, should-we-call-an-ambulance sick. Again: Who could plan for these variables? Frankly, I'm astonished that we're all here to talk about it."

"And don't forget the Donna variable," Ellen pointed out quietly. "She had everything ready to go: false IDs, paperwork, a reasonably good exit strategy, proof if Kovac got cute . . . only she died before she could do much more than send Delaney a letter. No one could have predicted that, either."

"I'm terribly sorry about your friend. And your mother, Lillith. Perhaps the silver lining is that the accident set all of this in motion. And brought you to us," Mrs. Tarbell added, hugging Lillith. "And . . . maybe accomplished something else."

"Nonna, it's a lot more subtle if you say something like that and *don't* wink."

"Oh, subtle." Mrs. Tarbell waved it away. "Tosh."

"This *is* the woman who clipped your wings and emptied your bank accounts," Delaney teased. "And your brother's. Overnight. After having you followed. Why were you expecting subtle, again?"

"Point. So you got Donna's letter, found Lillith, and then found my grandmother?"

"Yes. And she agreed to help finance the Big Pipe Dream—conditionally, of course. But since there was a kid in play, she wanted to give you the monetary equivalent of a brisk shake first."

"Blake, too, since Lillith's presence would permanently impact his life as well."

"That is an insane way of prepping me for fatherhood," Rake announced. "Not just me. Anyone. It's an insane way to get anyone ready for unexpected fatherhood."

Or unclehood, Delaney thought. *And I see we're still not mentioning that possibility to Lillith. Perhaps the Tarbells think she's had enough uncertainty in her short life. Either way, I guess it's not my problem. Donna wanted her well looked after, but she was vague on specifics. . . .*

Which was problematic. This dinner looked like the last scene in a sitcom where everyone talks about lessons learned and then leaves, only to reappear a week later for the next episode. For the first time in her life, Delaney didn't want to disappear, never seen again by the mark(s) in question.

Maybe I'm catching gastroenteritis? It does *seem pretty warm in here. . . .*

"Insane!" Rake was still bitching, which she thought was kind of adorable. "Who does that? And how are you going to explain yourself to Blake when you see him in a couple of days? Don't give me that look, Nonna. You had a ridiculous overreaction and treated your grown grandsons like adorable morons."

"*Se la scarpa si adatta . . .*" Teresa murmured with a smirk.

"I'm going to ignore that snipe with dignity and grace," he retorted. Then: "Oh, come on. Stop laughing. All of you!"

"Yes, don't pick on Rake," Delaney said, patting his arm. "He did the best he could with the tools at his disposal."

"*Thank* you. Wait . . . no, hell with it, I'm taking your words at face value."

Delaney laughed. "Oh my God, you're still an adorably naïve doof, I love you."

Pretty immediately, she felt the blood rush to her face. *Whoa. Right out there in front of everyone.*

Um.

What the hell do I do now?

Nothing, she decided. Because even if she'd blurted it out, it was true. She had no idea she could fall in love with Rake in just a week, but there it was. And the strangest/best thing was, no one at the table seemed to think she'd said anything strange, or that Rake was doing something odd by reaching out and taking her hand in his.

"So! I don't know about you guys, but I don't think eight desserts are enough."

Which, happily, was something else they could all agree on.

Fifty-three

After far too much pasta and wine and sorbet and cookies, they were ready to go their separate ways. Ellen and Teresa handed out hugs all around before taking off, leaving the Tarbells with Delaney.

Lillith cleared her throat. "Will you be okay, Rake?"

"At any other time, that would seem like a condescending question," he replied. "And I don't blame you for wondering. I'll be fine—I'll be with Delaney."

"Hmmm." From the nuclear option.

"Oh, stop it, you've got a dirty mind."

"As do you, dear. But never mind. I'll take Lillith back to the hotel and get her settled, and we'll see you in the morning. Do *not* keep us waiting. This isn't a flight you want to miss."

"Noted." He reached down, his daughter reached up, and they hugged.

"You'll *love* America," Mrs. Tarbell promised, taking Lillith's hand.

"Grandma, I was born there. I actually live there. For my whole life. This was just a dangerous field trip."

"Right, right, I keep forgetting—your Italian is so *good*, dear." And they were off in a swirl of tweed and Chanel and Lillith's fake belly, which currently held crackers and Tootsie Roll pops.

Rake spotted what he'd been looking for and tugged Delaney's elbow. "C'mon, my treat. Well, Lillith's. She lent me a thousand euros."

Delaney was already rolling her eyes as they approached the dock. "So corny, Rake, c'mon—really?"

"Shut up, darling. I wanna! It's our first night on the town as a couple, dammit—"

"We're a couple now?"

"—and we're being romantic."

"We are?"

"Oh, yeah. C'mon, here's a guy ready to make our night unforgettable. *O solo mioooooo . . .*"

"Stop. Just stop."

But he didn't. And then he and the gondolier sang together. It was the most awful, wonderful thing ever.

Much later, naked and sweaty

("Oh my God, how are you *doing* that?"

"Martial arts and yoga."

"Liar."

"You're right. I've never done yoga.")

she rested her head on his shoulder and tried to slow her breathing.

What is it about love and sex that can make people so completely, dangerously irrational? To take risks they'd never, ever take in their right mind?

Well, now she knew. She'd risk everything for a man she'd known a week. It was insane. Wonderful and insane.

But now what?

"You never told me where you live." Rake's voice rumbled out of his chest and through hers, *yum*. "Just that you roam the world, grabbing random pickpockets and scaring the shit out of scammers and reuniting lost children with their lost fathers."

Well, there was the hotel in Chicago. And the condo on Cape Cod—not hers, technically, but Mr. Marsh had been in the nursing home for two years, and loved when she stayed there. And sometimes she stayed at Sofia's apartment. But as far as a *home* home—

"Because I was thinking, you could move in with Lillith and me. In Vegas." When she sat up, he added, "If you don't like Vegas, we could live somewhere else. Anywhere. I don't give a shit, if you're there."

"*Live* together?" she asked, astonished. "All three of us?"

"Well, yeah." He blinked up at her. "What'd you think?"

"I haven't even said I love you! On purpose! It just slipped out earlier. . . ."

"But you do."

God, the insufferable confidence. "How do you know?" It was true, but she'd spent a lifetime not letting people see into her. She'd been taking home poker pots since she was eleven.

He sat up, kissed her. Held her hands, turned them over, kissed her palms. "It's all right. Don't look so scared. I love that you blurted it in front of everybody."

"But how d'you know?"

He let go of her hands and lay back down, like he didn't want to crowd her.

"You put yourself in danger for my sake and, more

important, my daughter's. And you hated keeping your word to my grandma, but you did it anyway, and you still managed to find ways to help me whenever you could without betraying her trust. You went way, way above and beyond the job description. And you don't fuck for fun."

"I don't?"

"No." He smiled. "And you haven't been with anybody for a long time, and I'm enough of a pig to be glad."

True, but . . . ? "All right, you're correct, you confident schmuck, but how—"

"Because you don't know you still sleepwalk. If you were boning on the regular—"

"Good *God*."

"—whoever you were with would have mentioned it to you before now."

"I—" Sleepwalk? No. Not for years. Not since she was a little girl. Except . . . Rake wouldn't lie. Not about this. "I do?"

"When you're upset about something, you sleepwalk that night."

"What do I do?" She was fascinated and mortified. The fact that he was acting like her nocturnal rambling was no biggie was the only thing keeping her from leaping from the bed. And possibly the window. *He never said a word. Not once. He was fine with my being a freak. He* likes *when I'm a freak.*

"You go to the window." His hand was stroking her naked back. "You're upset until I tell you that you're an adult and can go wherever you want. Then you're happy and go back to bed."

She *stared* at him. "You never . . ."

"No."

"But now? You're telling me now?"

"No more secrets."

"No more secrets," she repeated like an idiot, and God, if that were true? That would mean everything. That would be too good to be true. But it seemed that was a Tarbell specialty: things that were too good to be true.

"So, back to why you love me," he said calmly, like he hadn't just blown her mind, "You did all that, why? Because you felt sorry for me? You hate pity. You went to all that trouble for a job? No. You love me. Which works out nicely," he sighed, snuggling into her, "because I love you."

She laid back down and put her head on his chest. Her head was spinning, and she'd think about what had just happened for a long time. Years. But for now . . . right now this very minute . . . "Say that again. I want to feel it *and* hear it."

"I love you, I love you, I love you. I love Claire Delaney, I love you more than I love Peeps— Ow!" It all rumbled through him—and her!—and that wonderful deep voice filled the room. Guy could've been in radio, if radio were still a thing.

She rested her chin on his chest so she could look up at him. "I've never been to Vegas."

"Oh, good. You'll hate it."

She laughed. "Really?"

"Oh, yeah. Everyone does. It'll be great. And the scammers in that town? It'll be like Christmas for you. We're gonna make some new rules, though. Family-friendly rules, so you can still stomp scammers but Lillith and I won't ever worry about you going to jail."

"Okay," she agreed. It wouldn't be that simple; she wasn't used to having someone outside the family worry about her. There would be a period of adjustment. Possibly lasting years. There would be arguments in their immediate future. Plenty of them. But also Rake and Lillith. And the Big Pipe

Dream. Their relationship wouldn't be simple, which, if anything, made it more valuable by far.

Las Vegas, sure. And maybe she'd take him to the Cape,
show him the condo, take him to meet Mr. Marsh, who loved
telling the story (to everyone, alas) of how Delaney saved
him from con artists and predatory prostitutes (the man was
pushing eighty, and that had been five years ago; what had he
been *thinking*?). She wouldn't bother with the Chicago hotel
room—she and Rake had seen plenty of those—but he could
show her Vegas, she could take them to Minnesota, get some
proper milk into Rake's diet, take Lillith fishing, keep an eye
on their dairy regimen . . . They had . . . everything, really.
Their lives, their pocketbooks, the world.

USA: Dead Ahead!

Epilogue

"Little brother," Blake said by way of greeting.

"God, you're *so* uptight. Who answers the phone like that?" Rake bitched, purely as a matter of form. Delaney and Lillith were in the lobby, saying one more good-bye to Sofia, Ellen, and Teresa and demanding that they come to Vegas pronto. That left Rake time to knock the last thing off his "To Do" list. "Listen, I've started a family and I'm in love and stuff, so. Just FYI. Her name's Claire Delaney and she's awesome."

"Congratulations!"

Weird. Blake sounded genuinely happy for him. And not surprised at all.

"Nonna told you all about her, huh?"

"In breathless detail. I particularly like the part where she's a master of the martial arts and can beat you mercilessly if the mood strikes. And beautiful, of course. Nonna said she has fog-colored eyes and a talent for aggravating you."

"Yeah, she's almost as good at it as you are. Which I didn't think was possible. I definitely didn't think it would make her hotter to me. And you haven't even heard the best part; Delaney had an old friend who—"

"Come to my wedding," his twin coaxed.

"Wedding! Why do I have the feeling you should have been the one doing all the talking during this call?"

"You'd never have let me get a word in edgewise. I had to interrupt you just to issue an invitation. Yes, I am getting married. I, too, have been pierced by the dart of love."

Rake made vomiting noises into the phone, which, oddly, seemed to please his twin, who continued happily: "And so I want to see you. I want Natalie to meet you."

"Of course, you flapping asshole. Wouldn't miss it."

"Excellent."

"So . . . you're okay? You've got your dough back, I've got mine, we're in love, happily ever after, blah-blah-blah?"

A sigh. "Never change, little brother. Yes, blah-blah-blah. I was ill for a bit but have recovered. You were taken prisoner—Nonna was vague on details and you *will* share the entire story before much longer—"

"No prob, since I finally have the entire story."

"—and have likewise gotten over that. I'm not sure if Nonna anticipated the consequences when she hatched this plan to knock us into poverty and force us to become better human beings."

"Speaking of Operation Fuck with You, I have more news: I'm a dad!"

"I don't think that's the name of the Op— What?"

"You heard me. I'm a proud papa."

"That's . . . that's wonderful! Congratulations?" Blake's bewildered and slightly panicked tone was as soothing as a massage. "How did—when can I—that means I'm an uncle."

"Yep! Or possibly a father."

"*What?* Rake, what are you talking about?"

"I'll explain later, but you're definitely an uncle. And even if you're a father, it's only on a biological level."

"What does that even—"

"Listen, I can't miss this flight—"

"*Rake Tarbell.* You will elaborate this minute!"

"Bye!"

"Rake? Rake? Don't disconnect, you miscreant!"

"Gotta go!"

"Raaaaaaaaaaaaaake!"

Index

About the Author

MaryJanice Davidson is the internationally bestselling author of several books, including the Betsy the Vampire Queen series. Her books have been translated into several languages and are available in fifteen countries. She writes a biweekly column for *USA Today* and frequently speaks to book clubs and writers' groups, teaches writing workshops, and attends conferences all over the world. She has published books, novellas, articles, short stories, recipes, and movie reviews.